Special thanks to Amy, Barbara, Don, George, Melissa, Nikki, and Pati.

THE JACK NOBLE SERIES

The Recruit (Short Story)
The First Deception (Prequel 1)
Noble Beginnings (Jack Noble #1)
A Deadly Distance (Jack Noble #2)
Ripple Effect (Bear Logan)
Thin Line (Jack Noble #3)
Noble Intentions (Jack Noble #4)
When Dead in Greece (Jack Noble #5)
Noble Retribution (Jack Noble #6)
Noble Betrayal (Jack Noble #7)
Never Go Home (Jack Noble #8)
Beyond Betrayal (Clarissa Abbot)
Noble Judgment (Jack Noble #9)
Never Cry Mercy (Jack Noble #10)
Deadline (Jack Noble #11)
End Game (Jack Noble #12)
Noble Ultimatum (Jack Noble #13)
Noble Legend (Jack Noble #14)

Get your very own Jack Noble merchandise today! Click the link below to find coffee mugs, t-shirts, and even signed copies of your favorite L.T. Ryan thrillers! https://ltryan.ink/EvG_

Receive a free copy of The Recruit. Visit:
https://ltryan.com/jack-noble-newsletter-signup-1

CHAPTER 1

JANUARY 17TH, 2010

The following takes place between Thin Line and Noble Intentions, books 3 and 4 of the series.

I stood at the corner of East 72nd and Third Ave. A frigid wind whipped from the direction of the Park. The cold rendered my nose useless in picking up the smells from the bakery behind me. Even the exhaust from the line of cabs didn't register.

The message had come in late last night from a random 212 number to meet Charles at this location. The big oaf acted as a buffer between me and the Old Man whenever he needed me for a job. I figured by now trust would've been earned. For the past couple of years I'd taken every job thrown my way. It didn't matter the target or the scope of work. Whether information or extermination, I completed each without a single thought otherwise. No hesitation.

The moral compass that once guided me had faded into the nether. Not much of a conscience ever existed, but at least there was some semblance of right and wrong guiding my actions. As long as I could justify taking a life, I did it. After being set up one too many times by those I trusted most, I'd had enough and decided that no one else mattered. The size of the paycheck was often the driving factor now.

The white Mercedes screeched to a stop in between two yellow cabs. A woman driving a blue minivan laid on her horn as she swerved to miss the back end of the luxury sedan. A cigarette butt flew out of the cracked window, soaring end over end toward me. The wind intervened and sent it fluttering to the ground.

"Getting in?" Charles said from behind the glass over the high-pitched wailing of an opera singer and a heavy club beat. "Or do I gotta open the door for you like I do the Old Man?"

I stepped off the curb, crushing the lit cigarette in the process.

Charles hiked a thumb over his shoulder. "In the back, asshole."

I peeked through the window and saw one of Charles's new goons occupying the passenger seat. The rear seat was empty, and so far neither man made any move to disarm me. So I opened the door and slid to the middle. Charles looked up at the rearview and made eye contact for a moment. His gaze shifted and the Mercedes jolted forward to a chorus of horns. I glanced over my shoulder and saw two cars behind us stopped at an angle, inches from one another.

"Jack," Charles said. "This is Matt, he's new to the inner—"

"Yeah, I really don't give a shit." I stared out the window at a woman jogging in shorts and a vest, her cadence almost in perfect time with whatever weird techno music Charles was blasting. "The hell are you listening to?"

Charles swatted his goon on the shoulder. "You believe this guy? I swear, what the Old Man sees in him, I don't get it. You could do the work he does, and do it better."

"Then why am I here?" I said. "You wanna replace me with this chump, then let me out now. I got plenty of other people I can get work from."

"Chill your damn goats, Noble. I'm just bustin' your balls, man."

Twenty minutes later we pulled to the curb in front of a renovated brownstone on Hicks Street. A stack of bricks piled as tall as a man stood to the left of the sweeping steps leading to the entrance. The salvaged windows wavily reflected the bleak day.

Charles led me inside the building while Matt remained with the car. He'd been given instructions to cooperate should a cop poke his nose into their business. Usually they'd do so looking for a handout. Even the ones on the Old Man's payroll were always on the lookout for a few bucks more. The old guy didn't mind. He used it as a qualifier to know who he could trust, and who he could consider killing.

We huffed it up three flights of stairs and stopped in front of an unassuming apartment. Charles placed one large hand on his belly, the other on the doorframe, sucking in deep breaths of air. I knew of at least five properties owned by the Old Man, and was sure he had several others. Some for meetings. Others for out of town associates to stay when they visited. And at least a few used as safe houses for his guys, and himself, when necessary. While I had no desire to run a business on the scale of the Old Man's, I adopted his practice of buying real estate. Together with my old partner Bear, we owned seven residences spread throughout the city, and a few houses in northern New York.

"You know the drill." Charles had one hand on the knob, the other extended toward me. Collecting my pistol was a formality. We both knew that once inside, I'd be out-manned and outgunned. No chance I'd reach for my backup piece.

He cracked the door, put his big hand on my back and pushed me inside. Two bodyguards dressed in black and wearing black gloves with cutout fingers turned their attention to me. The third remained perched at his lookout spot, watching the road below. The Old Man spun a quarter-turn in his office chair. A lit cigarette dangled from his fingers. Smoke slipped from his parted lips, catching the sunlight and creating a haze between us. As the smoky veil lifted, his yellow teeth shone through his crooked smile.

"Mr. Jack," he said, tipping his ash into a ceramic tray. "So good to see you. Feels like it's been forever since we last met."

"A month," I said. "Last time we saw each other was a month ago. Remember, you needed help making that woman disappear. Something about a paternity suit, if I remember correctly."

"So recently?" Smiling, he shook his head and gestured for me to take a seat opposite him. "Perhaps I am slipping in my old age."

"Perhaps." I stood firm, waited to see if he'd get to the point of the meeting.

The Old Man waved at his bodyguards and they dispersed, leaving him, Charles and me as the sole occupants of the room. The door slammed shut, and we waited amid the thundering silence.

I broke the first rule of negotiations. "What's this all about?"

The Old Man took a final drag off his cigarette, then extinguished it in the tray. Exhaling, he said, "An associate of mine, a businessman, made a rather large and costly mistake, putting himself at risk in the process. Which puts me at risk. And when I'm at risk, my entire organization, including my contractors, is at risk."

"What kind of dealings do you typically have with this associate?"

Charles leaned forward. "That's not for you to worry—"

The Old Man sliced his hand through the air between us. "Please, Mr. Charles, allow Mr. Jack to ask whatever questions he wants. After all, he is the one who is going to help us solve this problem."

"Yeah, Chuck," I said. "So back to my question."

"He's a businessman, so business dealings. As you know, a good portion of what I do is on the right side of the law. I have many associates who do not delve into or share our view of the world."

"And this guy?" I said. "What's his worldview?"

The Old Man smiled, answering the question in the process.

"What do you need me to do?"

"Find him. Find out what he knows, what he's said, and what he's planning to do." The Old Man reached into his breast pocket, producing a bullet. He placed it flat on the table, spun it with a flick of his finger. "And once you've got every last bit of information out of him, kill him."

I nodded, said nothing.

"One more thing." The Old Man lifted his eyebrows. He spoke through clenched teeth. "Before killing him, Mr. Jack, make him hurt."

CHAPTER 2

THE REST OF THE MEETING WAS MORE OF A FORMALITY THAN anything else. Matt showed up around this time. The guy stood in the corner and kept his mouth shut while Charles, the Old Man and I continued on with the kind of mindless banter that occurs in boardrooms across the country. Throughout our bullshit conversation, the missing details of the job nagged at me. What had this man done that left the Old Man wanting him not only dead, but also tortured? I preferred hitting hard and fast and getting the job done. Torture wasn't my thing, but for the payday the Old Man was offering, I couldn't refuse the job or his requests.

After we wrapped up, Charles led me out of the building. His new associate Matt stayed behind. Perhaps he had his own private meeting upstairs. What was his role within the organization? Had it been coincidence that we were in the same car together that morning? Or did they want him in there with me for a reason?

"Everything you need's in here." A worn leather messenger bag dangled from Charles's fingertips.

I slung the lightweight bag over my shoulder and protected the zippered opening with my left arm. I felt a pistol inside the bag.

"What do you know about this guy?" I shot him a sideways glance to judge his reaction as we stepped out into the cold.

Charles's expression revealed nothing. It rarely did. His face was made of stone. "Just some guy who got on the Old Man's bad side."

"You never met him?"

Charles shrugged, his bottom lip poked out, pushing his upper lip into his nose. Was he telling me something, or was it a reaction to the frigid air freezing his nose hairs together? "What's it matter? Guy could be my best friend's cousin's lover and he'd still be gettin' whacked. Know what I mean?"

Once the wheels were in motion, there was no stopping the hit from taking place. It was only a matter of deciding on the trigger man. For some jobs it could be anybody. Others required a specific assassin. I'd take just about any job these days. That hadn't always been the case, though. Morals and ethics, as shifty as they could be, played a part at one time. Too much had happened to me over the years to care anymore. But I still had two no-gos. Kids and dogs. Not a chance I'd harm either. Everyone else? Better not do something that gets me sent to your front door.

"True enough," I said. "Anything I should be aware of with him? Military background? Security?"

He pointed at the bag. "It's all in there."

We slipped into the idling Mercedes. The heated cabin was a relief from the arctic assault happening outside.

"You believe this flippin' weather?" He blew a puff of hot air into his clasped hands then rubbed them together before slipping on a pair of black leather gloves. "Where's this crap come from?"

"Canada, I guess. Maybe Alaska."

"Weatherman Noble." He looked at me. "You'd be real cute on television. You know that? Maybe get you one of those skirts to put on, maybe a wig to help cover up that ugly mug of yours."

"I don't think I could sleep at night if I knew you were jerking off to me on the eleven o'clock news."

Charles chuckled. "You wish, Noble."

We headed back to Manhattan, the Upper West Side this time. As we approached the drop-off point, I scanned the street for threats and flagged anyone who looked out of place. On this morning where temperatures had only just reached zero, that was pretty much everyone. In the end, though, no one stood out enough to warrant concern.

"This job could go a long way for you in our organization," Charles said as he pulled to the curb, rubbing the tires against the concrete. "Maybe get you a full-time gig."

"Why would I want that?"

"Why wouldn't you?"

I acted as though I mulled it over for a couple of seconds. "For starters, I don't like following the orders of underlings. I can handle a boss, some of the time, as long as he leaves me the hell alone. So really, the only job worth having would be yours. My first act would be to take you down so I could slide into your position. From there, I'd work on taking over the whole organization."

Charles laughed. "You? Right. A guy who likes to live in the breeze and pick up work when it suits you. You wouldn't want to take on the Old Man's responsibilities." He paused a beat. "Mine either."

"Like you do anything important on a daily basis."

"You got no idea, Noble." He shook his head. "You really don't."

"Just busting your balls, man. I don't want your job. I certainly don't want to run an enterprise like the Old Man's." I cracked the door open, inviting a steady gust of wind inside. "And I have no desire to be a part of your organization."

"Solid pay for a guy like you. No more drifting. And you'd have the full protection of the Old Man. Right now you're pretty much in danger every second of every day. With his backing, you'd be almost untouchable."

"Untouchable…right. Except to the same people I already have to watch out for. Like you said, every second of every day, I'm watching my back for the criminals I put away, and the agency I put them away for. Let's not get into other organizations and the Old Man's rivals I've weakened in the past."

"But if you're with us, you'll be avenged. If someone got you right now, you'd be a dead asshole with no one mourning you."

I sat there for a moment, my grip loose on the door handle. He was right. If someone took me out right then and there, no one would mourn my passing.

And I was happy with that.

CHAPTER 3

I TURNED A SIX-BLOCK WALK INTO A HALF HOUR ORDEAL FULL OF wrong turns and narrow alleyways. The route was designed to make a tail easier to spot. The Old Man knew plenty about me, including the locations of some of my real estate, which was fine. But I couldn't compromise the one I was headed to now.

I first caught sight of the guy on the corner of 96th and Amsterdam. He wore a brown bomber and black scarf wrapped to his chin. Dark glasses shielded his eyes from view, and were unnecessary on the overcast morning. He followed me on two successive turns, maintaining a fifty-foot gap between us. He was sloppy, though, and failed to use the sparse crowd as cover.

The next alley was littered with dumpsters and grease traps. The foul stench was the first odor able to pervade my senses outside that day. How the bums drinking and napping in the narrow corridor managed to remain there I had no idea. I figured that maybe the only thing that smelled worse than them was that stretch of cracked asphalt.

The short road tee'd at the end. I turned right, casting a quick glance back toward the street. The guy stood in the open, cell phone in his hand, looking up at the brick facade of the building.

Who had he called? Backup? Charles or the Old Man? Maybe my new friend Matt?

I scanned the lane behind the buildings and realized I'd made a mistake. The map in my head told me this path would intersect with a narrow walkway between two apartment buildings, dumping out on W 98th Street. It didn't, though.

Dead end.

I swung my head around and saw that the other direction offered no outlet either. I tried three nearby doors in an attempt to find another way out. All were locked. It was time to get a little creative. Across the main alley was a fire escape that ran to the top of the building. The access was low enough to reach with a running start and a hop up the wall.

I reached into the messenger bag and retrieved the pistol. I released the magazine, verified it was full, slid it back in, then chambered a round. I held the gun close to my side and lowered my head as I stepped into the opening.

The man was waiting there.

I wasn't surprised by the sight of him, but he had the drop on me. He was positioned like a receiver on the line, knees bent, arms dangling, ready to explode. He slammed into me like I was an undersized cornerback. I absorbed the hit and whipped my left arm around, driving a fist into his upper spine. Somehow he managed to get his left leg around my right knee. His right arm slipped down and grabbed hold of my left thigh. He was a trained grappler, wrestling or jiu-jitsu.

I pushed my mid-section forward, but it was too little too late. He drove me to the ground, landing with his shoulder square in my gut. The combination of my back slamming on the asphalt and all of his bodyweight coming down on my diaphragm knocked the wind out of me. My mouth filled with blood. I'd clamped down on my tongue when I hit the ground. He had me in a perfect position to take me out. And then he reached for my bag and tried to yank it off me. I managed to hang onto the bag despite feeling as though I was drowning, my oxygen-starved lungs burning for air.

The guy was there for the information I had. Was he a Fed? Someone working for my undisclosed target?

"C'mon man, let it go." He'd reared back on his heels and tugged hard enough to lift my torso off the ground. The bag's strap was bound to rip at the stitching.

I desperately choked on the air rushing into my lungs. I caught my breath after a series of heavy gasps and coughs. A moment later adrenaline-fueled strength flooded my body. I tightened my grasp on the bag, wrapping the strap around my wrist, and felt along the ground for my pistol.

"Not worth dying over, dude." The guy delivered a weak kick to my shin.

"Who are you?" I said.

He jerked forward and threw a punch to my gut. I tightened my abdominals a second ahead and absorbed the blow. He grabbed the bag with one hand

and my wrist with the other. With every passing second he wrenched it further from my possession.

I gave up on my search for the pistol and focused all my attention on my assailant. I knew one thing for certain. He was an amateur. The only reason to get that close was in an effort to gain control over me. He'd gone all or nothing for the bag, leaving himself vulnerable.

I flung my right arm around and came crashing down on the side of his face. One hit to his jaw was all it took. His head snapped back, body went limp. His grasp on me and the bag relinquished as his body slumped over.

I got to my feet, spotted my pistol and snatched it off the ground. My hands and arms shook from the adrenaline coursing through my body. I dragged the guy into the shadows and searched him. I found his cell phone, a knife, and a money clip that contained two twenties, a five, and an expired driver's license. But he didn't have a firearm on him. I held his ID up and angled it to catch the light.

Nathaniel Spencer.

Spencer groaned as he rejoined the land of the conscious.

I slapped him across the face, aiming for the red mark where I'd decked him a minute ago. "Who the hell are you?"

His eyes fluttered before honing his gaze in on me, then at his license. "Looks like you already know."

"Who do you work for?" I paused a beat, waiting for him to reply. "I have the means to find out."

He looked at me like I was crazy.

"Are you FBI? DEA? You work for that bastard?" Sure, the last part was vague, but all underlings would at some point refer to their boss with the phrase.

"The hell are you talking about, dude?" He propped himself up on his elbows. Blood trickled down his chin from the corner of his mouth. "I spotted you getting out of your boyfriend's Mercedes. You looked like an easy mark."

"What?"

He jutted his chin toward the bag dangling from my left hand. "I was trying to rip you off, asshole."

I aimed the pistol at his chest. "You really think this is the best time to play the tough guy?"

He averted his eyes while shaking his head.

"You're a thief?" I said. "Nothing more?"

"I'm tellin' you, dude. I figured you had some cash and decent credit cards in your purse."

I lifted the bag. "It's not a purse. And if you had gained possession of it, you'd be in some serious trouble."

He scooted back until he reached the wall. I kept the pistol trained on him as he rose.

"Who are you?" he said.

"Not who you thought I was." I tossed his money clip to the end of the alley. "And I know who you are, Spencer. If I see your face again, you're dead."

CHAPTER 4

A CAB OFFERED THE BEST CHANCE OF GETTING OUT OF THE AREA as fast as possible. I had the driver zig-zag through a network of streets until I was sure no one was following. Under no circumstances could anyone discover the location of the apartment, which meant I had to play it safe with the driver. The cabbie could be on the Old Man's payroll, with instructions to always be on the lookout for certain individuals, taking note of pick-up and drop-off locations. So far the guy had paid little attention to me, but that meant nothing. I had to assume he was keeping track.

I had him drop me off a few streets over from the apartment. After paying my fare with cash, I hustled the two blocks through the cold. The building's foyer was only a few degrees warmer than outside. I peeled off my gloves and rubbed my hands together before unlocking my mailbox and pulling out a stack of envelopes and adverts. It was all for previous tenants. Once inside the apartment, I dropped the mail and the bag on the small square kitchen table and pulled a bottle from the freezer. The first swig of whiskey stung where I'd cut my tongue during the fight. The second swallow numbed the pain. The third warmed my frozen core.

I sat down at the table, shoved the mail to the side, pulled the files from the bag and had my first look at the target.

His name was Marcus Hamilton Thanos. Six-three, two hundred eighty pounds. He looked soft now, but I was sure at one time he was a tough bastard. Had to be with that name. It was the kind of name that led to endless bullying while growing up. Aside from the personal details, there was little additional information. I wanted to know more, and help was a mere phone call away. Curiosity could be a bitch, and often had unintended consequences attached to it. I had to resist the urge to find out more about the guy, as it had little bearing on the job I'd been tasked with. Thanos had been marked for death. The part of executioner was to be played by me, after I'd gleaned whatever info I could from him.

Find out what he's planning on saying. Make him hurt.

Thanos had done something to piss off the Old Man. Was it betrayal? Or was he planning on testifying against the Old Man, or maybe revealing something about their dealings that could land the old crime lord in jail?

I considered calling in a favor to Brandon. The former analyst was the best I'd ever been paired with. He'd never failed me, no matter what task I set him on. Since striking out on his own, he'd been an invaluable resource. But I'd used him less after an incident that left him and Bear for dead.

I decided against bringing him in. At least at this stage of the game. There was no need to raise red flags by having a few top secret databases searched for any intelligence they contained on Thanos.

The next folder contained my destination. Chicago. Thanos had an office by the lake. His house was in the suburb of Naperville. Satellite imagery of the surrounding neighborhood told me I wouldn't have to worry too much about meddling neighbors. The lots were large and sprawling. A long driveway cut through a manicured wooded area. It'd be hard for anyone to see me. On the other hand, it'd be hard for me to surveil the place and get an idea of what I was up against. And considering what had happened earlier in the alley, I wasn't entirely positive that this job was on the up and up.

At least as far as assassinations went.

I sorted the papers into a single folder and then locked the dossier in a safe under the kitchen sink before making my way to the master bedroom. I got out of the clothes I'd brawled in earlier, grabbed a hot shower, and changed into a pair of boxers after shaving off my beard.

I wasn't done, though. Inside the closet were three additional safes, one biometric, one electronic, and one old fashioned. I kept enough cash to survive for three months, two full-sized pistols and one subcompact, and plenty of ammunition. I was traveling by air, so they were all staying behind. I also kept four false identities in a safe, complete with driver's licenses, credit and debit cards, and even AAA memberships. I grabbed the packet for Jonah Lamb, an identity I hadn't used in over three years. Jonah Lamb was a claims adjuster from Albuquerque, New Mexico who was divorced with no children. He lived on the road forty-four weeks a year. Poor guy didn't even have time for a pet.

I put on a pair of khakis, a button up checkered shirt, brown oxfords, and grabbed a pair of black-rimmed glasses to complete the look.

Back in the kitchen I retrieved an unused burner phone from underneath a drawer. I used the phone to call an associate in Chicago, someone who went all the way back to my days in the Marines. We'd travelled in different directions during the years since. I wasn't reaching out to involve him in my assignment. In fact, the less he knew the better. But what he could provide was weapons, and I would need a few.

We chatted for a couple of minutes, the kind of bullshit two old associates might throw at each other when they hadn't spoken in three years. When I told him I'd be out his way sometime tomorrow morning, he carefully told me he'd have a solid selection for me to choose from.

After the call, I booked my flight for five am, then managed a few hours of shuteye. Things were looking up. For me, that was. For poor Mr. Thanos, the end of the road was quickly drawing near.

CHAPTER 5

I RENTED A SILVER CAMRY AT THE AIRPORT AND WOVE THROUGH downtown Chicago until I reached Thanos's office. The dark concrete and mirrored-glass building stood ten stories tall not too far from Printer's Row. A parking spot opened up on the curb in a location that gave me a great view of the main entrance, which offered the only area to catch a glimpse inside as people came and went.

I settled into my seat as a steady stream of warm air blew from every vent, leaving me feeling as though I might slip into unconsciousness at any moment. I'd managed four hours of sleep the night before. Not a big deal, I thought at the time. After all, I had an hour-and-a-half long flight I could doze through. Turned out to be wishful thinking. Relentless turbulence left the 757 in a state of constant flux as it tumbled through pockets of choppy air.

The rising sun burned off a thick layer of morning fog. Sunlight reflected off a nearby building, directing an intense beam in my direction. The glare made it impossible to see in front of the building. I lowered the visor and sat up to shield my eyes. Within a few minutes, the car felt overly warm and sweat formed on my brow. I cracked the windows and prepared for an arctic assault. It had been cold in New York, but on this morning Chicago might as well be Moscow. The sounds of the city slipped in through the open windows. What had been a soft murmur tempered by glass morphed into the urban jungle I'd grown accustomed to.

I hadn't spent much time in Chicago, and was unfamiliar with the intricacies of the city. Figured it'd be a good idea to familiarize myself with my immediate surroundings, so I trekked the four blocks surrounding the office building during morning rush hour, the perfect time to assimilate with the crowds hurrying to work. They were sparser than I'd imagine them being when the temperature reached springtime levels. Still, people had to get to work, and there were enough of them to offer ample cover.

The scouting mission revealed a few possible vantage points should the job require a long-range attempt on Thanos as he left the building. I noted two egress points in addition to the building's main entrance. There was little information on Thanos, and for all I knew, he travelled with a security detail, which he might if he had caught wind of the attempt on his life. I couldn't shake the thought that he had an idea what was coming. The fight in the alley the previous day still had me off my game a bit. The encounter was too random to actually be random. I couldn't silence the nagging voice in my head that told me Nathaniel Spencer had something to do with this job.

The mob thinned out, signaling that it was time to return to the rental car. I grabbed a hot cup of coffee from a cafe a block away. By the time I reached the car, it barely passed for luke warm. Back behind the wheel again, I settled in for a stakeout. The urge to get the job over with nagged at me, but I was unarmed, and this wasn't the right setting. I needed to know more about Thanos. I had to get a visual on him, really get a feel for who I was dealing with. There was only so much that could be gleaned from a photograph. But seeing a man in person, watching how he carries himself, holds his head, juts his chin, that was how I'd get a read on him. How I'd determine my approach to the job.

The chatter in my head subsided after a few minutes. I settled into the zone, keeping my thoughts to a minimum. Going down the rabbit hole of people and past events never led to a positive outcome. Especially with my history.

I finally caught a break an hour later when three men emerged from the covered entryway. None were my guy. Two of them were too young, and the third guy had the look of a soldier. They were all of similar build, big and thick and about six feet tall. The older guy had red hair and fair features. The two younger men had brown hair and pasty winter skin, and the only thing that differentiated them was that one had a beard. They were dressed the same, black suits, no ties, sunglasses. None of them wore a coat, which indicated they planned on only being outside for a few minutes. Not a one of them bothered to conceal the fact they were carrying a weapon.

The jumpiest of the three, the bearded guy, glanced in my direction. They must've made me when I'd returned to the car with the coffee and stayed put.

The bearded guy remained at the corner while the other two crossed the street diagonally. The guy with red hair raised his hand to slow oncoming traffic, never taking his gaze off me.

There was plenty of time for me to leave. I didn't, though. I wanted to hear what they had to say. After all, they'd come out into the cold to talk with me, and there was little chance of them making a big scene in public. There were cameras at every corner, and in most of the shops along the road.

The redhead came around to my window while his associate stood in front of the car. I glanced in the rearview. A minivan had pulled up a few moments ago. One of theirs? I figured if I wanted to get out, I had to go through the guy, and he was banking that I wouldn't. Too bad he didn't know me.

The redhead rapped his knuckles on my window, pulled back his unbuttoned coat, revealing his sidearm. I hesitated a beat, then pressed the button, rolling the window down a couple of inches.

He leaned forward so his eyes were level with the opening. His nose and cheeks were bright red from the cold. "Need some help?"

I shrugged him off, said nothing.

He knocked on the glass with the barrel of his pistol. "Maybe it's time you move along, fella."

"Why's that?" I said. "Guy can't sit in the sun and enjoy his coffee?"

"Gonna be straight with you, buddy. We don't like the way you look. We don't like that you've been here over two hours. And we don't like that you took a walk around our building, making sure to do it during rush hour so you blended in with the surroundings. Fact of the matter is, you only see three of us. What you don't see is a building full of guys just like me and him."

I kept my gaze fixed on his. He was starting to impress me. I'd taken them for hired goons, nothing more. But it sounded as though he had a background similar to mine.

"Now, here's how it's gonna go," Ginger said. "You're gonna start this piece of junk tin can, put it in gear, and get the hell away from our building. If you're not gone by the time I get to the other side of the street, you'll be tailed. And before you think I'm kidding, realize that we employ one of the best drivers in the business. You won't even know he's there, especially if you try that grade school level evasive technique you used to scout the building." He straightened up and reholstered his sidearm, then bent forward again. "You might think you know me, but let me assure you that following your instinct is gonna lead to a really bad day for you. So do the smart thing and get the hell out of here."

I pressed the button and the window squeaked all the way down. Ginger backed up a couple feet, out of striking distance.

"We gonna have a problem, buddy?" he said.

"No problem," I said. "Just want you to realize you don't scare me. And while I may not see all of your guys, I can assure you, you don't see all of mine." I tapped the steering wheel, then pointed across the street. "We're onto what's going on inside your office. So here's my advice. When I pull away, don't give me a reason to send my men in."

His blue eyes narrowed to slits and he stared at me as though he was trying to decide whether to take me seriously. I didn't look like your everyday schmuck. At least I didn't think so.

"All right, buddy," he said, smiling. "Get the hell out of here."

I turned the engine over, shifted into drive and pulled away from the curb, making sure to come close to the other guy's knee. He hopped out of the way and flicked me off.

It was a risk going in hard like I had, but I wanted to gauge Ginger's reaction. He didn't back down, which told me something was going on in there. Question was, did these guys work for Thanos? Or someone else?

My finger itched to call Brandon for some answers. I resisted.

I stared into the rearview. The three men huddled together, walking toward the building's entrance. They glared in my direction. Ginger was on his cell phone. Figured he was either talking with the boss, or another of his guys stationed further down the road. I shifted my focus to the upcoming intersections and alleys, looking out for an incoming tail.

Once far enough out of sight, I turned right, then left, then worked my way toward I-90. It was time to pay a visit to an old friend.

CHAPTER 6

I FIRST MET SHANE CARRINGTON IN OCTOBER OF '98. HE WAS A career Army Ranger who'd entered the CIA-sponsored program later on following an incident with his CO that left the old bastard wanting to prosecute. Fortunately for Shane, someone higher in the food chain in the Pentagon recognized all Shane had done for his country, and saw that the incident was nothing more than an old coot exerting his power, and eventually he recommended him for our program. He joined me and Bear in Eastern Europe, and we worked together up until 9/11. Shane retired a month or two later and went to work for a security firm that was nothing more than a front for a black-op run by a crazy old prick that narrowly avoided jail time himself. Shane and I fell out of touch for a couple of years, then reconnected in '04. This pattern continued over the next half-decade.

I drove past his house, pulled to the curb, hopped out. The little house couldn't have been more than a thousand square feet. It fit in with the rest of the neighborhood. Light gray siding, white shutters, red door. The grass was brown, like everyone else's, but looked as though he took good care of it during the growing season. A Honda Accord rested peacefully in the short driveway.

The front door opened and a guy I hadn't seen in years stepped out. I stopped on the walkway. Tried to hide my surprise.

"What? You ain't ever seen a guy with no legs walking?" He lifted his robe with his cane and revealed two metal legs before taking a couple clunky steps to the edge of the porch.

He'd made it three months with the security firm before being sent to

Afghanistan. They were ahead of everyone else, even my unit, part of the Special Activities Division, with members in place before the end of September. Shane's team was chasing down a lead in the rugged mountains when the guy next to him stepped on a two-decade-old IED. A relic from the Afghan-Soviet war. The guy who'd discovered the explosive was ripped in half, dead before he could blink. Shane took a hell of a beating and ended up losing both legs, one mid-thigh, the other closer to his knee.

"Well, you coming in?" He propped the screen door open with his elbow.

I shook off the surprise and went up to him and shook his hand.

"Good to see you, Shane."

"Likewise." His staccato, Chicago accent had only intensified since returning home. "And glad to see I'm still the more handsome of the two of us."

"Now, I distinctly remember those three women in the Philippines saying otherwise."

"Jack, I didn't have the heart to tell you back then, but those weren't women." He smiled, then jutted his chin toward the door. His smile faded as his eyes danced back and forth, studying the street. "Let's get inside."

"Everything all right?"

"Yeah, I just get a little spooked when someone from the old days shows up. Know what I mean?"

I'd had that same experience multiple times. It seemed for every old friend that came back into my life, there was another waiting in the shadows ready to cut off my head. Guys like Shane and I had seen a lot and done even more. Things that had been redacted and crossed out with black marker, if not shredded and burned. Only a handful of folks in the Pentagon had access to the truth ten years ago. At least half of them were now dead, and not all by natural causes. I tried not to dwell on what might have occurred in the hours since I reached out to Shane. It had been years since that particular slice of my life had brought any problems for me.

"You don't have to worry about me," I said. "I don't keep in contact with anyone from those days."

He pulled a bottle of Wild Turkey from the cabinet and set two glasses on the counter. "Not even Bear?"

He was referring to the guy who'd been by my side since we were eighteen-year-old know-it-all assholes in Recruit Training. The big man and I had gotten off to a rocky start, but quickly became best friends. When we said we had each other's back, it wasn't a figure of speech. He was the only guy I knew would take a bullet, hatchet, machete, or speeding train, for me. And I'd do the same for him.

"Bear and I still work together," I said.

"Just not on this job." He slid the bottle and a glass in my direction.

I poured a couple ounces of the whiskey. "You fishing for details?"

He shrugged. "I dunno. Looking for a little excitement, I guess. Gets boring sitting in front of a computer typing code all day. Don't get me wrong, the pay's good. Especially combined with the hush money the government gave me." He tapped his cane against his prosthetic. "I mean, I was a Ranger for years before I got in the program. I spent two years out there with you. Even after blowing my legs off I'd have gone into Baghdad in my wheelchair if they'd have let me."

"I know you miss the action."

He stared into his glass and nodded, lifting his chin off his chest. "You got no idea, man."

I could only imagine how he felt. I'd taken my share of lumps over the years, occasionally resulting in a month or two out of commission. And during those times I went stir crazy. It wasn't in my nature to sit still. I sure as hell couldn't stare at a computer all day long, cooped up in an office cubicle. I'd end up being one of those guys that walks in and shoots up the damn place because they took the tuna roll off the cafeteria menu.

"I imagine I would, too," I said.

"Damn right you would." He downed his drink and exhaled loudly, gritting against the burn of the alcohol sliding down his throat. "Enough of that talk. What do you need?"

"Two nines, full-size and a sub-compact, a knife, and a takedown rifle if you've got one. Couple holsters. Extra ammo."

He turned and started toward the hallway with no rhythm to his steps. "Follow me."

At the end of the corridor was a door with a keypad deadbolt. He punched in the code, pushed the door open and left me alone to gather what I needed. He had a nice selection to choose from. I took my time searching through his armory. For my main piece I chose an H&K VP70. The full-size semi-auto pistol was capable of firing in a three-round burst. A sub-compact Springfield XD-S .45 worked perfectly for my concealed, as it was the same firearm I carried in New York. A custom made .308 takedown rifle that disassembled into five parts and fit in a small black duffel bag. Finally, I grabbed a five-inch survival knife with a leather-wrapped hilt and ankle holster.

"Find everything you need?"

I looked over my shoulder to see Shane in the doorway, seated in his wheelchair.

"Yeah, thanks. As always, you came through big time."

He looked over my selections and nodded. "Looks like you're gonna have some fun, huh? Is this something I'm gonna see on the evening news?"

"Not if I do my job right."

"I'm envious. You know that, right?"

"Well, like you said, you get to be the handsome one. I gotta have something, right?"

Shane's cheeks rose and his face crinkled as he laughed. "I miss you, man. I wish you spent more time out here."

I glanced toward the window and took in the barren scene outside. The wind was whipping the bushes and tree branches around. "Not a chance. Too damn cold out here."

"It's the lake, man. Wind comes whipping off it and makes it feel twenty degrees colder than it really is."

I shoved a shoulder holster and the HK in the bag with the .308, and secured the .45 in a holster on my right hip.

"Gonna get going?" he asked.

I nodded.

"How 'bout one more drink?" he said.

"I think I can manage that."

We returned to the kitchen and I poured a healthy dose in each glass. We toasted to old times and loose women in Dubai and each took a swig. I felt the alcohol taking the edge off and considered hanging around a bit longer. It'd do me as much good as it would Shane. He eased back in his chair, smiled.

"This is good, man. It really—"

Someone banged on the front door and his smile faded.

CHAPTER 7

DIM LIGHT CUT THROUGH FLOATING DUST AND CAST A LONG BEAM across the floor. A shadow moved across it. The pounding on the door started up again.

"You expecting someone?" I said.

"Was gonna ask you the same thing," Shane said. He wheeled a few feet toward the foyer and stopped.

"Not a soul knows I'm here. I'm traveling on an alias so tight it's squeaky clean."

Shane moved forward a few more feet and stopped next to a tall vase near the corner. He stuck his arm in the vase shoulder deep. A moment later he pulled out a revolver with a six-inch barrel. He motioned for me to get out of sight before disappearing into the foyer

The knocks continued, loud and forceful, the way a cop would bang on a door. I second-guessed whether I had been followed from Thanos's office building. Had I been distracted enough by Ginger that the guy who blocked my exit by standing in front of the rental car had managed to place a tracking device on the vehicle? Had I completely underestimated who I was dealing with?

"Christ almighty, Lexi," Shane said. The door groaned on its hinges as he pulled it open. "You scared the crap outta me."

"Scared you?" she said. "You took so damn long to open the door I thought I was gonna have to break it down."

She had the same hard-edged accent as Shane.

He emerged from the opening first with a smile on his face. He looked relaxed, calm. The revolver rested on his lap. A long, lean shadow stretched beyond his on the floor. A moment later Lexi appeared. Her gaze swept across the room left to right, stopped on me. Her dark eyes matched the roots of her dyed hair. She had a pale complexion, but didn't most people this time of year?

"Who the hell is this?" she said, keeping her focus on me.

"You knock on the door like a cop," I said.

Shane chuckled.

"Not a cop," she said.

"Good," I said.

"No, it's worse." She smiled as she pulled back her black coat revealing a holstered Glock. "FBI."

I glanced over at Shane and shrugged as though to say what gives.

"Don't worry," Lexi said. "I've got no interest in busting my cousin. So whatever you two derelicts are up to, just don't let me see it and we'll all be fine."

"Cousin?" I said.

"Don't see the resemblance?" she said.

"Well, just with how handsome he's always saying he is, I expected his relatives to be a little more…"

"Homely?" she smiled.

"Lexi definitely got all the looks," Shane said.

"So, you're finally admitting I'm the better looking one?" I said.

"Don't flatter yourself," Lexi said. "Neither of you is that good looking." She let her coat fall back in place, covering her sidearm. She crossed her arms over her chest and narrowed her eyes while staring at me. "How do you two know each other? You look familiar, but don't sound like you're from around here."

"Military," I said.

"Ranger?" she asked.

"No, later in his career." I wondered how much she knew about Shane's time after the Rangers. Considering her job, he might not have felt comfortable confiding in her.

She nodded slightly. "Pencil pusher, huh?"

"Yeah, you could say that."

"What brings you to Chicago?"

"On my way to L.A., but my flight out of New York was delayed. Missed my connection. So, I booked a non-stop for tomorrow morning and figured I'd come see my old buddy."

"What'd you say your name was?" she asked.

"I didn't."

She waited a moment, eyebrows arched. "You gonna tell me?"

"I was hoping you'd frisk me for my wallet."

"Keep dreaming, office boy."

I ditched the smile and gave her my alias. "Jonah Lamb."

Her gaze cut toward Shane, perhaps looking for any sign on his face that I'd lied. A moment passed. "Anyway, would you mind if I had a couple minutes alone with my cousin? I need to run something by him."

I stepped out on the porch and pulled out a cigarette. The lighter wasn't too cooperative in the cold, hardly generating more than a spark. I snapped the smoke in half and tossed it in the bushes. I'd cut down recently, but still needed the nicotine jolt every once in a while. It'd have to wait.

Lexi's car was parked in the driveway. I had no doubt she'd run my plates and called the rental agency to get my name. Probably had someone running my alias at that moment to gather any intelligence on me. I knew what would come back. Nothing much at all. It would show I was a Marine, but the files would be inaccessible. Depending on what she knew about Shane, she'd accept this as the way things were, or she'd dig further. I didn't care either way so long as she didn't take a further interest in me.

The door opened and Lexi stepped outside. She extended her hand. "It was nice meeting you, Mr. Lamb. Shane really appreciates it when his old buddies stop by. Doesn't seem to happen enough. I guess you can imagine it's hard to get involved with the community in his current condition. He doesn't look at himself as handicapped, doesn't look for support from others with similar problems."

"I can see that. I know I'd feel that way."

"If you keep in touch with any of the others—" She paused a beat. "If there are any others left, tell them to give him a call. He'd like that."

"Will do." I pulled her hand closer to me. "Why don't we grab a drink later?"

"Not a chance."

I shrugged. "Maybe some other time, then."

"Not likely," she said with a quick lift of her eyebrows and a smile.

"I didn't get your full name."

She released my hand and pushed past me on the way to her car. I watched, half-conceding that she might be a problem, half-excited over the same prospect. I found myself drawn to her and wanted to run into her again.

"She'd flip your world upside down, man." Shane wheeled himself next to me. "And her last name's the same as mine."

Lexi Carrington.

"Think she'll figure out who I am?" I said

"Would it be a problem for you if she did?"

Lexi backed her vehicle down the driveway into the street. She pulled even with us, waved, then drove off.

"I don't know," I said. "Probably in some ways. Maybe not in others."

"Still thinking with your dick. Good to see some things don't change." He laughed. "Come on back inside. Let's finish those drinks."

CHAPTER 8

I LAID LOW FOR THE NEXT THIRTY-SIX HOURS. THE PLAN WAS TO wait almost a week, let the encounter in front of Thanos's office blow over, then complete the job. A cheap motel room close to the Wisconsin border took cash. I paid for three days upfront. It kept me out of sight and off the grid. I slept and read and thought about Shane's life since his injury. I spent too much time thinking about his cousin Lexi. The last thing I needed was to get involved with an FBI agent.

A small diner across the street provided breakfast, lunch, and dinner, and plenty of cheap coffee. The front and sides were floor-to-ceiling windows, offering a view from the parking lot to the motel. The waitresses didn't engage in small talk. The regulars left me alone. It was the kind of place I could snag a meal that was so greasy and salty it could've been made from road kill and I'd never know.

The motel room's curtains did a decent enough job of blocking the sunlight. I managed a decent night's sleep, woke up around nine and headed to the diner for a late breakfast. The same corner booth that afforded me with a view of my door was available. I slid in and looked over the breakfast crowd. There were a few new faces. Nobody stood out as a threat.

My room was dead center on the second floor of the U-shaped motel. The cleaning lady emerged from the room next to mine, her long black hair pulled back in a high pony tail. It lifted off her back as she leaned her head forward to check her phone before rapping on my door. After a few moments, she pushed the door open, then turned and flicked her cigarette over the railing before entering the room. Courteous. The door stood open, darkened like an entrance to a bear cave.

The waitress set a plate filled with eggs and bacon down in front of me, then returned a few seconds later with a carafe of coffee. It was the same meal I'd had for lunch and dinner the day before, minus the carafe. Guess she was tired of running back and forth for coffee. She wasn't kidding when she said I drank it like water. I coated the meal with an extra layer of salt and pepper and dug in. It was the kind of dish that fueled me with energy all day. The American Heart Association didn't like it, but I was on a shorter timeline than most. Might as well enjoy myself.

I wrapped up my meal and remained seated while waiting for the cleaning lady to finish with my room. Once she left, I paid the bill and headed back across the street, stopping in the office to extend my stay another day. The cleaning lady was standing near the top of the stairs, smoking another cigarette. She smiled and spoke to me in Spanish, asking something about my day. I nodded, said nothing. I scanned the walkway past my room, then glanced down at the parking lot. A new car, a four-door Mercury sedan, had arrived while I was in the office. Two shaded figures occupied the front seats. Couldn't make out whether they were male or female, but they were both large. Their arms practically rubbed together. Exhaust billowed in the cold air. Maybe they were picking somebody up.

Or perhaps they'd acted on a tip and were waiting for me.

I put my head down and made my way to the room. Once inside, I parted the curtains an inch with my thumb and forefinger and checked the parking lot again. My view was now cut in half. The car was there, but I couldn't see the windshield. They'd cut the engine. Extending their stay?

The .45 on my hip only provided so much comfort. Five rounds and a pretty strong kick meant it wasn't the most reliable weapon if I was facing a two-on-one situation. I grabbed the VP70 and set it to single-shot. For a moment, I wondered if I should have brought a third sidearm.

Was it possible my location was compromised? The only ways I could've been tracked to the motel was if my ID had been compromised, or if they'd managed to put a tracker on my car while Ginger was playing tough guy. Lexi had fished the alias out of me, and I had no doubt she'd run the name through the databases. But Jonah Lamb was squeaky clean. No one knew about him outside of a small circle. And they weren't the type of people who'd show up in Illinois in a Mercury to stake out a motel room.

There was a chance, as slim as it was, that someone at the diner recognized me. No one looked familiar, and I didn't see that spark of recognition in anyone's eye when they glanced in my direction. No one got up and abruptly or frantically left the place. If they *knew* me that's how they would have reacted.

"Get a grip, Jack," I muttered. "Just a couple guys swinging through on their way to Kalamazoo, Michigan, or some damn place."

I went to the bathroom, set the VP70 on the vanity, and filled my cupped palms with cold water. I splashed it on my face. My heart rate decreased. My abs, chest and shoulders loosened. I studied my soaked reflection. Water dripped off my face.

How had I gotten here?

It was one of those existential thoughts that comes out of nowhere, often at the wrong time, or when you wake up at two in the morning when it's easy to slip back into the dreamland and forget. That wasn't happening now though. The question seemed to be burning itself into my consciousness. I didn't want to dwell on it. Couldn't afford to, not with a job in progress. This was not the time to question my life and career choices.

A sharp rap at the door shifted my focus. I wiped off my face, grabbed the HK, and slid through the room toward the window. I didn't peel back the curtains. That'd be too obvious. Instead, I placed my ear against the wall and waited. A dozen seconds passed. I heard nothing. The light filtering in through the door was broken into three sections, shadows indicating someone stood on the walkway.

Three hard knocks echoed through the wall. I pulled my head away from the wall and aimed the pistol at the door.

"Sir, are you in there?"

CHAPTER 9

"SIR, PLEASE, I SAW YOU GO IN." SHE PAUSED A BEAT. "I LEFT MY cigarettes in there."

I glanced through the peephole and saw the cleaning lady. She fished through her apron and produced a key. I tucked the pistol in my waistband and covered it with my t-shirt.

"Hang on a sec," I said, looking back to see if I could spot her smokes. They weren't in sight, so I unlatched the door and opened it.

"I'm sorry." She held her gaze firm as she walked past. Her eyes were wide, wet, like she had been crying.

I stuck my head out the open doorway and checked in both directions. Empty. Letting the door fall shut, I turned and watched her head into the bathroom. "You OK?"

She shook her head. "It's just cigarettes. I think I left them in the bathroom."

"I was just in—"

The sound of a pump shotgun will stop anyone in their tracks, even if they've only ever heard the exaggerated stock clip they use in the movies. A chill raced down my spine. Two shadows stretched across the floor. This wasn't a robbery or chance encounter. Who the hell was I dealing with? First thought was that Thanos's goons had found me. But how? Random coincidence? Someone drove by the motel and spotted my rental? No chance.

The cleaning lady peeked out from the bathroom. Her lips trembled. Tears streamed down her cheeks. The men had forced her at gunpoint to get in the room, but were smart enough to stay out of sight. They could've simply taken her keys, but then I'd hear them coming and have time to get ready. They'd played it well. And now the woman feared for her life. She'd seen the men, seen them commit a crime. How much of one was still to be determined.

"Don't move, asshole, except to get your wallet outta your pants." His neutral accent gave me no inclination as to where he was from, only that he hadn't grown up in Chicago. Couple of thieves passing through, pegged the motel, and more importantly, me as an easy mark? I didn't buy it.

The cleaning lady averted her eyes and started crying. One of them had probably turned a weapon in her direction. She needed to get in the tub and lay down, hope they'd forget about her. But I couldn't tell her that. Poor thing was about to wind up a statistic.

I pulled my wallet out, careful not to reveal my concealed Springfield. There was nothing I could do about the VP70 on my hip. If these guys had any training at all they'd have already spotted it.

"Good boy," the guy said. "Now toss it back on over here."

I needed to make a move, but they weren't giving me much to work with.

"Nothing worth taking in there," I said.

"Who said we're taking?" the guy said waving his pistol. "Now toss it, or I'll shoot you."

"If you were gonna shoot me, I'd already be full of holes." I lowered my arm, pulling the wallet tight to my body. "So, if you want this, you'd better come and get it."

"Please, mister!" the cleaning lady shouted. "Do what they say. I don't wanna die."

Every muscle in my body clamped down over the next few seconds. I braced for impact, whether a bullet or a fist. One of the shadows on the floor shortened as the guy approached from behind me. His steps were slow and deliberate. He racked his handgun's slide. I turned my head slightly to the right to get a read on how far away he was. He was smart enough to keep an arm's length between us. Had he come too close, or touched the weapon to my head like in the movies, it would have made it easy for me to gain control of his weapon, and use him as a meat shield against his partner.

"We just wanna know who you are and what you're doing here," he said. "Now, we can do this in here, or we can bring you someplace special."

Either way the outcome remained the same. They'd kill me. Forcing them to take me with them would at least provide an opportunity for me to catch them slipping up.

"So, what's it gonna be?" he said.

Before I could answer, his partner exclaimed.

"Shit!"

"What?" the guy behind me said.

"Cops," the other guy said.

The cleaning lady glanced at the door, blue strobes bounced off the ceiling and over her face. I could see her debating whether to make a run for it. She shifted her gaze in my direction for a moment. I nodded at her, encouraging her to do it. Her lips drew tight. She burst out of the bathroom and started toward the door with an apparent plan to bull rush the guy with the shotgun.

This was my chance. They hadn't taken my VP70. I dropped my wallet on the floor and turned right while pulling the pistol from my waistband. The man behind me stood about three feet away. I lunged in his direction, my arm whipping toward him, my hand wrapped around the pistol's barrel. I drove the butt into his larynx.

The guy's head snapped back as he dropped his piece and raised his hands to guard his throat a second too late. A guttural, choking scream escaped his gaping mouth. He wrapped his hands around his neck, tearing at his shirt collar as though that would enable him to breathe again.

I drew the .45 from behind my back and aimed it at the guy with the shotgun. He swung his weapon like a baseball bat, nailing the cleaning lady in the gut. Her torso bent forward as her rear flung back. She looked like a parachute suspended in the air for a moment before crashing to the ground. Her body writhed on the floor. Her face reddened. In a few moments, she'd regain the ability to breath. But I knew at that second she thought she was dying.

The guy swung the muzzle of his weapon toward me, chambering a fresh round along the way. Before he could take aim, I lunged across the room and placed myself between him and the weapon, wrapping my left arm around it to wrestle away control. I slammed the pistol open-handed against his cheek three times. He dropped to a knee. I wrestled the shotgun free from his weakened grasp, drove the buttstock into his nose. I searched his pockets, grabbed his cell phone, then dragged him into the bathroom, leaving behind a trail of blood.

The man with the crushed larynx had stopped fighting. His face blue, he laid almost motionless on the ground, drawing in short breaths like a guppy out of water. His eyes bugged from his head, bloodshot, staring up at the ceiling. I searched his pockets and came up with two extra magazines for his pistol and a money clip containing cash only. I pocketed the cash, the rounds, and took his pistol. Neither guy had an ID on them. It was intentional in case I turned out to be who they feared I was.

The cleaning lady looked as though she were about to explode. I went over and placed my hand on her diaphragm.

"Slow down," I said. "You have to relax to let the air back in."

Her eyes were big and wide, and fixated on mine. It took a moment for her to calm down. After she did, she choked on the air rushing into her lungs. I helped her get to a seated position against the wall near the door.

"Who are they?" I said.

"I don't know, Mister." Her voice was gravely. She rubbed her neck. "They approached me on the walkway and made me go to your room."

"My room specifically?"

She cradled her stomach with both arms. "Yes. Your room. They showed me a picture of you and everything."

"A picture?" I'd searched both men and hadn't found a picture. Perhaps they'd disposed of it outside.

The sirens drew close enough that the sound echoed in the room. The only way out was through the rear window, and that was a thirty foot drop to a steep slope at least three times as long. Chances of coming away uninjured were slim. I could take my chances with the cops. My alias was clean. If they didn't let me go, I had other ways of getting released from custody.

I snapped a photo of each guy on my phone. As quickly as the sirens reached their peak, they started to fade. A moment later, an ambulance's siren overtook the police. I pulled back the curtains and saw a line of emergency vehicles streaming down the road past the motel.

"Get a load of that," I muttered. Bastards had saved my life. I offered my hand to the cleaning lady. "You OK?"

"Yes, thank you." She rose to her feet and shuffled toward the door.

I dismantled the shotgun, pocketed the rounds and tossed it over the railing. "Follow me out of the room, wait until I'm clear of the parking lot, then call the cops. Tell them nothing about me, all right? Nothing about my stay, and definitely don't give them a description of me. Got it?"

She nodded.

I exited the room. There were five people standing there, looking at me. Their mouths hung open at the sight of my blood-covered shirt. Fortunately, I had a change of clothes in the trunk. I turned toward the stairs and left the room.

"Mister, wait!"

CHAPTER 10

I HURRIED BACK TO THE THRESHOLD, ADRENALINE PUMPING through my veins. I expected to see that one of the men had snowed me, and was attacking the cleaning lady. When I reached the room I saw the cleaning lady standing in front of the bed, holding my wallet.

"You forgot this."

I couldn't believe I'd been so careless. The cops would've found it and the hunt would have been on. I was eight hundred miles from home, with few contacts to help me out here. I couldn't even rely on the Old Man for assistance. Chicago wasn't his territory. Every associate he had outside his organization was as much an enemy as a friend. There was always Frank Skinner of the SIS, but we'd been on rocky footing for some time now. I'd turned down every job he'd offered the past two years. He knew I would every time he reached out to me. I had no idea why he kept offering.

The cleaning lady pulled out her cell phone and punched 9-1-1. Her finger hovered over send. She gestured with her head toward the small crowd watching us. "You should leave now. There are witnesses."

I took a quick look at the crowd of onlookers who'd gathered. A prostitute, a middle-aged alcoholic, and three junkies. The police wouldn't put much stock into what they said. And since the motel took cash, I checked in under the most basic of names, John Smith. The cleaning lady didn't know who I was either. The wallet was clenched shut and latched.

"Make sure you describe me as older, and balding."

"And not white," she said, tearing up. "Got it. Thank you for saving me. I was so scared I wouldn't get home to my baby."

I ran down the stairs to the car. By the time I reached it the cleaning lady had her cell phone pressed to the side of her head. It wouldn't be long before a few of those patrol cars that had raced past a few minutes prior would be rerouted back to the motel.

The situation was bad. Leaving in a rush meant I left without erasing evidence of my stay. My prints were all over the room. Not too much of a problem given that there were at least twenty other sets in there. Cleanliness wasn't exactly a standard of the place. But if anyone matched my face with a set of prints, it would kick off a chain of events that started and ended in the Pentagon, albeit different sections. These days I had far more enemies in the building than people willing to stick their neck out to help me. Getting any of them involved wasn't a situation I wanted to deal with.

I headed away from the motel. The incident had sped up my timeline in Chicago. The job had to be finished soon. While I couldn't guarantee that the men I encountered at the motel were Thanos's guys, I had to consider the possibility. Dumb luck had led them to me. Carelessness on my part. I should've ditched the rental and grabbed a new one. Doesn't matter how large or small an area. Give yourself a chance to get caught, and you'll be caught. Perhaps they weren't Thanos's men. Maybe Charles or the Old Man had me followed and decided to take me out. In that case, was the job a ploy to get me in position? I saw no reason for the Old Man to concoct such an elaborate scheme to erase me. He could lock me up in his dungeon and let time run its course if he wanted. Charles, however, well, there was no love lost between us.

I rolled down the windows, let the frigid air wash over my body. Sweat froze and dried in place. My scalp felt like ice. I'd only made it a half-mile and already paranoia had me in its grips. That led to a slippery slope of self-doubt with every move I'd make if I didn't get things under control.

I hopped on the highway for a few miles, then exited and found a quiet residential neighborhood. Winding through the streets of two-story homes with square yards, I started to feel safe. I found a cul-de-sac, drove around the circle and stopped next to the curb between two homes with empty driveways. That didn't mean no one was home. This seemed like the kind of place where folks took care of their cars, parked them in the garage.

My heart had slowed to a decent rate, the sweating had stopped, and I breathed normally again. I had to forget about what had happened at the motel, at least for now. Every thought and every ounce of energy had to be directed toward taking out Thanos. The office was obviously off limits, too great a security presence there. His house was the next stop.

I needed a new car. Driving the one they'd seen at the office building was out of the question. And I had to wonder if it was being tracked right at that moment through telematics and the close-caption TV network throughout Chicagoland. Chances were Thanos's security presence extended to his residence, whether the same men from the city or a new group.

I found a rental car store, drove a few blocks past and ditched the car. They didn't have much for selection. I ended up downsizing to a compact car, a black Honda Civic LX. It was roomier than I had anticipated, and the heat worked immediately, but I wouldn't be using it as a weapon in a car chase. The thing was, it was new and I hadn't been seen in it. So long as my Jonah Lamb identity hadn't been compromised, I was a ghost once again. If I was tailed, or someone showed up unexpectedly, then I knew I'd have a problem to deal with back in D.C. or New York. Maybe both.

I decided the best plan of attack was to watch the house tonight. See how large of a security presence there was, and note any patterns in Thanos's evening routine. I stopped off to grab a bite to eat and plan my route. With my route to Thanos's house mapped, I set out on a forty-five minute drive. It was getting late in the day. The sun alternated between hovering behind the tree line and shining directly in front of the Civic. The intense glare reduced visibility to a few feet. The sun finally set below the horizon, and with every passing second, darkness pervaded.

CHAPTER 11

THANOS LIVED IN A FIVE-THOUSAND-SQUARE-FOOT HOME ON A private acre-and-a-half in the suburb of Naperville. The sprawling neighborhood was composed of custom houses on similar lots. No two homes I passed were the same.

I ditched the Honda at the end of a quiet street a half-mile away and jogged the rest of the way, keeping my head down. A few cars drove by, but no one paid any attention to me. Nothing unusual about a guy in his mid-thirties out for a jog.

The dimly-lit street offered a few places to hide for a while. Thanos's side was lined with a thin layer of pine trees, but in the house next to his, a family ate dinner in front of a large bay window that looked out on their front yard. So I chose a house across the street. Its empty driveway and darkened windows indicated no one was home, though with a three-car garage, I didn't expect the owners to keep their Mercedes or BMW exposed to the harsh Chicago winter.

The front of the house had a perimeter of waist-high shrubs, but there wasn't a single spot that offered me a view of anything other than the entrance to Thanos's driveway.

The sun had been down for a few hours now, temperatures had plummeted. I'd stopped on the way over and purchased thermals, gloves, a hat and handwarmers, figuring the gear provided a three- to four-hour window to stakeout the residence. But all of it did no good if I couldn't see anything.

It was time to test how secure Thanos's property was.

I backtracked a few houses, crossed the street, entered pine forest on a neighbor's property. There I waited for a few minutes for any signs of activity. After a while, nothing happened, so I moved to the property line. A long row of high hedges separated the two lots. The driveway stood twenty feet away. The front door another thirty or so past that. I had a decent view of the entryway and front yard. This was where I'd settle in. I dropped to the ground and did my best to blend into my surroundings by piling up leaves in front of me.

The first hour passed with minimal action. Motion sensors mounted to the corners of the house lit up a couple of times, revealing a masked furball scavenging for a meal. Random cars passed by, each time a different vehicle. Likely driven by a stuffed suit on the way home from a twelve- to fourteen-hour day of power-brokering in a high-rise in the city.

What a life.

A strong gust of wind came out of nowhere, blowing leaves and debris in my face and infiltrating every single chink in my thermal armor. For a second I considered that the suits in the high-rises might've had the right idea. Who would last longer in the other's position? I doubted many could stay alive for a week, let alone a day, in my line of work. But how long could I stand being a CEO or a lawyer or any other white collar job before I shoved my Beretta down someone's throat because their incompetence was screwing what I wanted done.

It'd been a long time since someone had given me an ass chewing. I couldn't imagine getting one from some neck-tie wearing middle manager.

Headlights swept over my position, lingering far too long. I buried my head in my arms for a moment. A black Escalade swung wide in front of Thanos's house, pulled into the driveway. The windows were tinted so dark I couldn't tell how many people were in the vehicle. It slowed to a stop ten feet from the garage and idled there with the headlights reflecting off the garage door windows. Why were they waiting there? Finishing up a phone call? Waiting on someone to come outside?

What I wouldn't give for a mobile bug to pick up on their cell phones at that moment. I pulled out a pen and notebook and took note of the license plate number. There were a few contacts I could reach out to who could get me registration information on the vehicle if I chose to go that route. I still wasn't keen on bringing anyone from the outside in on this job. I had too little information on Thanos.

The front door opened and Ginger from the office building stepped out wearing a brown leather bomber. He pulled a wool cap over his head, scanned the area, turned back toward the door while motioning for someone to join him. A moment later Thanos appeared wearing a long black wool jacket, black gloves, no hat. They slid into the back seat of the Escalade on the driver's side. The SUV continued to idle after the headlights cut off.

The front passenger door opened. A man hopped out, slammed the door shut, ran around the front of the vehicle. I watched as he went inside the house. A few seconds later, the front windows darkened, the guy remained inside. The Escalade's reverse lights illuminated a swath of driveway in white. The SUV backed out onto the street, whipping the tail end away from me. For a few moments, the ground around me lit up like downtown Chicago. Then it all went black.

Dammit.

I should've parked the Civic closer, then I could tail them. That would've been a bad idea. That car would've stuck out like a streaker in the ritzy neighborhood.

With Thanos and his main bodyguard gone, I decided to get a closer look at the house despite not knowing how many people were inside. I elected to cut through the hedges, mindful of the motion sensors. Halfway down the side of the house was a six-foot privacy fence. Was it to keep people out, or keep something in? I rapped on the gate a couple times and waited. The lack of response didn't leave me feeling good that there wasn't a dog back there. A well-trained canine wouldn't make a sound. He'd wait for the intruder to show himself, then pounce with the element of surprise at its back.

Was Thanos the kind of man to have such a dog? Considering he had dealings with the Old Man and a ton of security, I had to assume so. I straddled the fence long enough to get a view of the yard. I could see everything except for immediately behind the house. I hopped down and peered in through a side window. The main level was open with very few walls, allowing me to see clear to the other side of the house. If I planned the hit right, I'd be able to take out every guy on the floor before they knew what had happened.

At the moment, only one person was visible inside. The guy who'd exited the Escalade after Thanos and Ginger had got in. There was no wife or children present, and no sign they even existed. The walls were bare except for a couple paintings. No family pictures. No toys on the floor. Just a couple of white leather chairs that looked expensive. The carpet was also white. Definitely not a family house. I spotted a pair of chrome bowls on the kitchen floor. That presented a problem. I needed a plan to deal with the dog.

I moved down the fence to the rear corner where I climbed up again and peered over. A German Shepherd sat on the back deck, looking right at me.

His ears were perked. I whistled to him. He cocked his head. I banged on the fence. He rose up, rear legs bent, ready to lunge.

The hit couldn't take place tonight if Thanos returned, not without killing the dog. And that wasn't happening. Wasn't the pooch's fault he'd been adopted by an asshole who knew a bunch of other assholes and that led to the biggest asshole of all showing up at his door with a couple pistols and a rifle.

But I wasn't asshole enough to kill a dog.

I set off for the Civic with a plan half-formulated in my head.

CHAPTER 12

I ARRIVED IN THANOS'S NEIGHBORHOOD JUST AFTER NINE THE next morning, figuring everyone would be gone by then. At most there'd be one guard inside who could be dealt with easily. For the dog, I picked up a box of dog treats and prayed they'd do the trick. If they didn't I had a bottle of sleeping pills. Not ideal, but he'd be fine after suffering through a bit of a hangover.

I parked one street over, behind the house, in front of a large stretch of empty land. Through the trees I could see Thanos's rear fence. I secured the VP70 and Springfield .45 in their holsters. The .308 was in a bag strapped to my back. I pulled a ball cap down over my forehead and got out of the car carrying a bag of tools which I dropped after I'd cleared the tree line.

At the back gate I hopped up, my eyes just above level with the fence, and scanned the yard. There was no sign of the dog. I whistled. Still nothing. I climbed the rest of the way over and dropped to a crouch in Thanos's back yard. I pulled the VP70 out and aimed it toward the house. The French doors in front of the deck didn't whip open. No one moved behind the thin reflections in the windows of the clouds and trees.

I rose and sprinted toward the back deck. I was hesitant to be out in the open in broad daylight. Not my best idea ever, but I was left with little choice without a team to assist. If I had one, we'd go about this differently. We could take on the security detail, kidnap Thanos, and deal with him in a remote location. Solo, there was no chance of that happening. I had to hit hard and fast, taking out everyone in my path to Thanos, at great risk of losing the man.

I'd barely made it to the deck when I heard it. That deep growl of a dog warning me. The one that told me I had five seconds until he was gonna tear me apart. I froze in place, reached into my pocket, pulled out a treat. The German Shepherd stood off to the side. He took two steps toward me, hackles up, baring his teeth. I snapped the treat in two, tossed one half at him. He whipped his head to the side and snagged it out of the air. I tossed another, to the other side, and watched him lurch and catch it. Probably could have won another state championship if I had a receiver like that in school.

"Good boy," I said, low and soft. I dropped to a knee, facing him. "Want another?"

He made a slight whimper, cocked his head.

I lowered my pistol to the side as I reached for another biscuit, leaving myself completely defenseless for a moment. Pulling my hand from my pocket, I said, "C'mere, buddy. C'mon," and held the treat out in front of me.

He bared his teeth at me for a second. His ears dropped back flat against his head. A dog his size, I had no doubt he could leap from that spot and land close enough to sink his teeth into my neck. I braced for the impact. He took another few steps forward. I tossed the treat a foot above his head and immediately grabbed another. The dog had no trouble snagging it out of the air.

Again I held the biscuit out. "You're gonna have to come take this one from me, pal. Not gonna throw it." The feeling that someone was watching from the French doors nagged at me, but I couldn't take my eyes off the dog. It'd smash any trust I'd gained, and he'd likely attack without warning.

He took a few more steps, unsure of me. He whimpered, growled, cocked his head, ears laid back and then shot forward. I was in, or I was dead. His face was less than two feet from mine now. He craned his head forward, sniffed the treat. He was massive at this distance.

"Go ahead, buddy. Take it."

He opened his mouth, gripped it with his teeth and pulled it out of my hand. I reached in my pocket for another. There was nothing between this trained watchdog and me. He remained still as I pulled another one out.

"Sit."

He didn't move.

I pulled the treat back a bit. "Sit, buddy."

He stomped his rear feet a couple times and lowered his butt to the ground.

"Good boy." I inched closer toward him, motioning my hand toward the ground. "Down."

He alternated his paws outward until his chest touched the ground. I continued moving closer, shifting the treat around the side of his body.

"Over."

He complied. I palmed the treat and placed my hand in front of his mouth. He took it without issue. I made the bold move of scratching his stomach. It seemed I had won him over, so I hopped to my feet.

He did the same, but this time he looked up to me, waiting for my next command.

I reached into my pocket again and had him follow me to the deck. There I had him sit and stay while I checked the back windows. If there was a single bad vantage point for the house, it was here. The kitchen was huge, with a long, high island that spanned a good twenty feet. Though I could see the entire level, I only saw the top half of it. Waist down to the floor was blocked.

The breeze blew in from the side. It felt thirty degrees warmer than when I got out of the Civic. I took a moment and breathed in the air. I assembled the .308, loaded it, and set it next to the back door. The dog paced behind me. I pulled the cover off the phone NID, cut the alarm, popped the lock on the French doors, and pushed them open. A heatwave greeted me. It was like stepping into a cafe, all I could smell was sugar and coffee.

On the counter a half-full carafe waited, steam slipping through the top. The orange light on the coffee-maker indicated the warmer was still on. I was about to grab a cup when the front door burst open.

CHAPTER 13

I SWUNG THE .308 TOWARD THE FRONT DOOR AND AIMED AT THE empty space. The cold breeze blew past me. It struck me again how little I knew about Thanos. What if it was his wife or kid, if he had one?

"Thanos, are you in there?"

The woman's voice was familiar, but I couldn't place it. Who was she? Did she work for him? She called him by his last name, not something an employee would do.

I took a step back and reached around for the French door's handle. Before I managed to open it, the woman rushed through the front opening, her pistol drawn. She scanned the room, left to right and settled on me.

"Lamb? The hell are you doing here?"

Surprised at the sight of Shane's cousin Lexi, I lowered the rifle a couple inches, took my finger off the trigger. "Visiting an old friend?"

Perhaps as a courtesy, she shifted her sidearm's barrel away from me. "I knew there was something about you I didn't like."

"Look, I can explain this." Not entirely, I thought. "First you gotta tell me what you're doing here."

"I don't have to tell you a goddamn thing. Got that?" She refocused her aim on me. "So hurry up and spill before I shoot you, then arrest you."

I set the rifle on the island and lifted my arms so I wouldn't appear threatening to her. She was processing the scene, and as far as she knew, I either worked for or was there to meet Thanos. I hoped she wasn't connecting the dots for my true reason there based on some intel she had been fed. This job reeked of a setup, and this would be the perfect way to take me down.

Avoiding prosecution would be nearly impossible. But I hadn't communicated with the Old Man or Charles since the day of the meeting in New York. Once the job had been accepted, they had no bearing or input on how I went about terminating Thanos, and I wasn't required to keep them in the loop. Hell, if they asked as much, I'd refuse the work. I demanded complete and total autonomy. And I got it.

"I want you to call this number." I waited for her to pull out her cell phone. She kept her pistol aimed at me as she slipped her hand into her coat pocket. She punched the number in as I told it to her. "A man is gonna answer. You're gonna give him this code: alpha-gamma-romeo-eight-five-five-yankee-alpha."

She shook her head. "What?"

I repeated the code. "Do it, OK? You'll find out who I am and maybe figure out what I'm doing here."

She pushed send and waited with the phone to her ear. I heard the muffled sound of a man's voice. She repeated the code, slowly and deliberately. A long pause ensued. Her gaze remained fixed on me during the uncomfortable silence. Then she blinked a few times, glanced right, lowered her pistol. A few seconds later she ended the call and tucked her phone in her pocket.

"Passcode?" she said.

I nodded, cleared my throat. "Noble Man."

"SIS?"

I nodded, said nothing.

"That doesn't exist, right? I'd heard rumors, inquired about them, but their existence was always shot down. Why would the country have an intelligence group so secretive that even the FBI wouldn't know about it? I mean, that's what they always said to me."

"Not really an intelligence agency," I said.

Her cheeks reddened and she clenched her fists. "Right, a group of commandos looking to shoot first, ask questions never, and fuck up every other agency's ops."

I held up my hands. "Not quite like that."

"Yeah, then what is it like?" She took a few steps toward me, glancing around the kitchen. "Where's Thanos?"

"What's your business with him?"

"Me? Hell with that, Lamb. What are you doing here?"

"Scouting. Thanos's activities raised a few flags in D.C. I was asked to come check him out. Waited around here until everyone was gone."

"Everyone isn't supposed to be gone. He's supposed to be here, meeting with me." She turned toward the door, stopped, looked back at me. "Wait a minute. Did you know I would be here, that he would be here? You're not here to gather information, are you? You're here to terminate him."

"Hold on now." I placed my left hand on the counter near the rifle's stock. "I'm not here to terminate anybody. I don't know much about this guy, only that he's been mixed up with some bad people. Maybe that's a mistake, maybe he's a piece of shit. Not my call what happens to him in the end. But I'm not here to kill anyone."

"He is a piece of shit." She relaxed a moment. "And he's my informant. The fact that he's not here, and you are, concerns me. Makes me think that someone found out that he's been working with me."

The ceiling above us creaked. Could be the house settling, but I doubted it.

"Did you go upstairs?" she asked.

I shook my head. "Only got in here a moment before you broke the door down."

"Make yourself useful." She darted toward the staircase. "Cover me."

I followed her to the staircase, pistol drawn. We climbed up, stopped at the second-floor landing. She signaled for me to wait for her lead. She rounded the corner, cleared the hall. I moved around her and went to the first door. We went room by sterile room. Thanos clearly was not married and had no kids. The place was as boring as a coroner's office when there were no stiffs present.

"You good?" she asked.

"Yeah, the place is empty."

"We oughta check the basement."

We descended the stairs, moved through the kitchen looking for the basement entrance.

"I think this is—"

A loud eruption disoriented me. The window exploded into a thousand shards of glass. The wall next to my head burst into a white cloud hovering in front of a gaping hole.

I dove toward Lexi, tackled her to the ground.

Another shotgun blast tore through the back door, shredding the wood and glass, and slammed into the ceiling. Plaster rained down. Automatic fire followed, hundreds of rounds in a matter of seconds laying waste to everything over waist high.

"Friends of yours?" Lexi scrambled to her feet, crouched, and slid out of harm's way.

I followed her. "Was gonna ask you the same thing."

She held my gaze for a moment, shook her head. "How are we gonna get outta here?"

"Shoot our way through the backyard. Got a car parked behind the house."

She racked her pistol's slide. I did the same to the VP70 and the pistol I'd taken from the intruder at the motel.

The assault subsided. They were reloading. I moved to the kitchen sink. The jagged hole where a window once existed overlooked the backyard. I rifled through a nearby cabinet, found a shiny metal pan that looked as though it had never been used. I held it in front of the window and it acted as a mirror, providing a view of the outside. A man dressed in head-to-toe black darted across the brown grass.

I leapt up, aimed, fired. The round tore through the guy's thigh. He dropped to the ground, losing control of his automatic. I surveyed the yard for his partner, but could not locate him or any others. Maybe they were behind the fence, waiting for us now that I'd taken out the first guy.

"Jack, get down!"

I dropped at the same time a window on the side of the house exploded. The round nailed the refrigerator, tearing through it and ripping the door from its top hinge.

"I'm gonna start shooting," I said. "You run for the back door."

I rose, aimed both pistols at the side of the house where they had shot from and opened fire, sending a round every two seconds. The guy dropped out of sight. Lexi dashed to the door, bent at the waist, kept low. She had her firearm at the ready. I followed her with one pistol aimed at the front door, the other at the expansive bank of windows on the side of the house.

Lexi went out first. I waited at the edge of the deck while she sprinted across the yard, past the dog who looked like he'd been wounded. The spot offered the best vantage point. While I looked over it, my mind started racing in an attempt to put together the pieces of why this was happening. It was too soon to process it all. That would come later. We had to get away first.

Lexi signaled from the opposite end of the yard that she had me covered. I dashed a third of the way, stopped and dropped to a knee next to the man I'd shot. His face was pale. The glimmer in his eyes faded. Blood sprayed weakly from his severed femoral artery. He babbled something incoherent. I checked his pockets for identification or anything that might reveal who he was. There was nothing, and there wasn't much time to waste. On the other side of the house was the other attacker. Maybe more.

I scooped up the automatic and ran to the fence. Once there, I tossed the firearm over and didn't bother stopping. I jumped, planted one foot against the fence, grabbed the top with both hands, and swung myself over.

Lexi joined me through the gate a second later. "Please tell me you blew your ACL with that stupid move."

I squatted half-way. "Think I'm good. There's still time on the way to the car though."

"Time to get serious." She looked around. We were in pretty deep woods here, like much of the property surrounding Thanos's residence. "Anyone could be out here."

"Wasn't anybody here twenty minutes ago when I came through."

"A lot can happen in twenty minutes."

"Ain't that the truth."

I started through the woods, but stopped in my tracks when the dog barked. I couldn't leave him behind. I hopped the fence and saw him limping toward me.

"What are you doing?" She looked at me like I was crazy.

"Cover me." I dropped into the yard and knelt next to the dog. He'd been injured, a pretty nasty cut on his leg and back. I hoisted him up over my shoulder. The dog growled, then whimpered, seemingly letting go and letting me carry him. "Gotta trust me, buddy."

We worked silently through the woods as a team. It helped that some of our training was universal, and some was common sense. We reached the edge of the woods, a mere fifty feet from the Civic and our getaway.

"There it is," I said.

"And there they are," she said.

I followed her outstretched finger and saw the police car at the end of the street.

CHAPTER 14

WE POSITIONED OURSELVES BEHIND A WIDE OAK THICK ENOUGH that if Bear were with us, he'd be out of sight, too. I hoped the cops wouldn't get out. In fact, it seemed too soon for them to have even arrived. We seemed far enough away from the city that the sound of a shotgun wouldn't raise too much concern. An automatic, on the other hand, wouldn't be an everyday occurrence. With the neighbors spaced a good distance from each other, and it being nine-thirty in the morning, the time between a 9-1-1 call being placed and the police arriving should've been longer.

"This street doesn't connect to Thanos's neighborhood," I said. "That's why I chose it."

She nodded. "I know, which makes it more confusing that we're seeing this patrol car, but not hearing any sirens yet."

"Regular patrol?"

She peeked around the side of the oak, shook her head when she returned. "They're stopped in front of your car. One guy's on the radio, the other's reading him the VIN."

"All right, all right." I ran my hands through my hair. "Just go up to them, tell them you're FBI and it's your vehicle."

Lexi ignored me. "I'm parked about a quarter mile to the north from here. We can backtrack a bit, then head through the woods. We can get to it with minimal time in the open."

I wasn't keen on heading back toward the men who were trying to punch holes in us with their firearms. "Why don't you go tell them who you are?"

"After what just happened? You kidding me?" She leaned back against the tree. "We'll be caught up in paperwork the rest of the week. I don't have time for that. I gotta find Thanos."

"You and me both."

She eyed me after I made the statement. I could see the next question forming on her lips.

The sirens cut through the air like a hawk moments before it descended to snatch his prey. We both stiffened and readied our firearms. I eased around the side of the tree and saw the patrol car tearing down the street. The call had come in, and they were closest to the scene. I had feared they heard the chaos and that's why they were present. They must've only recently arrived.

"Let's roll." Lexi dashed toward the Civic. By the time I cleared the woods, she was at the passenger door.

I freed the fob from my pocket and unlocked the doors. A few seconds later, I had the dog in the backseat, the car in drive, and was following in the tire tracks of the police cruiser.

"No, not that way," she said.

"One way in, one way out," I said.

"No, it's not. There's a dirt road that connects to another dirt road that dumps off on a back road."

I left the car idling for a moment. A chill raced up and down my spine. Usually happened when I was about to enter a world full of hate and pain.

"I know what you're thinking, but you gotta trust me, Lamb. There's gonna be ten patrol cars and a couple detectives here soon. They're gonna block the roads. Even if we had gone to my car, we might not have made it out of Thanos's neighborhood."

There was something about the desperation in her voice that left me feeling like I could trust her.

"All right," I said. "So help me, if you're lying…"

She placed her hand on my forearm. "It's legit."

I followed her directions and turned onto the first dirt road. A cloud of dust plumed behind us, distorting the reflection in the rearview. If someone was going to move in on us, this was their chance.

The road led into the woods where it intersected with a smaller path that was nothing more than two narrow tire tracks almost overgrown with waist-high grass and weeds. I laid off the accelerator and slithered along the path. No telling what might be hidden in the undergrowth. Even a stump could cause the Civic to become stuck, leaving us to huff it out on foot in twenty-degree weather.

The steady drone of a helicopter approached from the north. The sound grew louder by the second. We were nearing a clearing in the woods, so I stopped the car to prevent us from being caught out in the open. The chopper hovered nearby for what felt like an eternity. The windows fogged as anxiety increased our respirations.

"Might be a good time to call your SA," I said.

"Not gonna happen," she said.

Why was she keeping her Special Agent in charge out of the loop here? Had she screwed something up? Miscalculated her plan? Had a major oversight on some detail or another? Regardless, rules were rules for her and she risked further trouble by not following them.

"At least not until you tell me what's going on with you," she said.

"Look at that," I said aiming a finger toward the sky. "The helicopter's moved on. Time to go."

I shifted into gear and sped through the opening. The little car bounced and banged and groaned, but it made it to the cover of the woods on the other side of the field without stalling or getting stuck.

"It's just a couple hundred yards from here," she said.

I didn't have a plan to follow anymore. This wasn't supposed to go down this way. I thought I would get in, kill whoever was in my way, deal with Thanos and extract any and all information I could from him. Then he'd die. A long winding trip back to New York would follow.

But now? I wasn't sure what the next ten minutes held for me, let alone the next couple of weeks.

Lexi aimed her finger to the right once we reached the asphalt. "About two miles that way and we'll turn left. That'll take us to the highway."

I lingered at the edge while searching the sky for the helicopter. It was nowhere in sight. I eased us out of the cover of the trees and pulled onto the single-lane road. Ten minutes later we were heading northwest on I-90.

I kept my gaze fixed on the rear-view more than on what lay ahead of us. In a land dominated by oversized all-wheel drive SUVs, the Civic felt like a copperhead hiding in the weeds. The compact would be a pain to tail due to sightlines, but I knew it could be done by a competent agent. I didn't begin to feel comfortable that we had escaped undetected until we'd traveled five miles on the highway.

Lexi broke the monotonous drone of the road. "Who was that guy I spoke with earlier?"

I glanced over at her. Her eyebrows were raised, lips slightly parted. Seemed she was genuinely interested.

"Just a guy."

"Come on, Lamb."

I glanced at the side mirror.

"That's not your name, is it?"

I shook my head.

"Didn't think so." She tucked her left ankle under her right knee. "Not even when you introduced yourself at my cousin's house."

"What gave it away?"

"Nothing you did." She adjusted the radio volume down a notch. "It was my cousin. Ever so slightly, he had a quick nervous glance when you said your name."

"He used to be better than that, you know."

She nodded, said nothing.

"I'll have to give him crap over that."

"You should. Especially considering what he does out of that little house. If he's ever picked up, someone like me will read right through him." She changed the station until she found one playing '80s music. Was that Madonna singing or Cindi Lauper? I couldn't tell back then, and I sure as hell couldn't now. "Anyway, given his reaction and the fact I had never heard or saw the name Jonah Lamb in any documents related to him, I had someone look you up that night."

"Find much?"

"I guess everything you wanted me to find."

"Not you, specifically."

"Right, well, it read like a false cover."

I shot her a look, and she nodded.

"I used to be involved in the DCO," she said, referring to the FBI's Department of Covert Operations. "Both in the field and at a desk providing support and intel. I lived deep cover for three years straight. Worked my tail off to take down this crime syndicate, only to have my cover blown when I was a week away from pulling off the biggest bust Chicago had ever seen."

"That's quite a statement."

"Damn right it is. You've got no idea what was about to go down." She took a deep breath, looked out the window, sighed. "Anyway, with my cover blown I had to leave that kind of work right then and there. Spent some time inside in the same unit doing support and intel again, but couldn't take it. Felt like a caged animal. So I switched to another boring desk job. I only recently found my way back into the field kind of on a trial basis to see how things go. If I can't cut it, it's back to cubicleland I go."

That explained a few things. And it made me wonder how well she kept her boss up to date on Thanos. If they were nervous about her being out in the field, then anything that wasn't perfect could be cause for them to pull her again. Presumably she hadn't informed anyone of her meeting today, otherwise we'd be downtown, safe in a high-rise building, in a corner office overlooking the lake.

"What about you?" she asked.

I shrugged. "Not much to tell."

"C'mon, Lamb, or whoever you are." She shifted in her seat so her torso faced me. "Who are you anyway?"

"Can't really divulge that right now, not with your contacts."

"I'll figure it out eventually. How many SIS agents could there have been in the last decade?"

I threw her a slight bone. "Call me Jack."

"Is that your real name?"

I shrugged. "I'll reply to it better than Jonah Lamb. I hate that name."

"Fair enough, Jack." She reclined her seat and closed her eyes. "Let's head up to Madison for the night and find a place to stay. We can regroup in the morning."

CHAPTER 15

WE REACHED OUR DESTINATION AROUND THREE IN THE afternoon and checked into a motel on the outskirts of Madison, Wisconsin. It was a great college town with the right amount of small town feel and plenty of bars. It put us about an hour from Milwaukee, and two and some change from both Green Bay and Chicago. If needed, the train station offered a way to get us to any of the three cities, or it could take us west.

With the way things had gone, I had to anticipate that at some point the Civic would be hot. I parked it on a street a block away from the motel in a spot I could see from the window in our room. If the car was found, we'd have a slight head start.

I laid down on the bed, window shades parted so I could see the Honda. The drone of the running shower lulled me into a meditative state. Steam escaped through the cracked bathroom door. Through it I could see the fogged up mirror and light bar above it.

Lexi still hadn't filled me in on all the details of her relationship with Thanos. I only knew that she expected him to be there this morning. At the time, I had thought Thanos had left with Ginger voluntarily, but now I was reconsidering it. Perhaps he'd been forced to leave. Was it for his own protection? Had they figured out that the car rented to Jonah Lamb was not a good sign?

Or was Thanos in even more trouble than if I had gotten to him first?

I propped a second pillow behind my head and stared up at the ceiling for a few moments. Why were we here? It made little sense that we were hiding out in the middle of Wisconsin instead of taking this head on in Chicago. Lexi was keeping something from me. She was smart to give me some information while holding back.

The water valve squeaked and the water slowed to a steady drip before cutting off completely. The last bit gurgled down the drain. Lexi's bare arm slipped past the cracked door, then her back, and half of her ass. She leaned against the door and it latched shut. I sighed and turned my attention back to the view outside, managing to clear my head of all thoughts for a couple minutes.

A few minutes later Lexi emerged from the bathroom wrapped in a towel that came down to her mid-thigh.

I turned toward her and soaked in the view. "Comfy?"

"Clothes are drying." She gestured toward the bathroom with her chin.

"Can't stand a day in them?"

Shrugging, she stepped over the dog on her way toward the bed. "They were covered in drywall and dirt and stunk like gunfire and sweat."

"Some guys like that kind of thing."

"Not the kind I like." She peeled back the sheets on the other bed. "If the towel's a problem for you, I can take it off."

My eyebrows arched as I mulled it over for a second.

"Kidding, Jack." She threw back the sheets and laid down. Her knees were bent, pointing at the ceiling. A drip of water slid down her thigh, disappearing into the towel.

I waited a couple minutes to see if she'd make a move. She did, but not the kind I'd hoped for. Her eyes closed and she appeared to drift off to sleep.

"What're we doing here?" I said.

She opened her eyes and took in a quick breath. I'd startled her awake. "What?"

"What are we doing here in Wisconsin?"

"I was napping." She looked over at me. "I can only guess what you've been doing with a woman in a towel in the bed beside you."

"Don't flatter yourself."

"I don't need to."

"Right, still doesn't answer my question. Why are we hiding in a motel room in Madison?"

"You're free to leave." She pointed to the door. "I don't need your help any more than you need mine."

I didn't move. Fact was, we both did need each other's help. Maybe not for long. But until our stories were reconciled, neither of us was ready to let the other out of their sight.

"That's what I thought." She closed her eyes and eased her head back onto the pillow.

"Lexi, come on. Level with me."

She rolled toward me, propped up on her elbow, stared me down. "Tell you what. You let me have a quick nap, and I'll fill you in on everything that's happened up till this point over dinner."

"Only if it's steak."

I noticed the dog's ears perk up.

"Deal," she said.

I waited a few minutes after she fell asleep, then got up and left the room. The cold air hit me with a jolt that carried me far enough to find a cup of coffee. I headed down the road on foot away from the side street I'd parked the Civic on until I reached a small store. The Mom n' Pop gas station had everything I needed. Fresh coffee, couple of sticks of beef jerky, and a selection of pay as you go phones. A burner that required no personal information to purchase, and could be bought with cash.

I talked with the old guy behind the counter about the Packers and how with Rodgers at the helm they'd see a Super Bowl soon. He agreed and relayed his dismay over Favre's betrayal by shacking up with the Vikings.

"Can't really fault him, though," I said. "Guy's gotta make a living, right?"

The old guy shrugged. "Some ways of making a living aren't all that honest, son. Know what I mean?"

"Yeah, you could say I do."

I continued a bit further down the road until I found a drug store. I went inside and grabbed a bottle of peroxide and some bandages for the dog, canned dog food, and a second burner phone. Though no information was required to purchase one, I'd be recorded on the store's CCTV, and a smart investigator could match up the purchase time with the phone and get the number. Having two bought from separate places might come in handy later if I needed to reach out to another contact.

I finished my coffee, left the store, and made my way back to the hotel. In all I was gone a little over an hour. The cold was bothering me less and less with every passing minute. All the time outside had started the adaptation process.

Lexi sat on the bed cross-legged, paging through a magazine. She lifted her eyes and nodded at me. The dog sat on the floor at the end of the bed. His ears perked up when he saw me. I knelt down and scratched his neck, then went to work patching him up.

"Have a good walk?" she asked.

"Have a good nap?" I asked.

She shrugged. So did I.

"Hungry yet?" she asked.

"Had some coffee, so I'm all right for the moment."

She hesitated a second, eyes on me. "I am too, I guess. Thanks for asking."

"I didn't."

She sighed and went back to the magazine. "Gonna be a long couple days."

"Couple days? The hell you talking about. We're gonna—"

"We're gonna nothing," she said. "Look, Jack, I'll fill you in soon. I prom-ise, I will. I'm waiting on some intel that might lead us to Thanos."

That shiver ran down my spine again. "Who've you been talking to?"

"No one that's going to try and track us down." She flipped to a new page in her magazine. "Trust me."

"You keep telling me to trust you, but you haven't really given me a reason to."

"Oh yeah, Mr. Lamb. Or is it Mr. Jack? Jack Jack? Just Jack? Will you still be Jack tomorrow?"

"Cut it out. I don't need this."

"You know, you're lucky you're not in jail right now."

"I'm calling BS right there."

"Why?"

"You won't even check in with your SA, yet you're telling me you're doing a favor keeping me out of jail?"

She remained stone faced. I could have hurled anything at her at that moment and I don't think she'd have blinked. Her predicament couldn't be as sticky as mine. Here I was, on a job to kill a man, and now I'm mixed up with what could be a rogue FBI agent. Then again, she was with me. Maybe it'd be worse for her.

"Fact is," I said, "if I end up in jail, you'll be in the cell right next to mine. Not for the extra punishment it'll provide me, which, let's face it, I probably deserve. But because you're in as deep shit as I am. The sooner you and I start working together, the sooner we can get this problem resolved."

She glanced toward the window. The sun hovered low in the orange-tinged sky, casting her face in its glow.

"On second thought," she said, "I am hungry. Let's go get that steak."

CHAPTER 16

WE LEFT THE DOG A CAN OF FOOD AND SOME WATER AND HEADED out on foot to find a place to grab a steak and a beer. The wind gusted from the south, carrying with it a warm front. Must've been sixty degrees out. Dark clouds raced north, blocking out the last traces of the setting sun. Half the town was on the streets in shorts and t-shirts. The reprieve from the cold only came so often, everyone had to take advantage of it. The globe-like street lights illuminated the sidewalk leading into the heart of the town.

We strolled along for thirty minutes until we came to Erin's Snug Irish Pub. Smoke piled over the building and the aroma of searing meat slipped through the open front door.

"Look good?" Lexi asked.

"Smells even better." Any place that had a sign with a lady doing an Irish step dance with a cow had to be worth a try. I nodded my approval and pulled the door all the way open for Lexi. As she slipped past, I caught a hint of her scent. No perfume or fancy shampoos, just her. I felt myself drawn to her.

A college-aged girl with pig-tails sat us at a table near the front windows. Not my ideal spot, but we were in Madison, Wisconsin. I didn't plan on running into anyone I knew here. Of course, I never did. Yet folks showed up out of the woodwork in the most unusual places.

The air between us was tense as we waited for the waitress to return with our drinks. Did Lexi have as much to say as I did? Was her mind overrun with questions? Were the tables turning on her over how she felt about me, like I was for her?

Shake it off, man. This isn't the time.

Lexi opened her mouth to speak but was interrupted by the server, who carried our drinks on a tray. I realized I hadn't paid the woman any attention aside from her hairstyle. Couldn't have picked her out of a lineup if someone had a gun to my head. I glanced at her, and the rest of the people occupying the small tavern. Aside from one large guy with a shaved head and a full sleeve seated at the bar, there wasn't much to worry about inside Erin's.

I lifted the pint of Yazoo Sue and inhaled the leathery, smoked tobacco smell. The first taste did not disappoint. Lexi sipped her Espresso Martini.

"That the best drink to go with a steak?" I asked.

She shrugged. "Best of both worlds, friend. Caffeine and vodka. Can't beat it."

"Guess not." I slid my glass across the table. "Try this."

She studied the black liquid inside my glass. "Not really a fan of dark beers."

"Drink it."

She took a swig, biting against the initial bitter taste. Her face relaxed as the subtleties of the brew set in. She lifted her eyebrows and nodded. "Not bad, I guess."

We finished our first round of drinks. I ordered the same while Lexi switched to the house red wine. After the second round arrived, I settled into my seat. Lexi's stiff posture eased some, and she leaned forward over her crossed arms. The tension between us was lifting.

She tore a chunk of bread off the loaf set in the middle of the table and lathered it with real butter. Her lips glistened after taking a bite. She licked the buttery oil off, took a drink, and leaned back in her seat.

"Level with me, Jack."

"About what, Lexi?"

She smiled slightly for a second, then her lips thinned, her brows lowered, her gaze intensified. "What were you doing at the house this morning?"

I remained still, one hand on my glass, the other draped over the top of the booth. I didn't avert my eyes, tick my head, or any of a dozen moves that would have given me away.

"You know I can't tell you that," I said. "Anymore than you can tell me your purpose there."

She sighed, crossed her arms. Her expression changed in an instant from stone-faced to pleading. "Seriously?"

"Hey, you wanna share? Then kick the party off by telling me what you were doing there, and why you were so concerned with Thanos's safety."

"You know why I was there."

"You fed me one line, Lexi. That's it."

She sat motionless, gazing off toward the bar.

"That's what I thought," I said.

"I was there because I got a tip," she said.

"About?"

"That someone was going to take—"

The waitress appeared with our food. She set the tray down and placed our steaks in front of us. Lexi had gone with a sirloin, medium-rare. It was a rare ribeye for me.

We each took a couple bites while the waitress finished up, then Lexi continued.

"—a contract on him." The steam from her vegetables created a thin smoky veil between us.

How I reacted to her statement was important. No shock or surprise and she might assume the SIS was behind it. Too much, and it'd look like I was faking.

"We heard the same," I said.

She set her knife and fork down, reached across the table. "From who?"

I shook my head, pulled my hands back out of reach. "Not from any of my sources. I'm working on someone else's intel here."

She took a deep breath and leaned back.

"And even if it was," I said. "I couldn't just reveal them. You know how this works."

Lexi resigned herself that the conversation wasn't going anywhere without her giving up information she wanted to keep close to the vest. She took a few more bites of her steak, finished her wine and signaled to the waitress to bring her another glass.

While waiting, she said, "Getting bounced from clandestine ops hurt."

I waited to see where she would take it, but she didn't say anything else. Her gaze was fixed firmly on me. "I can imagine. I've been in situations where I had to leave an op, leave a job that I... I don't want to say enjoyed, but one that gave me purpose. Know what I mean?"

She nodded, then said, "Why'd you leave?"

I took a drink, wiped the foam off my lip. "Which job?"

She laughed. "Guess the one you enjoyed the most?"

"Asshole boss." I paused a beat. "How'd you blow your cover?"

"Who says I blew it?"

I shrugged. "Assumption, I guess. Anyway, getting outed doesn't necessarily mean you can't ever go in the field undercover again. Switch regions or targets, yeah. But totally bounced?"

"You're right. I didn't want to move to the west coast."

"That's rubbish, Lexi. I can see how much the job meant to you. You'd have gone wherever they wanted you to go. Is staying in Chicago doing boring field work, or God forbid, being a cubicle dweller, better than doing what you love?"

Her cheek sucked inward as she chewed on it. After a few moments, she said, "My husband was a good man with a horrible sickness."

"Cancer?"

"No, not like that." She spun her knife on the table. "Addiction."

I could see how that could be a problem for an FBI agent. "Drugs?"

She shrugged and nodded. "And drinking, and gambling. Later I found out it was prostitutes, too."

I started to see where this was going . "So you got kicked because of him, something he did."

"I take full responsibility for my actions. I do not blame him. Like I said, he was sick."

"I'm sure the agency shrink loves that you've made so much progress, but you can cut the Al-Anon talk with me. What'd he do that got you in trouble?"

She shifted in her seat, wiped her hands on her napkin. "That's the thing, Jack. Nothing. He did nothing. He was sick, and his sickness led him into a very bad situation."

"And sucked you right into it, too."

CHAPTER 17

THE TAVERN THICKENED WITH PATRONS. EVERY SEAT AT THE BAR had been taken. All tables were occupied. There was a line out the building, stretching down the sidewalk. A guy with a thick brown beard and dark-rimmed glasses stared through the window at my steak. Every time the door opened, a warm gust enveloped me, carrying with it the smell from the bakery next door.

The waitress set a fresh beer down in front of me. I dipped my finger and swirled it around to take some of the life out of the head.

Lexi hadn't responded to my last statement, which told me I was close to the answer. She got up and excused herself and disappeared into the restroom.

I used the break to reassess the makeup of the crowd. It was a good mix of students from the University of Wisconsin, and the working class folks of Madison. No one stood out, which was a good thing. After nearly two decades in the business, a bunch of faceless people was the best present I could receive. The only one in the crowded room that stuck out appeared again. Lexi wove through the room like a dancer. Effortless.

"Gonna finish that?" I pointed at her steak and stuck my fork in it after she shook her head.

"How can you still be hungry?" she asked.

"Not so much that I'm hungry." I cut off a chunk and stuck it in my mouth. "I don't know when we'll get a meal this good again."

She sipped on her wine and watched me eat. A few silent minutes passed. I knew how to play this game, and so did she. First to talk loses, and that person would have to reveal more of their hidden past. I'd either hit the nail on the head, or had it all wrong. Question was how long she could go without letting me know.

It didn't take too long to get my answer.

"He didn't suck me into some strange problem or into the underbelly of society," she said.

"Is that right?" I said between chews.

"I had a choice. I could have left him to those sharks. Let them break his arms again. Or maybe his legs this time. Perhaps this would be the evening they'd pull the trigger."

I said nothing while waiting for her to continue. Her eyes were wide, bright, wet.

"I don't know how he got the number. I mean, when I was under, I was *under*. No one was supposed to be able to find or reach me. Not even my handler."

"Really?"

"With the group I had infiltrated? I had to keep everyone past arm's distance. These were the type of guys who wouldn't stop at me if I'd been made. They'd torture me until they had enough info to get to everyone."

"Not exactly folks on the up and up."

Lexi nodded. "You could say that, at least to the rest of the world. Truth was, they were in deeper than anyone would have ever imagined. Myself included. They weren't my original mark. I was introduced after some time. He was the one behind it all."

She had me intrigued. "Who?"

Lexi smiled and wagged her index finger. "Can't do that. I'm already on the verge of losing my job. I reveal that secret and I'm not only out of the Bureau for life, I'll be in lockup. How do you think I'd do in the pen?"

I studied her for a moment. She was slim and athletic. Pretty, but not overly so. She hardly wore any makeup. I imagined she'd be a knockout all dolled up.

"Yeah," I said. "You'd be taken out pretty quick."

"Or live my life in solitary confinement. I may be a good actress, but I can't stand being alone all the time."

"So back to the husband and this situation you got caught up in."

Lexi nodded, took a drink, continued. "He called me in the middle of a meeting. I ignored it at first. I mean, I was undercover, meeting with a mob boss and a politician. I couldn't even take a second to figure out how he had the number. But the damn phone kept buzzing and buzzing."

"What were you there for?"

"Pardon?"

"In the meeting," I said. "What was your purpose there?"

She stammered for a moment. "You know I can't reveal that. It's all classified."

"I've got clearance."

She laughed. "I'm sure you do. Tell you what, if you have the access and can find the non-redacted file, have at it."

I'd get it out of her sooner or later. Probably later. Not that it really mattered, I was curious though. Whose life did she pretend to lead? What did she do for a living, and how did it benefit a mob boss and a politician? For that answer, I had to think about what would bring two such people together.

Money and power and lots of both.

"You were some kind of finance guru, right?"

She turned her head slightly, said nothing.

"Why else would those two have you in a room. Unless you were posing as an assassin." I crossed my arms and looked her over for a moment. "Nah, that wouldn't be the case. Definitely a numbers gal."

"Good guess," she said. "That doesn't mean you're right."

"OK. Anyway, get back to what happened."

"I get out of the meeting, flustered as hell, and answer the next call. He's being held, said they'd beat the hell out of him already and were threatening to kill him. I tried to get him to calm down, tell me what they wanted. Next thing, he screams like I've never heard him do before. Guy gets on the phone, says he's holding my husband's middle finger in his hand."

"He cut it off."

She nodded. "Didn't start with fingernails or anything like that. Just cut the damn thing off at the bottom knuckle. So I ask them what they want. They hang up."

"Can't imagine what you were thinking right then."

"Well, I was pissed, but the guy's my husband, and I love him and all that. At least, I make myself believe I do. Anyway, I have to get him out of there. And here's where I made two major mistakes. First, I was supposed to meet again with the mob boss after he finished dealing with the politician. I blew him off."

"And second?"

She lowered her chin to her chest. "I called a contact at the bureau, had them trace my cell. The one I was using with my cover."

"They weren't part of clandestine ops."

She shook her head and took a drink. "Talk about breaking protocol."

"So what happened?"

"They traced the location of my husband's cell phone. Some dive in the projects, little three-room place. I went there, took out the lookout, broke into the dingy house. When I saw him, he was battered, bloody, missing two fingers. His right eye was swollen shut. His nose was broken in two places. Half his bottom lip was hanging off."

"Jesus."

"Right? So, anyway, I shoot the first guy I see. It's a fatal shot, guy goes right down. Then another man bursts out of the bedroom. I draw on him, got him dead to rights."

She'd already killed one man, and injured another, all while breaking rank and disappearing. "Kill him, too?"

"No," she said. "I froze."

"Why?"

"I knew him. And he knew me. Well, not me, but my cover."

"He was part of the organization."

She nodded. "Right hand man for one of the capos. Two steps down from the boss."

"What happened?"

"I shoulda killed him, but he was unarmed. He called me out by my under-cover name, looked around, saw his partner on the ground. I guess he figured out what was going on because he rushed toward the table for a pistol sitting there. I jumped on him and we struggled for a bit. The fight went in his favor. He had me pinned down. The pistol was almost in reach. He's sitting there, all his weight on my chest, my arms locked in one of his. His other arm was outstretched, feeling along the table. All the pressure is bearing down on my neck. My vision started going black on the edges."

"Your husband find a way to intervene?"

She forced a laugh. "That piece of dreck? No way." She glanced toward the window. The line outside the tavern had shrunk. "Sirens."

"Someone heard the round you fired," I said.

"Yup, and the police responded. Practically ran through the front door with their patrol car. So, Gav—I mean, this guy dives out the window and runs. But he's made me, right. Once they all get together, they quickly figure out I was undercover. Thankfully they only knew a little about my husband. FBI got him patched up and dispatched him to the witness protection program."

"He still in it?"

She shrugged. "I assume so. There's no contact with him. But after it was all said and done, I got my butt reamed. I mean, how many possible ways could I have fucked up in one night? Since then, we haven't been able to get close to either man."

I said nothing.

"I just want to make it right. Put them both away, and then deal with my ex-husband so I can put that chapter of life to bed."

I watched her as I eased back into the seat. Things started to make sense. She'd been handcuffed by the FBI. Probably pushing paper all day long. To do otherwise, they'd have to admit that they had an agent undercover who went after a politician. That could cause all sorts of problems if she didn't have enough evidence.

She had to have been acting alone and without permission now. Why? Was Thanos connected with the mob and the politician?

CHAPTER 18

A FEW MOMENTS LATER LEXI SAID SHE WANTED TO LEAVE. THE questions could wait. She'd unloaded a lot of information, and I wasn't sure I could get her to reveal any more at the tavern. We paid our check and headed outside. The temperature had dropped thirty degrees during the time we were inside. A biting wind gusted in from the northwest and arctic air worked its way through our light clothing.

Lexi stepped onto the street and flagged down one of the few cabs roaming the area that night. It pulled up next to us.

"Sure this is a good idea?" I said, pulling the door open an inch.

"No," she said. "But I'm freezing."

"Fair enough."

We climbed in and remained silent during the four-minute ride to the motel. The driver dropped us a block past it. We cut down a side street and came up to the motel from the road behind it. It was hard to tell if anyone was watching. It was dark and there were few streetlights.

Back in the room I checked on the dog, changed out his bandages, freshened his water. We had to find a place for him soon. Problem was clinics ask questions, and in a case where it looks like abuse had occurred, they called the authorities.

"We'll get him somewhere tomorrow." She placed her hands on my shoulders and squeezed.

I stood, turned. We were face to face. She reached for my chest, her fingers dragged down to my waist. She hooked her thumb in my waistband. I reached around her back, pulled her into me. Our lips grazed past one another a few times until they met. We fell onto the bed and disappeared into one another.

A few hours later, I pried her lifeless arm off my chest and slipped out of bed. I grabbed my bag and headed outside. The full wrath of winter was on display. Snow fell, accumulating on the grass below. The street and parking lot looked darker than before. Too warm for the snow to stick. But with the temperature in a free fall, the asphalt might ice up if it snowed all night.

I trudged through five inches of powder around the back of the motel. A section of the building bowed inward like the letter U. The wind didn't hit as hard there. I pulled out one of the phones from my bag and dialed a number by memory.

After three rings, the call was answered.

"Whaddya want?"

"Put him on the line," I said.

"Why?"

"Charles, so help me God, this isn't the time to screw with me."

He laughed. "I'd say it's the perfect time. See, this way I don't have to worry about cleaning your blood off my ring when you get your panties in a wad over me busting your balls."

I said nothing.

Charles sighed. "What? Nothing? Man, you need to lighten up if you're ever gonna join us." The line went silent for a moment, then I heard muffled voices. Finally, Charles came back on the line. "Here he is. For your sake, I hope you have good news."

"Good evening, Mr. Jack." It was after two in the morning in New York and the Old Man sounded wide awake. "I've been waiting for your call. From what I gather, our acquaintance has gone missing."

"That's something I don't get."

"What's that?"

"You'll use some damn codeword for the target, yet continue to address me by name."

"Mr. Jack, there are lots of Jacks in this world. Who could possibly figure out I'm talking to you?"

I knew the line was secure on both ends. Brandon, my go-to guy for tech and surveillance and intelligence, had set up a network of numbers for me to use. I gave each to one and only one person. I dialed into it, it dialed out to them through a network of switches that'd baffle the most experienced server geek. And the line worked both ways. All I had to do was update my number in the system. No traffic could be monitored, not even by the NSA or GCHQ.

For the Old Man's part, I was aware the lengths he went to in order to maintain silence. Still it was good practice to keep some distance on these calls. Sloppy habits and all that.

"Maybe the same people who figured out I was in town to deal with this guy," I said.

There was a pause on the line. "Are you saying that the disappearance has nothing to do with you?"

"I'm saying from the moment I arrived in this town, I've been hot. I had a security detail all over me in the city. I had a couple goons show up at a motel I paid cash for. I can't say for sure the two are related, but there has to be some connection. Then this morning I show up at the house to take care of the problem, and someone else has already cleared the drain. Not only that, they'd left behind a couple watch dogs to ensure any additional clogs were dealt with."

"I see." I could hear Charles in the background asking the Old Man what was going on. He muffled the phone for a few seconds, then came back on. "I can assure that I had nothing to do with any of these events, Mr. Jack."

The snow that had accumulated on my hair had begun to melt and seep through to my skull. "I'm finding it hard to believe you right now."

"Be that as it may, I'm going to reach out to a contact to see what they know. Can I reach you at your number?"

"No. I'll call you tomorrow morning. You better have some answers for me or I'm going completely dark. You won't know I'm there until it's too late."

I took a walk after the call. My relationship with the Old Man had been rocky since its inception. Those inside the organization held little regard for me, despite the work I'd done. Charles would just as soon kill me as work with me. Maybe the Old Man wasn't behind it. Perhaps Charles had done the dirty work, undermining his boss. After all, I still couldn't figure out what the deal was with Matt, the guy who had driven with us. Was he really part of the organization like Charles had started to tell me? I shouldn't have cut him off. Matt could've been a hired hand and had been tracking me since I left New York.

Someone had been a step ahead of me the whole time. It became increasingly clear that Thanos never returned home last night. His own security detail had sold him out, or they were taken out, too. I thought back to the guy I'd shot in Thanos's backyard. He didn't look familiar. Neither did the men at the first motel. How many groups were at work here? Three? At least that many between the Old Man, Thanos's security detail, and some other opposition of unknown origins.

And what connection did Thanos have with Lexi's previous life in the Bureau? With the politician and mob boss? I needed names in order to connect the dots.

That familiar chill raced up and down my spine. I glanced over each shoulder in search of a tail. I was on high alert, and the lizard brain was on repeat telling me to get out of town. I wanted to listen. But, then what? Would I always be on the run from the Old Man? It'd be better if I cut the head off his organization. And taking number two out as well. Life with Charles running that show would be a nightmare. The guy never thought before taking action. I often found it hard to believe the Old Man trusted him so much.

I worked my way through the storm and back to the empty covered walkways. The stairwell had iced up. Guess throwing out salt was too much work for the night crew.

The shades covering the windows in my room were faintly illuminated, as they had been when I left. I stopped at the door and listened for a moment, then opened it and saw Lexi, dressed, and picking her shoes up off the ground.

"Going somewhere?"

CHAPTER 19

I LOOKED AROUND THE ROOM TO SEE IF ANYTHING WAS OUT OF place. Nothing had moved, not even the dog.

"Jack, I, uh..." She set the complimentary writing pad and a pen on the bed. "It's all on there."

I closed the door and leaned back against it. "If this is about what happened tonight, you know there's no pressure here. Not like I expect us to start—"

She waved both hands. "No, it's not that, Jack. C'mon, I'm a big girl. I'm capable of handling any feelings that arise. I mean, we were both a little tipsy. It's only natural."

I looked around again, noted the car keys were missing from the nightstand. "Then why are you leaving in the middle of the night?"

She pointed at the pad of paper on the bed. "It's all on there."

"One or both of us might be in danger here. I'd rather talk this out than read about it."

She dropped her shoes and sat on the bed. "I can see you're not gonna make this easy."

"Wouldn't dream of it."

She took a deep breath. "Here goes. I'm basically AWOL from the Bureau right now. Do you know what that means for a federal agent?"

"I have an idea." We had leeway in the SIS, but failure to report would not be looked upon kindly.

She stretched her arms back and leaned into them. "I don't feel like it's safe for me to check in with my boss. Things got so out of hand."

"When are you gonna level with me, Lexi? What's going on here? Why were you at Thanos's house, and what's he got to do with your time in the DCO?"

She closed her eyes, dropped her head back. Her hair grazed the bed. Her breasts stuck out toward the ceiling. I shoved the thoughts associated with that aside and focused on the issue here. Was she leaving to get away from me? Or trying to keep me safe? But from what?

She turned her head toward me, leveled me with her stare. "Why are you interested in Thanos?"

I had to think on the fly. "We're concerned that he's funneling funds to a terrorist organization."

Her eyes narrowed and the skin above her nose crinkled. "Thanos? Terrorists?"

"I haven't seen all the intel. My job was to infiltrate his residence and his office, look for evidence. If possible, I was to apprehend him and conduct an interrogation."

"His office? Good luck. He's hired so much security that it's impossible to reach him there. Hell, even at his home most of the time. That's why we scheduled our meeting when we did, so he'd have everyone out of there. I can't imagine who found out."

"What's he do for a living?"

"You don't know?" She leaned forward, put her hands on her knees.

"Like I said, I was only given a name and a couple addresses."

"He's into a lot of stuff. Real estate, mostly. That's how he earned his fortune. He's got several other businesses."

"All legit?"

She shook her head. "Of course not. Think I'd have leverage on him if they all were?"

"Good point. He reached out to you, though?"

"He's mixed up in all kinds of things. Something happened, and he hasn't told me what yet. But he needed help getting off the grid. He knew someone was coming for him." She rubbed her chin. "You, perhaps."

I shrugged, said nothing.

"He was scared, I know that. He feared for his life." She rose and paced across the room, stepping over the dog, who'd decided his job was to block anyone from passing from one side to the other. "What I wouldn't give to know what he was hiding."

"What if I can help you there?"

"How? By interrogating him?" She shook her head and waved me off. "And what does that mean anyway? Like, you'll sit down and have a cup of coffee with the guy? Or…"

"I'd take the 'or…' there."

"You're a trained killer, aren't you?"

I had to phrase it delicately, otherwise I might lose her to the night. "I do what it takes to get a job done. You remember what it was like undercover, right? Didn't you have to skirt the law on occasion? Same here. Sometimes it involves getting information from a junkie. Other times I might have to make a purchase from an arms dealer to gain their trust, make them believe in my story. There are times when I've been tasked with neutralizing a target, an enemy combatant of the state. If my job was to take a life, there was a damn good reason for it. I'm not simply a murderer. Not a psychopath."

I couldn't tell by the way she stared at me whether she bought into my story. It wasn't entirely false, but I gave her the description that best described me up until two and a half years ago, when I was betrayed by the people I worked with and wound up on the wrong side of a rogue FBI agent who was working with a terrorist. The way that shook out, I knew there was no right or wrong side of the law. We are all bastards in the same game, only some of us used self-righteousness as an excuse.

"OK, we're gonna get out of town," she said. "I've got a place we can go where we can regroup. I've got a contact there who can make a few calls for us, maybe help figure out what's going on."

I reached into my bag and pulled out the unused phone and held it up. "Here, take it. It's clean. Why don't you make the call from here and save us some time."

She smiled, shook her head. "He doesn't work like that. Besides, this is a good place to take the dog." She opened the door and stood in the doorway. "Come on, Jack. Let's get going."

I grabbed a bottle of water off the nightstand, leashed the dog, and followed Lexi into the snowy night. She took the wheel and drove us toward an unknown destination.

CHAPTER 20

WE DROVE THROUGH THE REMAINDER OF THE NIGHT WITH THE radio buffering the silence between us. Every thirty minutes or so we alternated between Lexi's eighties station, and my jazz station. She got a kick out of my choice, said she pegged me for a heavy metal fan. Maybe once upon a time, but these days I needed something to calm the nerves and take the edge off. Nothing did that like Coltrane.

I dozed off somewhere around four-thirty and woke up as the sun crested the horizon in front of us. Shielding my eyes against the sharp rays, I attempted to figure out where we were. The dull, flat landscape gave little away. We'd ventured off the highway, traveling on country roads lined with dead cornfields.

"Where are we?" I asked.

"Not far away," Lexi said.

"Helpful." I glanced out my window in a second attempt to pinpoint us on my mental map, but still came up empty. "Welcome to Anywhere, Mid-west, USA."

"Pretty much." She adjusted the radio dial from the fading station. "We're just over the Illinois border about forty miles west of Indianapolis."

I traced a route along a network of highways in my mind. "You went back through Chicago?"

She shook her head. "Straight south from Madison, then east at Bloomington. Got off I-74 about twenty minutes ago. Takes about an hour and a half longer, but I think that's worth it to avoid Chicago. Even in the middle of the night all it takes is one person to spot you and it'd be over."

"Sure, we're more out in the open in the middle of the night. Fewer people on the road."

"Right. Anyway, we should stop and get some coffee before we reach the house."

She turned off a quarter-mile down the road, sped through a wooded area, and then pulled into the small parking lot of a diner that only had breakfast and lunch hours. A Ford F-250 and Chevy 2500 truck were the only vehicles parked in front. Two guys wearing jeans and flannel shirts sat at the counter with their backs to us. The woman working the line looked between them at us.

I pulled the door open for Lexi. Coffee and pancakes and syrup saturated the warm air that greeted us.

"Mornin' folks," the woman said.

The guy on the left looked over his shoulder at us, nodded once, looked away. His buddy didn't bother.

We took two empty stools at the other end of the counter. A minute later the waitress came to take our order.

"Sure thought it was gonna be a warm one today with the way it heated up last night." She wrapped her arms over her chest and shivered. "Guess that's too much to ask for this time of year, though, huh?"

I nodded, said nothing. Neither did Lexi.

"You folks are kinda off the beaten path here, aren't you?"

"We like to wander around between our appointments," Lexi said. "Never know what you might find, or who you might meet."

"What're y'all pitching?"

"Fluoroscopy equipment," Lexi said.

The woman's forehead folded upward, she scratched her chin as though she were contemplating purchasing something she had never heard of before.

"It's kind of a niche market," Lexi said. "Mostly for doctors."

"So you two," the woman wagged her finger between us, "you're not a couple?" Her voice rose as she said it.

I glanced over at Lexi. Her cheeks reddened a shade or two.

The woman nodded and winked. "Yeah, I know how it goes. All those hours in the car together, the hotel rooms, the late-night nightcaps at those fancy bars. So let me ask you, either of you got attachments back home?"

"You writing a book?" I said.

"No," Lexi said, waving her hand in front of both of us. "It's not like that."

The waitress shifted her focus to me. "Yeah, well, I can tell you, hun, you're missing out if you're not chasing after a guy like that."

"You've earned yourself a tip no matter how else the meal goes," I said.

The small talk shifted to taking our orders, then the waitress returned to the other end of the counter and chatted with her regulars.

I threw down two cups of black coffee before my bacon and eggs arrived. Lexi went heavier on the carbs with a meal consisting of grits, hash browns, and whole wheat toast.

Uneasiness held a tight grip over me as I kept waiting for something to happen. Maybe the cook would come out from behind the line with an AK and shoot up the place. Or some of Thanos's guys would block us in, take us into custody, torture us. Hell, perhaps Charles's ugly mug would stroll in through the door and he'd challenge me to a fight on neutral ground. That last one actually held some appeal.

But an hour passed without incident. We drank our coffee and ate our breakfast and did it in relative silence. We both had things we wanted to say, at least I did. I figured the things Lexi wanted to talk about weren't along the same lines as me. Or maybe they were. She was a hard woman to read.

I studied her for a minute, taking note of the hardened look of someone who'd come up in a male-dominated sector. She looked tough as nails. Was the interior as rough as the exterior? She'd let me in a little. What other secrets were hidden in there?

"You don't have to worry about me," she said, holding her loaded fork in front of her mouth. Steam rose off the pie in front of her.

"What?" I said.

"Christ, Jack, you've been staring at me the better part of five minutes. I told you, I'm a big girl. You don't have to worry about me."

"Who said I'm worrying?" I pulled out my wallet and dropped a fifty on the counter. "Just wondering what you're thinking about, and what's in store for us today."

She shook her head, dropped her fork, and walked out of the diner, leaving her mostly uneaten dessert behind. The waitress came over, collected the fifty.

"I knew there was more going on with you two." She smiled and winked. "Let me get your—"

"You can keep the change." I barely heard her thanking me as I left the restaurant.

The car was running. Lexi had already shifted into reverse, her foot pressed on the brake hard. The dog whimpered a couple times after I sat down. I reached around back and scratched his neck. He eased back down and closed his eyes.

The next twenty minutes were spent in painful silence. I had a hard time believing Lexi's attitude had to do with what happened last night. So what was it? Did she think someone was onto us? Should I open up about my past, make her understand we were OK?

She turned onto a dirt and gravel driveway that disappeared into the woods. The Civic sounded like a tank crushing the ground beneath it. We passed through the trees and into a clearing where I saw a small house. A long fence stretched to either side. The flowerbeds were barren. There were no cars out front. A porch swing and a couple of white rocking chairs were unoccupied.

The blinds in the front window parted a couple inches. I couldn't make out the figure standing behind them. After Lexi parked the car and shut it off, the window coverings fell shut again.

"Someone expecting us?" I said.

"Get the dog," she said, stepping out of the vehicle.

I pulled open the back door and helped him out. He limped next to me, doing his best to walk on all fours as we approached the front porch.

The door opened. A tall male figure was shielded by the shadowy screen door. He eased the screen door open and stepped out wearing faded jeans and a white undershirt. He was thin, but muscular. His silver-and-black hair was thick, as were his dark eyebrows. A thin mustache adorned his upper lip. He held a rifle by the barrel in his right hand.

"Who the hell is this?" He stared right at me. "I told you don't be bringing no strangers around here."

Lexi sighed, rolled her eyes. "Hiya, Pop."

CHAPTER 21

I GLANCED BETWEEN THE OLD GUY AND LEXI. "POP? THIS OLD spinster is your father?"

"Spinster?" He tensed up. The veins on his biceps stood out. "Figures she ain't told you nothin' 'bout me. My dear Lexi only comes by when she's in need of something. So what is it this time? This knucklehead knock you up?"

Lexi blushed and looked down at her feet.

"Let's try something easier," he said. "What's this fellas name?"

"Jack," she said.

"Jack what?" he said.

"I only know his first name, Pop."

"Can't say I'm surprised you're shackin' up with some fella when you don't even know his last name."

She stepped forward, went toe to toe with the old guy. "You listen here. You will not talk to me or my friend like that. I'm not shacking up with nobody. Jack is a professional associate of mine."

"Such a professional you know his full name, right?" He turned his back on us and went inside, letting the screen door fall shut.

"Come on," Lexi said.

I grabbed the door and waited for her to step inside, then followed her in. It was warm, at least seventy-five in there. A wood burning stove sat in the middle of a large square room. The smell reminded me of a month I spent in Vermont. Went there to get away from everything a couple of years ago while recovering from a waterboarding incident.

Lexi's father pulled a beer from the fridge, opened it, took a long pull, draining half the bottle. He didn't bother asking if we wanted one. Might have had something to do with the fact it wasn't even nine a.m. yet.

He drew a bead on me. "You undercover?"

"Something like that," I said.

"Something like that," he repeated with a roll of his eyes. "Pretty simple question if you ask me. Either you are, or you aren't. Now, maybe you don't want to tell an old curmudgeon like me. Might help if you knew I spent my whole damn working life in the Agency. Hell, during the eighties I practically lived on the other side of the Berlin wall."

"Cold War guy, huh?"

He nodded. "You young assholes don't know nothing about that."

"I remember watching the wall fall. I was thirteen, so I guess watching was all I could do at the time."

He shook his head. "Christ all mighty. You and her make quite the pair. What were you, Lexi? Eight? Nine?"

"Ten." She sat down across from him. "Jack's not undercover. He's with another agency."

Her father rested his elbow on the table and scratched at the stubble on his chin. "Oh yeah? Which one?" He crossed his arms over his puffed out chest. "Not my Agency. Not this guy."

"No, sir," I said. "I worked with those guys in Africa and the Middle East from '95 through '02. Part of a special program with the Marines."

"So you're a Jarhead, then."

"Was, sorta. Never spent much time in a platoon. Was pulled into that assignment during Recruit Training. Afterward I got into another agency and have been working with them since."

"Well, which one?" he said.

"Afraid I can't disclose that, sir."

"Well that's some bacon grease fried bullshit, son. Got me all excited to talk shop, and you're gonna hold out on me like that. Christ, I'm—and I hate to say this with Lexi present—but I'm liable to get blueballs sitting here wondering just what it is you do, and how that got you hooked up with my FBI agent of a daughter."

"Dad, come on. Enough of that talk." She got up, poured a glass of water, took a sip. "Are you gonna help us or not?"

"Guess that depends on what you need." He looked back at Lexi. "And why an FBI agent and a man who works for a yet-to-be-named agency can't gather this information on their own."

She rejoined us at the table. "It's not that we can't. Things are a bit, I dunno, tense at the moment. If we start asking a bunch of questions, it might raise suspicion. And you know as well as I do, once that happens, you can kiss all your plans goodbye."

"It might help if you stop talking in circles and tell me just what it is that you need, girl."

"There's a man named Thanos," I said. "Lives and works in Chicago. Lexi and I share a mutual interest in him."

"For different reasons," she added.

"Right," I said. "Thanos is our common thread. We both attempted to apprehend him at the same time. In fact, that's how we met. Problem was, someone had already gotten to him. No one has seen or heard from him in over twenty-four hours."

"Where and when did this go down?" he asked.

"Thanos's house," she said. "Yesterday morning, around nine."

"He was probably at work then," he said. "Hell, I bet he was in his own damn bed last night."

"Doubtful," Lexi said.

"Why's that?" He shifted in his seat to face his daughter.

"Someone shot up his house while we were in there," Lexi said. "And I'm not talking about a couple guys with plinkers, Pop. They were armed with shotguns and automatic weapons."

"Yeah, guess that could pose a problem," he said, frowning seemingly over the fact he admitted he agreed with us. "You think the shooters were there for you or him?"

"Good question," she said. "I've been playing it over and over in my head. Did someone get him out in time, or did someone take him forcibly and then waited around to clean up any mess that might arise? Did they know about his involvement with me?"

It was an angle I'd only glancingly thought about. Lexi didn't know about Thanos leaving the night before, and I wasn't sure now was the best time to tell her that the thirty minute head start she figured Thanos had could indeed be several hours more.

"So, again," her father said. "Why can't you get your people to look into it? They can check his cell phone records, telematics to track his car, look for credit and debit card transactions. Christ, you kids got it so damn easy now. When I was in the field, we had to work to catch somebody."

Lexi looked in my direction for several seconds without making eye contact. She didn't need my help, or for me to intervene. She couldn't or wouldn't answer his question with me present.

As fate would have it, the burner phone in my pocket started buzzing.

CHAPTER 22

L EXI STARED AT THE PHONE AS I PULLED IT OUT. "WHO'S CALLING you on that line?"

Staring at the number on the screen, I shrugged. "I didn't give it out to anyone. I'm gonna take it outside so you and your dad can talk alone."

I exited through the front door, blocking the dog from following with my foot until the door was secure. I answered the call as I stepped off the porch.

"Who is this?" The cold air froze my throat and lungs, forcing a stifled cough.

"Mr. Jack."

The Old Man.

"How the hell did you get this number?" I said.

"Please," he said. "You think you are the only one with friends in the spy business? How I got the number is of little consequence. What I am more concerned with is where things are with your job. Give me an update, now."

I headed down the driveway into the wooded area. "I don't have one to give. He's off the radar, and so am I."

A steady breeze rustled overhead limbs and caused the tall pines to sway side to side, sometimes slamming into each other with the sound of a baseball bat driving a triple over the left fielder's head. I continued to the other side of the woods where I had a view of the winding driveway all the way out to the narrow country road. It was deserted. Would it stay that way?

"My associates in Chicago are growing concerned over the disappearance of our friend," the Old Man said. "You say you know nothing of where he went and who he went there with?"

"If you've been in contact with someone who knows him, then you need to share what they told you."

The Old Man laughed for several seconds. "Mr. Jack, you see, this is what I love about you. So many men, they are, well I'll come right out and say it, they are scared to death of me. I don't know why. I'm a pretty decent boss, and a great friend to have on your side. I guess it's because if you cross me you won't have many more opportunities to do so. Even people who have simply upset me by not using a coaster for their beer have found this to be true."

"That's great, it really is. What's it got to do with me?"

"You don't screw around with me, Mr. Jack. You have something to say, you say it. You're not scared of me. You don't pussyfoot or tap dance around because you fear what I might do to you."

"Got news for you, Feng. You aren't the biggest badass I've ever been around. Hell, the DIs down on Parris Island bit harder than you do."

This elicited another round of laughter from the Old Man.

"So spill already. I'm tired of wasting time here in Wisconsin." Figured it wouldn't hurt to throw him off my trail. Although I had a feeling he had one of his contacts monitoring the call in an attempt to isolate my location. Until they did, he had no way to know I was in Indiana, which meant Lexi and I had a two-plus-hour head start. Then again, the Old Man was able to reach me when he didn't have the number, so it was plausible he already had my location, in which case, we were screwed.

"They are concerned over the involvement of a rogue FBI agent."

My gut tightened. "OK."

"Seems that this agent had infiltrated my associate's organization."

"Got to his men?"

"No, the agent was undercover and managed to get close to my associate and one of his most powerful allies."

"What'd they do to the agent when they found out?"

"They didn't do anything to the agent because the agent fell off the face of the planet after being outed. Word was that the FBI placed the agent on permanent leave and whisked her away into witness protection."

"Her?" I acted surprised.

"Yes, Mr. Jack. Women can become FBI agents, among other things, these days."

"So if this agent is out of the picture, what's the concern?"

"She resurfaced recently. Guess the FBI is so bad at their jobs they can't even keep track of one of their own. Well, when she resurfaced, she went straight to our friend. She had the goods on him."

"If that's the case, why didn't she just go to her superior at the agency?" I looked back through the woods to see if they'd exited the house. I only saw the dog wandering down the driveway toward me. "Seems to me that would have earned her some brownie points, at least."

"Ah, I wish I could answer that. I can only assume that she was thinking she could get back in the Bureau's good graces by pulling off a big bust. Put all the pieces together, then go to them with it."

I knelt down and petted the dog's head. "I suppose that makes sense."

"My associates believe that this rogue agent was coercing our friend into turning on them. And she may have our friend in custody at an unknown location at this time."

"It's gonna be tough to track that down," I said. "Unless you're holding back and have more info to give me."

"I'm sure it will be," he said. "I'm going to send you her picture, and some information about her. I hope you understand, you'll have to use your own contacts for additional intel. I cannot be linked to this in any way."

"How much?" I asked.

"How does an extra hundred thousand sound?"

"Come on." I lowered my voice. "This is a federal agent. That's a death sentence if I'm caught."

"OK, you win, Mr. Jack. A quarter, but no higher."

A quarter of a million dollars with the target less than a hundred yards away. Any other day, I might actually pull it off. But I knew half of Feng's story was rubbish, so I decided to play along for a while to get the missing intel.

"I'm going to have the details sent to you in a few moments," he said. "Let me know when you've located her."

I ended the call without responding and stood at the edge of the woods for several moments with my eyes closed. The distant hum of an eighteen-wheeler rose over the steady wind. I looked out over the property up to the road. Still deserted.

"What the hell have you gotten yourself into this time," I muttered as I turned back toward the house.

The phone vibrated a few times. I downloaded the attachments the Old Man had sent. If there was any doubt in my mind, it was now erased. I was staring at a photo of Lexi, taken recently. Someone had surveillance on her after she came out of hiding. How long had they been following her? When did she manage to lose them?

It hit me that she hadn't lost them. *We* had. They followed her right into Thanos's house. They were the shooters.

Son of a bitch.

What if the guy that got away had already reported that I was with her? The Old Man just played me like a two-dollar fiddle.

CHAPTER 23

LEXI STOPPED TALKING MID-SENTENCE AND SHE AND HER FATHER
stared at me like I was a crazy man busting down their screen door.

I took a moment to catch my breath following the sprint to the house.

"What is it?" she asked, walking toward me.

"We need to separate," I said. "And you need to get out of here."

"Jack, what are you talking about?"

I stood just inside the front door. The dog followed me in, nuzzled his head
against my outer thigh. I felt uncomfortable being in the house even with our
head start. They couldn't track me until they had the number, and chances are
they only found out about it recently, otherwise the Old Man would've called
sooner. I'd place my bet that whoever the Old Man was going to send was
based in Chicago, worst case would be Indianapolis, in which case we had
more than half-an-hour lead time.

"Look at this." I met Lexi halfway, pulled out the phone, and showed her
the pictures the Old Man had sent to me.

"OK," she said. "That's me. And...?"

"Someone sent those to me, and thinks you're involved with Thanos's
disappearance."

She put her hands on her hips and took a half-step back. "We both know
that's not true."

I had to spell it out. "Lexi, this person doesn't know that you and I are
working together. Get it?"

"Then why'd they send you my..." She leaned back against the wall and
wrapped her hands around the back of her head. "Shit."

"Shit is right," I said. "There's a contract out on your life, and they want me to fulfill it. And to make matters worse—"

"What could possibly be worse?" her father said.

"—they called *me*. On a burner phone. That means they know where we're at right now. I don't know how much time we have, but we can't waste any of it. Someone is gonna show up here sooner or later, and I'm betting all my money on sooner."

The old guy shook his head, spat into the sink. "Come on, girl. I can take you and the dog to my hunting cabin. Ain't no one gonna find us out there."

"I'm sorry," I said.

"Tell me who," she said. "Who's doing this?"

I shook my head. "Lexi, I can't do that."

"Is it the SIS?"

"SIS?" her father said. "Son, is that who you work for?"

I said nothing to him. "No, it's not them, Lex. Another organization. I can't explain right now. We don't have time for this, you need to get moving."

"You sure? I spoke to your guy, Frank. He might've—"

"No, he wouldn't have," I said. "A move against an FBI agent wouldn't come from him. He doesn't have that kind of power."

"But the people who control his budget do," her father said.

"It's not like that, sir." I reached for Lexi, but she pulled away. I walked over to the table and wrote down a number on a scratch pad, then tore a few extra sheets of paper off in order to eliminate anyone finding the indentation. "I want you to get a good distance from here and pick up a phone from a drug store. You call this number later and it's gonna ring to me. It's an untraceable line. Not even the NSA can hack it."

The old guy leaned in and whispered something to his daughter. Lexi looked at him and he nodded reassuringly while squeezing her hand.

"Jack, there's something you should know. It might help you make sense of all this."

I shook my head. "I already know. They washed you out after your incident while undercover and tried to put you in witness protection. You already mentioned you're AWOL. We don't have time to get into it right now. We each need to create some distance from this place. But I need you to tell me the names of the two men from that meeting and what Thanos's connection was to them."

The dog started growling. All three of us turned toward the front door. Somewhere beyond the trees, tires crunched along the gravel driveway.

"I got an ATV parked out back." Her father leashed the dog and led him to the back of the house. "Lexi, let's get moving. Jack, I got an AR-15 behind the fridge. It's ready to go, thirty rounds and a spare mag on top of the fridge."

"Jack," Lexi said.

"Go. I'll take care of whoever's out there." I grabbed her wrist and placed the paper with my number on it in the palm of her hand. "Don't stop at the first place for a phone. I guarantee if there's cameras, they'll get a hold of the footage. If they can spot you, they can get the number of the phone you purchased. It'll be game over then and you won't even know they're coming."

She leaned in and kissed my cheek. The lingering wetness absorbed her hot breath. "I'll call you tonight."

As they exited through the rear of the house, I heard her father say, "Nothing going on between you two, huh?"

I pulled the refrigerator out a foot and grabbed the rifle. It was equipped with a red dot scope. I flipped the safety off, chambered a round. The soft hum of an idling engine was all I could hear. I moved to the front window, hoping the layer of dirt and grime would hide me from view. Scanning the front yard, I spotted the car in the woods, made out the grill and hood. Looked like a black Chevy Tahoe.

A door opened and slammed shut three seconds later. The engine cut off. Another door opened and closed. Two men emerged from the trees. They wore long black coats, black pants, sunglasses. They had arrived too quickly for the Old Man to be involved. Even if he knew my exact location, it'd take time to get his guys here.

Were they Feds?

It made sense only if the FBI knew where Lexi's father hid out. Considering his background, I assumed someone kept tabs on the guy. Old spooks make for nasty skeletons when they get lost in the closet. The Bureau wouldn't actively monitor him, though. Sharing was the buzzword in this day and age of real and immediate threats of terrorism. But the kindness only went so far, especially without hard evidence. Chances of the Agency revealing the locations of retired operators to anyone not on a need-to-know basis were slim to none.

Could the FBI have been tracking Lexi, and by proxy me, the whole time? Why wait until now to take her down, though? They could have easily nabbed us last night in the motel.

A diesel engine chugged to life in the distance, maybe a quarter mile away. The guy in a wool cap signaled to the other and they slipped back into the woods. The SUV's engine turned over. A few seconds later I lost sight of them, and not long after that it fell silent.

I pulled up the snapshot of the area in my mind. From what I saw on our drive in, there wasn't another road other than the ones we came in on for miles. Lexis's father would have other ways out, of course. He might even have a way to get to that hunting cabin using trails and fire roads. Would be better for the both of them if that were the case. It seemed they'd be OK for now. If somehow they ended up in a shootout, I placed the odds in Lexi and her father's favor. They knew the terrain here, knew what spots offered the best vantage points.

I exited the house, rifle in hand, and set out on foot into the woods. I made my way through the tangle of brush and trees. The clearing beyond was empty. The road, too. Whoever it was had gone, and I figured it was time I did the same.

The rental wouldn't make it across the land behind the house. The only available route out was the way we had come in. My plan was to get to the highway and start back toward Chicago. I put the rifle in the trunk then headed out with the windows down and the radio and fan off. The frigid air intensified, but it was necessary for a few miles. The men could be waiting, hidden on a driveway or tucked in behind a cluster of trees. If that V-8 roared to life, I needed to know so I could create as much distance as possible between us.

By the time I reached the end of the narrow country road, I couldn't feel my face. I checked the rearview, holding my gaze steady for several seconds. No one had followed me out. I rolled the window up and blasted the heat on high.

A quarter-mile later the car dinged at me a couple times and the gas light cut on. I recalled a gas station not far from the diner where we'd eaten break-fast, ten minutes away at most. I passed five cars and two eighteen-wheelers during the ride over.

The gas station lot was empty except for a late-eighties model Buick parked on the side, in front of the propane tank cage. The sun reflected off the store's glass front. I shielded my eyes but couldn't see anything inside. I pulled up next to the pumps. A sign said, "Cash Only - Pay Inside First."

The glare intensified as I walked up to the store. Heat radiated at me so intensely that by the time I reached the entrance it felt close to sixty degrees. I went inside where I was greeted by an elderly woman who didn't bother to look up from the tabloid spread across the counter.

"Twenty dollars on two," I said.

She raised her hand and nodded without making eye contact.

"Coffee fresh?" I asked.

She nodded again, said nothing.

"Go ahead and add that as well."

"It's on the house, hon," she said.

I poured a cup, dropped a twenty and a five on the counter, and left the store. The sun prevented me from seeing anything. At least the canopy over the pumps would provide a little relief.

I was halfway across the parking lot when I heard the sound of a vehicle traveling at a high rate of speed. The black Tahoe I'd seen in the woods swerved onto the shoulder and was headed right for the gas station. Its outer wheels crashed against the curb. The driver slammed on the brakes, skidded across the parking lot, and came to a screeching stop on the other side of the rental, blocking the front escape. Doors opened, boots hit the ground. I couldn't tell how many men there were.

To either side of me was nothing but road shoulder and woods. Behind me was the store, and behind that, more trees. The fastest path to cover was the store. I had to hope there was a back exit. I dropped my coffee, lowered my center of gravity a couple inches and turned to sprint.

"Don't move, Jack!"

CHAPTER 24

Two silhouettes stood out in the brightness on opposite ends of the SUV. I couldn't be sure, but it looked like a third person remained inside the vehicle behind the wheel. The Tahoe's engine gurgled over the silence.

"You're covered, man," the guy said.

Would they get into a shootout here, gas pumps between us? Hell, all I had to do was shoot one and hope I could run fast enough to get out of the explosion. I reached for my hip. A gunshot tore through the still air. Whatever birds had remained for the winter booked it out of there, squawking as they hauled off in fifth gear to get away from the gas station. I grimaced, waiting for the searing pain to set in.

"That was just a warning shot," the guy said. "One more move, you die."

I held my hands out wide. "You wouldn't go through all this to kill me."

"You're right," he said. "But I've got no problem shooting you in the knee cap, so put 'em up, man."

I had little choice with no escape path and two armed men honing in on me. I lifted my arms upward, palms to the sky. One of the men approached, told me to turn around and face the store. He put his hand on my back.

"Don't try to be a hero, man." He worked through my jacket, pulled the pistol on my hip, and the one behind my back. "What the hell were you up to today?"

"Was hoping some ugly bastard would give me a reason to kill him. I'd say you're pretty damn close if you don't put my pistols back where you found them."

The guy chuckled. "You're not a fucking legend, are you?"

"What're you talking about?"

"You're every bit the asshole I heard you were." The guy yanked me back by my collar and pulled me around to face the SUV.

There in front of the rear passenger door of the SUV stood a man I hadn't expected to see in Indiana.

"The hell are you doing here?"

"Good to see you, Jack." Frank Skinner blew into his cupped palms, then pulled on a pair of black leather gloves. "Sorry we had to do it this way. Figured it wouldn't be a good idea to just walk up to you."

"These assholes your new recruits?" I said.

"You could say that." He pointed at the guy who'd frisked me. "Gary there is former Army SOF. Miguel's from Mexico, worked on a cartel task force. We brought him in for his expertise in that area."

I glanced at each man, then back at Frank. "Nothing better to do today than screw with an old friend?"

Frank laughed. "Friends is kinda harsh, isn't it? I mean, maybe in the beginning, but...ah, who'm I kidding. I think you're a sonofabitch and you think I'm a sonofabitch. One of us is right."

"Maybe both of us." I jutted my chin toward Gary. "Now that we're all acquainted, how about returning my pistols."

Frank nodded at his understudy and held out both firearms, handles toward me. I holstered them then walked up to the SUV. Frank pulled open the rear door and waved me in. After speaking with Gary and Miguel, Frank joined me in the back.

"So what's this all about?" It was a dumb question. One meant to irritate him. We both knew why he was there. Partially, at least.

"You have a suspended FBI agent call me to verify you and you don't think I'm gonna follow up on that?" Frank motioned for Gary to pull out of the parking lot. "Christ, Jack, you have any idea what you've gotten yourself into? Do you know, and I mean really know, who this new girlfriend of yours is and what's she's done?"

I wanted to spend as little time as possible in the SUV with Frank and his guys, so there was no point pussyfooting around or trying to piss him off moving forward. I needed additional intel that he might have. Screwing around with him would only encourage him to withhold that information. I took a deep breath to settle my heartrate.

"She went AWOL while on assignment, on a covert op. Her husband got into trouble and she had to make a choice. His life or her career. She chose him even though he was a heartless bastard who didn't deserve her. Ended up blowing her cover. Because she'd been made, they put her into the protection program, but she couldn't take it. Too much left undone. I'm not entirely sure on some of the details, the men she was after, or what Thanos has to do with them, but it's starting to come together."

Frank stared hard at me for a good five seconds before offering any input. "Close enough."

"What am I missing?"

"Nothing too important." He reached into his bag and pulled out a folder bound with red string. He unwound the string, opened it and set it on his lap. It contained a series of photos. The first of which I recognized as Thanos. "OK, you know this guy. How about him?"

It was Ginger, the security guard. "Yeah, I had a run-in with him."

"Get his name?"

I shook my head.

"We don't have it either. Best we can tell, he's from Russia."

"Sounded American to me."

Frank altered his accent. "And I can sound like a bloody Brit, can't I?"

"Point taken."

"We assume he's hired security for Thanos."

"You'd be correct," I said, leaving out the fact that the last time Thanos had been seen was with Ginger.

"Might be a good idea to track this guy down, see what he knows." He raised his hand and cut me off. "I know, easier said than done. We've got a team working on his location. As soon as we have it, you will, too."

"Who else you got in there?"

He pulled out a photo of a middle-aged man, maybe fifty. His hair was mostly grey, minimal wrinkles. "This is Will McGrath. He runs the Chicago mob." He shifted to another photo.

"I know him," I said.

Frank nodded. "Figured you might recognize him. That's Jarred Denton, a local politician. Probably seen him in the news being investigated for fraud a year or so ago. DA couldn't make the charges stick. That's when they got your FBI friend involved. She worked the mob for eighteen months and finally made it in with McGrath's inner circle. He secured the meeting with Denton. It was actually their second meeting, the one you referenced. He finally felt comfortable enough with her to hear the pitch."

"And she blew it." Another piece in place. "What's Thanos have to do with this?"

"What we know about Thanos is that he's a money guy. Doesn't get his hands too dirty, though. Uses someone like that redheaded security guy, who uses his own guy. That way there's no direct connection between the underling who carries out the activity and Thanos."

"If Lexi was trying to protect Thanos—"

"Hold your horses there, partner," Frank said. "We don't know what she was doing there. But I'd like to know exactly why you were in his house when those idiots shot the place up and drew every eye in the Midwest to this clusterfuck."

"He was my mark."

Frank cleared his throat. "Who gave the order?"

I held his gaze, said nothing.

"Right," Frank said. "Can't tell me."

"You wouldn't want me to reveal you in a similar situation, right?"

He didn't answer. "I can also tell you that as of eight this morning a contract has been placed on your friend through unofficial channels. But believe me, it is as official as it comes. You better hope her interest in this jackoff is solid, or the first time someone has her in their crosshairs, she's done."

I needed to warn her that the threat to her life was legit, if the pictures I showed her hadn't done the trick. It was too soon for her to have tried calling, but I needed to get a phone soon. I'd already trashed the phone since the Old Man had compromised it.

"I assume she was back at that house?"

I didn't answer.

"Would have been better if she hadn't run. She could've helped us fill in these blanks, get things moving." He paused a few seconds. "There's still time for that, Jack. If you can reach her—"

"I can't," I said. "And the only phone I had is gone, so unless we bump into each other at the grocery store, it ain't happening."

He nodded, but I knew he didn't buy it. Frank knew me too well. And it was the same with me in regards to him. They wouldn't accept her with open arms. One of the reasons the SIS was created was for the kind of job he was talking about. All of its agents were essentially off the grid ghosts and could move about the country with ease. Few cared how dirty their hands got, so long as what they were doing was sanctioned. And the jobs were sanctioned at the highest level of the Pentagon, even if those giving the OK didn't truly know what was going on.

I looked up as the SUV veered onto the interstate heading east toward Indianapolis. "Where are we going?"

"Here's the deal. You're reactivated as of three days ago." Frank swatted away my objection before I could voice it, and tossed me a set of credentials. "And don't even try to wiggle out of this. You know the charges that can be brought against you over this Thanos thing. I figure three days gives you enough time that everything you've done up till now is covered."

There was little I could say in retort. "One condition. I'm gonna need—"

"First of all, you are not in a position to give me conditions," Frank said. "Second, I figured sooner or later you were gonna ask about a partner for this, so I took the liberty of getting Logan on a plane to Indianapolis. He's landing in less than an hour. Gonna drop you off at the airport. There's an Audi in long-term parking in the terminal garage. It's already outfitted with everything you'll need. Firearms, couple of phones, a laptop, a GPS tracker you can stick under a wheel well of a car, and plenty of cash. I want you to check in with me at five p.m."

I was officially an SIS agent again. The taste that left in my mouth nearly caused me to vomit. At the same time, Bear was on a plane to Indy.

And that was the first bit of good news I'd heard since arriving in Chicago.

CHAPTER 25

FRANK AND HIS GUYS DROPPED ME OFF IN FRONT OF Indianapolis International Airport around eleven a.m. near the arrivals gate. The place looked like something out of a sci-fi movie, shaped like a giant alien craft. The front and sides were floor-to-ceiling windows, spanning almost a hundred vertical feet.

I made my way inside and found a coffee shop where I grabbed the largest travel mug they offered and filled it with the darkest roast they had on tap. The warm brew took me away from the moment, eased my tense lungs, cleared the dull ache in my head. It only took the Audi's keys pressing into my leg to bring me back to the current situation. I wondered what Frank hadn't told me about the car. Why was it in long-term parking? Had it been sitting there for a while? Had he resorted to resource sharing with another agency? After all, why Indianapolis of all places? This wasn't a major hub for the SIS. And I was sure the vehicle had additional capabilities beyond what he told me. Tracking of the vehicle was bound to be in place. Before starting, hell, before unlocking the doors, we had to check underneath for anything obvious.

With the coffee in hand, I wove through the meandering crowds en route to the gate. I found an empty spot on the wall and settled in. Wave after wave of travelers arrived. Some weary from business, others excited to see their loved ones. I only had to toss a glance in the pack's direction to know that Bear wasn't in their midst. After fifteen minutes, I saw him poking out, a head above the others, shaggy mane and beard. He pushed through the middle of a Japanese family, he was dressed in jeans and a brown leather jacket, and headed toward me with a broad grin.

I left the SIS in '02, and Bear retired from the Marines a couple of years after. We started a little business venture in the following months. Mostly work-for-hire for various government agencies in the US, UK, western European countries, and a few in Central and South America. Business had been good, but after an incident involving Frank Skinner, a double-crossing FBI agent and a terrorist, both Bear and I realized we were suckers for doing only their dirty work. There was no good guy or bad guy in this business when you reached the level of operations we had. Didn't matter who backed you, you were nothing more than a cog in their machine, and when you freelanced, that was a bad thing. So we changed our philosophy, worked for the highest bidder.

He grabbed my hand and pulled me in for a quick one-armed hug. The kind where guys beat each other over the back, somewhere between a hug and a brawl.

It'd been a couple months since I'd seen Bear. He'd taken off for the winter for some time in the Keys. He needed to unwind. I stuck around New York and picked up a few easy jobs to keep the funds coming in and to watch over our interests. It was a nice break for the both of us, but after spending the majority of my adult life with the Bear by my side, I was used to having him around. God forbid one of us ever decided to start a family. The poor wife would hate us.

Bear had traveled light. Everything he needed was in his backpack, so there was no need to go by baggage claim. We followed the signs for long term parking and walked the aisles until we found the Audi. Could've used the key fob to honk the horn, but that would draw unnecessary attention to the vehicle.

Frank had spared no costs on this one. The black S8 looked brand new. I popped the trunk and pulled up the floor. There were compartments on both sides of the spare. I worked my hand down the side until I found the latch. Inside were two Beretta 92FS 9mm pistols, which we were both more than familiar with. He'd also provided two cell phones, and a bag with approximately thirty-thousand dollars in mixed bills. There were two black duffel bags embossed with corporate logos on the back seat containing clothes for both of us.

"Check underneath," I said.

Bear dropped to the ground and wormed his way under the vehicle. "Looks good, man."

I felt around each wheel well for attached devices but came up empty. Under the hood everything looked normal too.

"Think it's clean?" Bear asked.

I shook my head. "Doubtful, but we don't have much choice. Besides, I'm starting to think Frank is our ally on this one, for some reason."

"Do you remember what happened two years ago?" Bear draped his arms over the roof and leaned forward. "I mean, all that time in the hospital, Joe the FBI terrorist, Skinner? It was a total cluster, man."

"I know, Bear," I said. "Frank had me, man. Had me in a damn SUV with two of his guys. They could have taken me out in a gas station parking lot in the middle of nowhere. They could've detained me in the car and taken me to a field station instead of the airport. He knows what I was doing in Chicago."

"Which was what, exactly?"

"I'll get to that," I said. "Point is, he brought you out here, took me to you, and gave us this ride, loaded with everything we need."

"So what you're saying is that we're gonna do his dirty work for him, which by the way is something he won't have his own guys involved in, and then he's gonna kill us."

I pulled out the ID Frank had given me in the SUV. Most people wouldn't be able to differentiate it from their own identification. There were only a few who knew better, and when it came down to it, I was better off with the credentials than without. I tossed it to Bear. "He reactivated me."

Bear shook his head, pulled his door open. With one foot inside, he stopped and said, "Here we go again."

CHAPTER 26

AS WE DROVE TOWARD CHICAGO I CAUGHT BEAR UP ON everything that had happened, starting with my meeting with the Old Man and the alley encounter, all the way up to sending Lexi and the dog off with her father. He nodded along with my story, let me finish before offering his input.

"Sounds to me like we need to start with Thanos's security guys," Bear said. "They were there the night before you planned on finishing the job. I'd like to know where they took him, and why. I guess you don't have any idea how he usually spent his evenings, do you?"

"Unfortunately, no." I hit the blinker and moved into the far left lane to get around a long line of white pickup trucks. "I had little to go by on this one. My thinking at the time was that if he left at night, it was for a meeting. Something hastily thrown together, maybe even unplanned. Certainly not the type of get together they wanted the public aware of."

"He the kind of guy the public would care about?"

"No," I said. "But the men Lexi dealt with while undercover are."

"So for him to go with his guys had to be with someone he didn't completely trust. Someone he feared didn't have his best interests at heart."

"Could be. Or maybe he just wanted to match firepower with firepower."

"Lexi's mob guy." Bear drummed his fingertips on the dash. "Do we know who that is?"

"I don't have a name, and haven't tried to find one, but I'm sure it's not hard to figure out."

"Right, but we need to be careful there. Can't go scaring a bunch of thugs and wind up with this guy breathing down our backs. How heavily do you think you can lean on the Old Man now?"

"Now that I'm officially SIS again? Hardly at all. I can probably get away with feeding him some disinformation to see what he'd throw back. But we're in recovery mode now. If we find Thanos alive, we need to take him into custody. I'll deal with the Old Man later."

"That's a big if at this point, partner."

That had been my feeling since the morning Thanos's house was shot up. There was still the lingering question of whether they were there for only her, or had they intended to take Lexi and Thanos out at the same time?

"You got a way for her to reach you?" Bear asked.

"She's got the number. Just need to pick up a phone to redirect to it. Hopefully she hasn't tried and given up yet."

"Let's stop and get one."

I patted center console. "I don't trust this car, man. My gut tells me there's something in it that'll allow Frank to check for cell signals. We can use the city, tall buildings, to our advantage. But out here on the highway, not a chance. I don't need him coming down on us. Remember, Lexi's got a contract out on her that originated somewhere in the Pentagon. For all we know, Frank is in on it."

"He's probably hoping you find her." Bear held up his hand like a pistol and pretended to take a shot. "Do his dirty work for him, then cut you loose again." He paused a beat. "Or use her life as a bargaining chip to get you to stay in the SIS."

"That's what I'm afraid of, Frank using this situation to gain control of me. When it comes to Lexi, he could put it simply. Do it, or die."

"Or take my hand," Bear quipped. "Ever wonder why that guy's got such a hard on for you?"

"Not really." I tapped the mirror and leaned toward it. "I mean, can you blame him?"

Bear laughed. "Don't get so full of yourself, man. Without me, you're nothing."

"Nothing?"

"Even your fanboy Frank knew he had to haul my hairy ass in from the Keys to Indianapolis to make sure this job gets done right."

"Nah, he's probably got something in store for you too. Wanted to make sure you got a bit of a workout before he put you to task. Good thing, too. You look like you softened up a bit."

"The beach and beer." He patted his stomach. "Does it every time."

We went back and forth for a little bit then settled into the ride. My mind kept tracing over the same basic questions as though they were written in sand and the waves kept washing them away. It helped to get Bear's perspective, and giving him a bit of time to mull things over might uncover something that hadn't crossed my mind. Together we'd solve this. We always did.

We reached Chicago a little after three that afternoon and found a garage to park the Audi about a quarter-mile from Thanos's office. We took a walk, grabbed a couple burgers at Beacon Tavern, then made our way to the building.

A bus stop two blocks away provided good cover. It was near where I'd parked a couple of days earlier. The sun bounced off windows across the street, creating a hell of a glare. It'd also affect those sitting in the offices. I banked on it making it more difficult for Ginger and his guys to ID me and Bear. Plus, turnover was constant at a bus stop. People came and went all day long, sometimes waiting as long as twenty or thirty minutes for their bus. It was a waste of resources to dedicate a lookout for the location.

I grabbed a newspaper off the bench and covered my face with it while focusing on Thanos's building's entry and roof. A guy positioned on top wearing sunglasses and a heavy coat walked the perimeter. He hadn't been there last time I was here. Were they anticipating me, or someone else?

Bear kept his gaze at street level, studied anyone that wasn't moving at a decent clip.

"Anything interesting?" I said after the other couple at the stop boarded a bus.

"Not really. Couple old ladies and a few homeless stand out for no good reason. Everyone else looks like they belong."

"Yeah, so far I've only spotted a rooftop watch. Everyone else? Guess they're keeping security close."

"Or loose because they know they don't need it right now." Bear stood up and stretched. "Or they've gone home 'cause they know there's no point in showing up."

"We need to go for the head. We need to find Ginger and put him to the fire." I looked around at an out-of-place gothic building across the street that looked as though it had been abandoned for some time. "Come on. Let's go for a walk."

I knew Ginger wouldn't get on the bus, and there was little chance he was staying in a nearby apartment or hotel room. Thanos lived a good thirty minutes away. Maybe the head of his security rode with him, possibly acted as his driver. Or maybe he went back to his own place, which I figured was temporary, so likely a hotel near Thanos's house. Either way, he had to have a vehicle. And there wasn't anywhere to park a car all day long in front of, along the side of, or behind the office building.

"That's gotta be it." Bear aimed a finger at a black sign with white vertical letters that spelled out PARKING. We stopped underneath it.

"There's gotta be an entrance somewhere on the other side, too." I peered into the cavernous garage and made out a wide opening catty-corner to us. "Come on."

We made our way through the shadows, used parked vehicles for cover.

"Any of them look familiar?" Bear asked.

I scanned each row for the Cadillac SUV I'd seen a few nights ago. "Not really. Keep a lookout for a black on black Escalade. I've got the plates memorized."

"Good thing," Bear said. "Those things are everywhere."

He should know. That's what he drove.

Bear continued. "Let's get to the other side and wait in the shadows for a bit."

"I got a better idea." I looked through the opening to the street. "They haven't seen you."

"Gotcha." Bear swung his leg over the concrete barrier. "Hang tight and wait for my call."

CHAPTER 27

ASIDE FROM THE SMELL OF EXHAUST AND THE OCCASIONAL GUST
of frigid wind, the parking garage wasn't that bad. Every couple of minutes I
moved into the sunlight, careful to keep my face hidden in the shadows. Made
it feel twenty degrees warmer. Bear had phoned to let me know he was in
place across from the building. From his vantage he could see the front
entrance, the side doors, as well as the street perpendicular to the other end of
the building. The man he was looking for was six-foot tall, thick, and
redheaded. He stood out in a crowd more than Bear.

I kept myself occupied by matching passing faces with the internal database tucked away in a far corner of my brain. Never knew when someone from
ten years or ten hours ago might show up. For now I was most concerned with
recent history, starting on my last day in New York. From the beginning,
nothing seemed right about this job. Anything billed as easy was certain to be
a major pain in the ass. I knew it, and I still signed on for this. The more I
thought about Charles's associate, Matt, the more I became convinced he had
something to do with this. Since I now had Frank and the official SIS channels
in my back pocket, it might be time to put them to good use.

My dealings with the Old Man were a tricky subject with Frank. Though I
carried out similar tasks for the two men, Frank had the Pentagon on his side.
To him, Feng was a ruthless killer who had no problem profiting off the vices
of others. Drugs, gambling, dealing with foreign governments, the Old Man
found none of it untouchable. It was my involvement with him and a few
others that led Frank to recently cease communications with me. It didn't
bother me, as I'd been turning him down for a while. I'd never trusted and

distrusted someone at the same time as much as I did Frank Skinner. From my last days in the SIS, I questioned whether he had mine or any of his agents' best interests at heart.

My phone buzzed and I quickly answered.

Bear's voice piped in through the bluetooth earpiece. "Your guy poked his head out of the building."

"Where's he now?"

"Back inside."

"Sure it was him?"

"Pretty sure. Went to get a pic, but he was already gone."

"He didn't see you, right?"

"The hell, Jack, you think this is amateur hour up in here?"

"No offense, big man, but you've been on vacation. You might be a bit rusty."

"Screw that," he said. "I'm well-rested and ready to kick someone's ass. So you keep that talk up and you'll be first in line."

The line went dead. I shoved the phone back in my pocket and went back to watching the street and garage.

It felt good to have Bear on board. While having Frank around left me feeling like something was gonna go wrong at any moment, Bear countered that and even had me somewhat optimistic that we'd figure out where Thanos had been taken.

Movement from the other end of the garage caught my attention. I turned toward the distraction. Two men had stepped out of the stairwell. I couldn't make out their faces, though, still too dark. They had on heavy coats. Hoods atop their heads. They stepped around a mini-van and walked down the aisle toward me.

I pulled out my phone and called Bear.

"Might have an issue here," I said.

"What is it?" he said.

"Couple guys showed up, came down the stairwell."

"And?"

"They're headed for me. How long you think it'll take you to get over here if something goes wrong?"

He laughed. "Too long. Besides, I ain't going nowhere. Just saw your guy again, and this time he had on a coat. Seems like he's getting ready to move."

I threw a quick glance toward the men again. One had a cell phone pressed to his head. The other hid both hands in his coat pocket. It occurred to me that they might be on their way to meet Ginger. Maybe I'd been looking at it the wrong way. What if Ginger was Thanos's associate, not the head of his security? If the guy was second in command to Thanos, he might be next.

"All right," I said. "I'm coming to you."

"What?"

I hung up the phone and made a line toward the exit. Going out in public put our operation at risk, but if those two men were connected in some way, there wouldn't be a chance to take Ginger down.

The first floor of the gray building across the street was a wall of tinted windows. I dodged traffic, minding the reflection of the garage behind me. The two guys exited through the same opening. They looked up and down the street. One pointed across toward me.

"Christ," I muttered.

The guy slapped his buddy's shoulder, and they hit the blacktop, huffing it in my direction.

I hurried toward the corner, hugged it tight as I turned right. Foot traffic ahead was light, ten or so people directly in front of me, half of them coming my way. Like any typical big city, they kept their gazes fixed ahead, ignoring everything around them. I pushed forward until I reached a spot where the Gothic building I'd noticed earlier indented. A narrow tunnel that led me to an overgrown courtyard. It was a mix of concrete and dead grass and weeds and rusted playground equipment. Broken windows with thick iron bars on every floor overlooked the area. Was it an apartment building? A school? An old psychiatric hospital?

I waited just inside the area, out of view from the tunnel. Thirty seconds passed, then a minute. I waited some more. Cold air whistled through the corridor. It felt as though a hundred sets of eyes gazed down at me, but every time I glanced up I saw no one.

And no one came through the tunnel.

Had they stopped following when they reached the street? Were they waiting on the other side? Maybe they knew I had no way out. Why not apprehend me here, though? There'd be no witnesses.

I called Bear again.

"You in position where you can check out the cross street for me? Tell me if a couple of goons are hanging out in front of the Gothic-looking building."

"Hang on a sec." Bear breathed heavily into the mouthpiece as he covered some ground. "Looks deserted, man. What'd they look like?"

I'd only seen them in the shadows and their reflection in the window. "Never got a good look. Heavy coats with hoods."

Bear laughed. "All right, then every person I see walking around right now is suspect."

"Stay there for a minute. I'm coming out."

I kept the line open as I headed back through the tunnel. Once we made eye contact, Bear moved back into position. The garage wasn't safe anymore, and if the guys were who I thought they were, I figured that Ginger would be spooked by now.

"You think they made you?" Bear asked.

"When I saw them in the window, they pointed at me. So, yeah, I think they know."

"Your boy's gonna be on the move soon."

I had to come up with a plan pretty fast. They stopped following, which meant they had to be tracking me somehow. I looked up and down the street. There were plenty of places they could be watching and I'd never know it.

"I'm gonna take over for you," I said. "They'll see me and either confront me, or leave as a team. You go get the car, pull it up here and wait for my signal."

I put my head down, pulled my collar up, hurried to the corner. Bear passed without batting an eye in my direction. They might already know about him, know we're together. But they might not. Either way it felt like our chances of catching up to Ginger today were diminishing by the minute.

I rounded the corner and placed myself in full view of Thanos's building. I looked up at his office, sunglasses reducing the glare off the window. I saw movement, a couple guys at least.

A black Escalade pulled up to the curb in front of the building. A man sat behind the wheel. His stainless watchband glinted in the sunlight. The passenger seat was empty.

"Where you at, Bear?" I said.

"Almost at the car," he said.

"Anyone watching you?"

"Just the ladies."

"This isn't time to fool around, man."

"It's clear." The S8's supercharged engine revved. "What's going on there?"

"Maybe something." I noticed the man in the SUV put a phone up to his head. "Hang tight for me."

"All—"

The line went dead.

CHAPTER 28

AT THE SAME MOMENT THE CALL DROPPED, THE DOOR ACROSS THE street opened and two men stepped out. They were medium height, lean, angry looking, and definitely armed. Behind them a third man emerged. Even with the beanie on his head, I could tell it was Ginger.

I pulled out the phone and hit redial. The line clicked, rang multiple times and then stopped.

"Dammit," I muttered. "Where are you, Bear?"

One of the angry men crossed the sidewalk, opened the passenger door and leaned in to speak with the driver, who stretched his arm out and shrugged twice. The angry guy looked back at Ginger and nodded. I was barely a hundred feet away, standing in plain view, and they paid no attention to me even though I was sure I'd been made by the two guys in the garage.

My finger hovered over the redial button on the phone in my pocket. I pressed it and waited while the phone rang eight times, then cut off again. I started to worry that they'd reached Bear before he could get out. I held on as long as I could. Once the rear passenger door on the Escalade opened and Ginger crossed the sidewalk for it, I turned and backtracked. I could only hope that Bear was waiting there and that he'd arrive in time for us to follow the SUV. We had to find out what Ginger knew, and we needed it today. Every second mattered now.

I reached the corner where I was mired in a group of powerwalkers all wearing neon tights and bright shoes. They scattered around me, tossing nasty looks as they passed. I scanned the street and walked ahead, saw the two men from the garage approaching. They were less than fifty feet away. I unzipped my jacket, pulled the right flap back a few inches. A shootout in downtown Chicago was less than ideal. Hell, brandishing a weapon would land me in jail. I glanced around at the network of CCTV cameras positioned on the traffic lights, on the sides of buildings. Shops had their own surveillance systems. Whatever was about to happen, it would get caught on video.

As I drew near, the men paid no attention to me. They slowed and stopped in front of a store window. I passed, throwing a nonchalant glance at them, saw them holding hands. I grew tense over the next few steps, my back to them, but after I passed they did nothing. I thought back to the window when I saw their reflection, saw the guy pointing at me. I searched my mind for a better description of that building. Letters stenciled on the window. Visa and MasterCard and AMEX logos on the door. It was a shop of some sort, and I recalled seeing the faint outline of a suit behind the glass.

All that energy wasted for nothing, and on top of that I potentially outed myself in front of Thanos's office.

Bear pulled up to the curb in the Audi. The lock clicked. I yanked the heavy door open and slid into the front seat.

I aimed a finger ahead. "Hurry, they're probably halfway to Sheboygan by now."

Bear didn't wait for me to pull the door shut. He cut back across the street and floored it to the intersection.

"Having fun?" I said.

"I'm trading in my beast for one of these as soon as we get back to the city."

"This car doesn't suit a guy like you. Too fancy."

He matted his beard down with his hand. "You saying I'm not classy enough?"

I shrugged as he hit the brakes at the corner. A group of people blocked the way. We caught the tail end of the Escalade as it was making a left a block away. Oncoming traffic made it impossible to turn in time. "Go straight. We'll turn right at the next intersection and hopefully have a better shot."

Bear gunned it before the light turned green. We raced down the block at seventy miles per hour, weaving left. He slammed the brakes and started turning twenty feet early, cutting in front of three cars. Tires squealed, horns honked. Bear collectively gave them the finger.

"We don't have enough to deal with up ahead?" I said. "You wanna anger some punk with a death wish, too?"

"You're getting soft," he said.

I hoped that wasn't true.

"There they go," he said. "Straight through. Shouldn't have much trouble now."

The light at the next intersection was blinking. Bear rolled through, wedging us in between a couple oncoming cars. My focus now was on the SUV half a block ahead. We had to get closer or risk losing them at a stoplight. There were cameras everywhere. I figured that meant cops were less concerned about basic traffic violations. They probably had license plate readers and a computer programmed to sort out where to send the ticket.

On cue, the light ahead turned yellow as Ginger and his guys cleared the intersection.

"Get through that light," I said.

Bear grinned, hit the gas, and used the lane marker as a center line. We squeezed between a mini-van and a classic Camaro painted black with flames on the hood. The light turned red. Bear pushed harder. I looked out my window at oncoming traffic. I could see the expression on the old guy's face as he tossed his coffee onto his passenger and gripped the wheel with both hands. His mouth was twisted in a scream as he stomped on his brakes.

We got through unscathed, but the sound of cars avoiding impact with us was sure to draw the attention of others.

"Need to be careful here," I said. "They might start evasive maneuvers to draw us out. Settle in a few cars back."

The next few minutes were tense. Sweat beaded up on my forehead. Every ounce of focus I had was spent in an attempt to see through the Escalade's heavily tinted rear window. Were they watching us? Armed and prepared to lead us to a location where they would have the upper hand? We still knew relatively little about Thanos, and nothing about his security guy. How big was their team?

Finally, the SUV turned right.

I pulled up the navigation unit. "They're headed to the interstate."

Bear followed the SUV, which continued on at the same pace. "I think we're good, man."

"I'd feel better if we could track this thing at a distance."

"Call Frank." He looked over and nodded.

I thought about it for a minute. This was an area he could help. But at what cost? I always had to keep Frank's ultimate motive in the forefront. It'd be nice to say he'd lend us all the support we needed. But I'd be lying. Frank Skinner would do whatever benefited Frank Skinner at that moment. If that meant helping, fine. Or it might mean him leading us down the wrong path while he took over and dictated how things would end up.

"Let's just stay on them for a while," I said. "If they're looking for a tail, I doubt this is the car that's gonna catch their attention."

"Wishful thinking," Bear said.

If they were trained properly, the make and model of the vehicle would mean nothing to them.

We merged onto the interstate heading north and fell six cars back, moving up and down the line as necessary. Bear did everything he could to make every move appear natural. Traffic was thick but moved ten miles per hour over the posted speed limit. Twenty minutes passed. My fingers hovered over the phone the entire time. I had to find a way to reach out to Lexi. By now she had likely called. Hopefully she'd continue to try because at that point I had no idea when I'd get my hands on a new burner phone.

The Escalade exited, and one other car in front of us followed them. Bear and I pulled down our sun visors and sat tall in an effort to stay out of sight.

"I doubt they'd recognize your ugly mug," I said.

"You're kidding, right?" Bear said. "You know as well as I do that they subscribe to MERC Monthly magazine. I was the damn centerfold three months last year."

It was good to have his off-beat sense of humor around again. But it did little to ease the anxiety that had built up over the past couple of days.

We dropped back further after turning onto the three-lane road. Bear pulled into a turnoff that entered a shopping center, then merged back on the road at the last second. Little things like that added up, made it seem like we were looking for something. At least that was the hope.

"Looks like they're about to turn," Bear said.

I studied the map. "That's a neighborhood. One way in, one way out." I looked up, waited until they made the turn. "Drive past and pull into the first parking lot you find."

We cruised through the intersection in the middle lane.

"For Christ's sake," Bear said.

The SUV had pulled to the curb a few blocks down. The front doors were open. One guy was on his phone. The other was looking in our direction.

CHAPTER 29

WE PULLED INTO THE FIRST PARKING LOT ON OUR SIDE OF THE road in front of a barbecue restaurant, gas station and drug store, all in one. Bear kept the S8 in gear while we waited next to a pump for the SUV to show up, or one of the men to emerge through the thick hedges surrounding the perimeter of the lot. My heart beat in time with every second that passed. Cars and trucks and SUVs streamed by in a steady pattern following the traffic light half a block down. A line of school buses drove past filled with kids no older than seven or eight. I figured they were on a trip to visit the Field Museum in town.

"They'd have come by now," Bear said.

I nodded, said nothing, kept my gaze fixed on the oncoming traffic.

"I can double back, see—"

"Nah, don't put yourself out there yet," I said. "They're following a protocol. Probably trying to sniff any followers out. Hang tight here. I'm going inside the store."

The first few steps in the open were agonizing. There was no cover, leaving me an easy mark. I clenched my jacket tight to my body and jogged across the parking lot. Behind me the Audi pulled away from the gas pump and into an open parking spot along the side of the building. I nodded at Bear, then entered the store. There were cameras positioned everywhere. No chance I could get in and out without having my face filmed.

First thing I did was fill two large cups with coffee. The brew smelled hours old. Didn't matter. We both needed the jolt. I grabbed a couple premade hoagies, some bottled water, and headed to the counter. The young woman there barely acknowledged me.

"I need a couple phones, too," I said.

"Which ones?" she asked, eyes still glued to her magazine. It was an article about ten things your boyfriend secretly wants you to do in bed, but would never tell you.

"You ever done any of those?" I figured if they had me on camera I might as well make an impression.

She looked up at me, cheeks turning a dark shade of red. A slight smile formed on her thin lips. "Maybe half."

"The cheapest ones you got."

She jerked backward as though I'd swung at her. "What?"

"The phones," I said. "I'll take the two cheapest you got."

Her smile broadened as she turned and grabbed two Nokias from a hanger and set them next to the coffees. "You get sixty minutes free on each."

"I'm heading up to Kenosha for a couple nights if you're free later." I tapped the magazine. "Maybe show you the rest of those moves."

Her cheeks reddened again as she held up her left hand. "Thanks for the offer, but I'm married."

I gave her a wink as I paid the bill, grabbed the goods, and exited the store, convinced I'd made an impression on the lady. And now if someone came questioning the clerk, she'd tell them I was headed to Kenosha, and Bear and I would have at least a few hours to work undetected.

I handed Bear a coffee and hoagie. The big man scarfed down his sandwich while I talked.

"As soon as you're finished let's get out of here and find a spot across the street somewhere. I don't want to lose sight of the entrance to that neighborhood."

He discarded the sandwich wrapper in the grocery bag, then pulled out of the parking lot. We found a nice spot a few blocks away on the other side of the neighborhood, located on the opposite side of the street. The view was perfect, allowing us to see every car, driver, and passenger that left.

While waiting I slipped out of range and powered on a phone. A few button pushes later it was connected to my server and calls to a specific number would route to the cell phone. All I had to do now was wait. Temperatures were dropping, so I decided to take a chance and leave it powered on in the car.

Bear glanced at the device. "You sure you wanna take that risk in here?"

"What's he gonna do? Fire me? Even if they can lock onto this, I'm using it once and dumping it. They won't be able to reroute the call or gain access to the conversation. At most, they'll figure out where we are, and I'm pretty sure they already know that."

Bear lifted his finger off the steering wheel. "Look at that."

Across the street a white Chevy Malibu waited at the stoplight. The driver was a thick silhouette behind the windshield. "Think that's him?"

"Pretty big dude," Bear said. "You said he's a big guy, right?"

"Yeah, somewhere between you and me on the goon scale."

He started the Audi and put his hand on the gearshift. The light turned green and the Chevy pulled out and accelerated past us. There was no mistaking the driver. Big guy, red hair. It was Ginger, and he was alone.

"Let's move," I said.

Bear was a step ahead of me, having already shifted into reverse. He peeled back, slipped it into drive, and merged onto the road without stopping.

Ginger had a four-car lead on us. We had to get closer. Without a spotter in his vehicle, I was less concerned about him noticing us. If he did, so be it. We'd have at least a five-minute window to corner him.

"I've seen this guy up close," I said. "We need to be ready for a fight."

"I've got two months of pent up grappling in me." Bear had been a state champion wrestler. He had offers to Michigan, Ohio State, and others. He'd also studied Brazilian Jiu-Jitsu over the years. The best chance against him was with a two-by-four. Or a gun. If he got within arm's reach, his target wasn't getting away.

Ginger's driving became erratic. He swerved across all three lanes, only to swerve back and make a sharp right turn into a parking lot. We cruised past and pulled into the next entrance. I kept an eye on his car. He idled, taking up four spots.

"Keep a sight line between us," I said.

"What do you think he's doing? Meeting someone here?"

"That'd be pretty damn good luck on our part."

"Yeah, scratch that, I guess." Bear cracked his window. Cold air flooded the car and dissipated the smell of burned coffee and oil and vinegar and cheap lunch meats. "Much better. You could use a shower, you know."

"Screw you."

"Only after you've showered." Bear grinned, amused at himself. His look of contentment gave way to concern as his brow furrowed and his eyes narrowed.

"What is it?" I tried to follow his gaze but came up empty.

"Who's that approaching his car?"

I scanned the lot. "Don't see anyone."

"It's a woman. Well, shaped like a woman, at least. Can't see her face."

She came into view for a moment before ducking into the passenger seat. Only a sliver of her face had been visible between her hat and scarf. Not nearly enough to make an ID.

"There was a camera in the trunk." Bear popped the latch before I could say anything. He opened his door and stepped out.

"Stay low," I said. "Don't let him spot you."

He draped one arm over the roof and leaned his head in. "They don't know me."

"But they know me, maybe. Doesn't take much to connect the dots between us, big man."

He nodded and slipped around the rear of the vehicle. The car bounced up and down a couple times as he put his weight on the trunk. A few seconds later, the lid slammed down and he dropped back into his seat.

"Nice rig," I said, admiring the Canon camera and lens.

Bear put it together, then powered the unit on. He set it on the steering wheel to hold it steady. "There we go."

"They looking our way?" I said.

He shook his head. "Just sitting there talking."

I leaned over to get a glimpse of the viewfinder, saw two figures partially hidden by the glare on the windshield. "Can you get in any closer on the woman?"

He shifted the camera slightly and adjusted the lens. "Yeah, but it doesn't do no good. Take a look."

I leaned in a bit more. She had removed her hat, but the grainy image made it impossible to make out a single detail. "Has to be someone he doesn't want his crew to see him with, right?"

Bear shrugged. "Could be his wife, bringing him a casserole."

"Always with the food."

He patted his stomach. "Ain't had a decent meal today. Anyway, yeah, I'd say it's someone he shouldn't be meeting with. Think this Thanos guy sent someone to him?"

"Depends," I said. "On whether you believe Thanos was taken against his will, or he fled. If it's the latter, then yeah, this could be the person they delivered Thanos to after ushering him from his house in the middle of the night. Now she's reporting to Ginger."

"Fill me in again on that. Did you see him with Ginger that night?"

I recalled hiding in the woods near the hedges, out of camera view, waiting there in the frigid cold. The SUV pulled up, a couple minutes later Ginger exited the house with Thanos and led him to the vehicle. Whoever had driven the SUV went into the house and never came out.

"So what if that wasn't one of Ginger's guys with him that night?" Bear said.

"Valid point," I said. "I've only seen a few of them up close. It's possible that Thanos utilized another group, or someone else's security team, to move him. All I know is this somehow ties into the mob boss and politician that Lexi was working on when she blew her cover."

The passenger door on Ginger's car opened and the woman emerged. Her hood was down, but her back was toward us. In a flash she covered her dark hair and then disappeared from view.

I flung my door open, put one foot on the ground. "Don't lose Ginger. I'm going after the woman."

CHAPTER 30

BEAR CURSED ME AS I WALKED AWAY FROM THE CAR. I'D LEFT HIM with no choice. We couldn't lose Ginger, whether he went back to the house following his meeting or moved onto another location. We also had to find out who he met with. She had to know something, was involved somehow.

I kept my head down and used every truck, minivan and SUV to shield me from view. The woman weaved through rows of cars. Keys dangled from her hand, glinting in the sunlight. I had no plan other than to confront her. What happened if she made it inside her car and out of the parking spot before I reached her?

As soon as I thought it, it happened. She stopped in front of an early '90s Ford F-150, white with blue trim wrapped around the lower third. The door slammed shut. The big V-8 roared to life. I started checking handles of cars parked nearby.

The truck rolled forward out of its spot.

I spotted a woman carrying a baby, ran up to her. She flinched back at the sight of me.

"Ma'am, I'm a federal agent. I need your car."

"Go away!" she screamed.

I couldn't recall a single time that had ever worked for me. I threw my hands up in the air and backed away from her. Last thing I needed was a good samaritan intervening because they thought I was assaulting the lady or trying to take her kid.

The truck had reached the end of the aisle, fifty feet away from the exit.

A police cruiser patrolled by the storefronts.

The woman with the baby was jogging toward the cop.

"Come on," I said, my words forming into a heavy vapor that lingered in front of my face.

Bear was gone, took off after Ginger. The woman in the truck was getting away. She was stopped eight cars deep in the left turn lane out of the parking lot. One, maybe two light cycles at the most, which left me with a minute and a half to find a vehicle.

The woman with the baby was nearing the police cruiser, which had pulled up to the curb and stopped. The officer rolled down the window and leaned out, his bald head glistening in the sunlight.

I moved a couple rows down in search of a vehicle. Modern cars were a pain for me to steal. I needed something old and easy to get into. A soft top Jeep would have been perfect. Problem was, there weren't many choices in that department.

And then I saw it.

I cringed, but I knew it'd work.

Someone was either crazy enough to drive their motorcycle in sub-freezing temperatures, or they'd abandoned their ride. I ran my hands through the saddle bags in search of a spare key. The only thing I found was a change of clothes and some tools, which left me questioning whether I was right about it being abandoned.

The light turned green. Six cars made it out. The woman was still there, along with seven cars behind her. No worries there with the bike if I could get it started.

I straddled the seat. It wasn't the most sophisticated motorcycle. Only took about ten seconds to hardwire the ignition and get it running. It sounded like a chainsaw cutting through concrete, but it managed to shift into gear, jerking away from the parking spot.

Glancing back, I saw the cop standing in front of his cruiser, looking out over the parking lot. His gaze swept right past me. Shaking her head, the woman shrugged and then patted him on the shoulder. Guess they'd given up on finding me.

Even at five miles per hour the wind felt like a block of ice hitting me square in the face. I wouldn't be able to last long on the bike. Hopefully the woman didn't have far to travel.

I reached the line of cars waiting to exit. The light turned green. I swerved inside between the vehicles and curb and sped past them, drawing a few honks along the way. To hell with them. We made it about a hundred feet before another light turned red. I settled in a couple cars back from the F-150, reached into the saddle bag, and pulled out some clothing. I exhaled a sigh of relief which nearly froze in front of me. The bundle of clothes included something I could use.

A heavy, woolly, purple scarf.

I ditched the rest and wrapped the scarf around my face, leaving only my eyes exposed. As the light turned green and I pulled away, the wind no longer felt like a sledgehammer against my skin. My eyes watered, but that I could deal with.

I kept to the driver's side of the Honda Odyssey in front of me, swerving to the lane divider on occasion to check the position of the F-150. A few minutes passed, we hit a stop and go spot, then the road opened up and the little bike was humming along at fifty-five.

The wind managed to find every chink in my armor. My hands and feet went numb. Even my face, clad in purple wool, was not immune to the effects. I couldn't tell if I had lips or a nose anymore.

After ten minutes, I caught a break. The F-150 signaled and moved over two lanes to the right. I followed suit and continued into the turn lane. There was no one in between us now. We pulled into a parking lot that contained a small grocery store next to a pizza place, and a Hardee's on the corner. My stomach grumbled even though I'd had a sandwich not that long ago. I shrugged it off. There'd be time to eat later.

She navigated through the restaurant's parking lot and pulled up to the drive-thru menu. I backed the bike into a parking spot and waited while she ordered her food. There was a line of three cars leading up to the window. When the F-150 pulled forward, it was just outside the point of no return, the spot where it would be locked in with a brick wall on one side, and high concrete median stacked with hedges on the other.

I hopped off the bike, leaving it idling, and dashed across the lot. I held a pistol in my right hand, pressed tight to my side to keep it out of view.

The exhaust around the truck was heavy. I sucked in a deep breath of gas fumes and kept myself from coughing it back up. I leaned forward to stay out of view, reached for the passenger door handle. It was unlocked. I flung it open and jumped inside the cab.

The woman froze at the sight of the pistol in her face. Then her gaze traveled upward and met mine.

"Jack?"

CHAPTER 31

I SAT THERE STUNNED, UNABLE TO FORM THE SIMPLEST WORD. The last two days raced past in my mind's eye. Had everything been a lie? Was I set up from the start? If so, by the Old Man, or was it after that point?

"Jack, how did you find me?"

I had the pistol pointed at her face and she didn't blink.

"What the hell, Lexi?" I slammed the passenger door shut. "You wanna tell me what the hell is going on here, because right about now, I couldn't be more confused."

She shifted the truck into reverse and backed out of the drive-thru line. A car swung around the curve from the mic and honked at her.

I tightened my grip on the pistol.

"Relax, Jack," she said. "I'm backing into a parking spot is all. Tell me, what did you see?"

My phone buzzed in my pocket. I ignored it. "I saw you get into a car with that Ginger, the same damn guy from outside Thanos's office. The guy I assume had something to do with Thanos's disappearance. That's what I saw."

She leaned away from me, one hand on the wheel, the other stretched out over the seat between us. She didn't appear scared, rather she was bracing for what was to come. "I know how it looks, but—"

"Oh, you do?" I lowered the pistol, shook my head. "Tell me, truthfully, did you try to contact me before you rushed back to Chicago?"

She said nothing, held her gaze steady.

"That's what I thought. OK, then, did you know they were gonna show up at your dad's place?"

"I have no idea who that was." She paused for several moments. "What happened there? Did you confront them?"

I chewed on the inside of my cheek for a few seconds. "Don't worry about that. I'm here now, right?"

She nodded slowly. "Look, I know this seems bad, or that I didn't trust you enough to let you know I was coming here. But, Jack, you gotta realize, I've got a lot riding on this. Thanos, he's the key to—"

"Clearing your name."

"Yes, and no." She sighed. "It's complicated."

Making her aware that I knew more would derail my purpose in the truck. "Back to this conversation you just had with Ginger."

"His name's not Ginger. It's Kozlov."

"Kozlov?" I rubbed the stubble on my chin. "Russian?"

She nodded. "Mitya Kozlov is a former KGB agent who defected and now makes his home in Canada along the Wisconsin border where he can slip in and out of the US without detection. He's a contractor, to put it simply. He was hired by a certain individual to keep dibs on Thanos. After my snafu, it became apparent that Thanos required more than someone watching from afar, and Kozlov was tasked with putting together a security team."

"So this whole time, you've been working with Kozlov?"

"Make no mistake about it, Jack. He and I are not on the same team. Nowhere close to it. If I were still working in an official capacity, that meeting back there would have never taken place. But through my time in the DCO, I got to know him and had him as an open channel."

"He works for the mob boss."

"Not exactly."

"Who, then?"

"You don't need to involve yourself in this." She looked out the windshield and paused.

I followed her gaze, saw a young, round woman trudging through the wind toward us. Lexi rolled her window down.

"You still want your order?" the girl asked.

Lexi pulled out a wad of cash and handed her a twenty. She rolled the window up, stared down at her lap. "There's enough for both of us."

"Because, really, that's my biggest concern right now." I searched for words that hid themselves well in the recesses of my mind. It wasn't that betrayal was a foreign concept to me, I just couldn't figure out Lexi's angle here. "So what the hell did Kozlov tell you? Where's he hiding Thanos?"

She gripped the wheel with both hands, took a deep breath, looked at me. "He doesn't have him, and he doesn't have a clue where he went. A few nights ago, his men left with Thanos from Thanos's house and never made it to their rendezvous point."

He hadn't told her that he was driving the car Thanos was in. "Why were they taking him? And where?"

"The where I'm unsure of." She licked her lips and took another breath. "The why was because they had very credible intelligence that someone outside their sphere of influence was about to make an attempt on Thanos's life." She leveled her gaze at me, drew her lips thin.

I sat still, said nothing, peered at her, waiting to see where she was taking this.

She hiked an eyebrow. "Would you know anything about that?"

I shrugged and remained quiet.

"I don't know a whole lot about the SIS. Hell, no one does, at least no one who'll talk to me. Is this the kind of thing they handle? Assassinations of US citizens?"

How much of what she had told me was truth, and how much was a fabrication? She had every reason to lie to me now, especially if she didn't trust me. Which, face it, neither of us had any reason to trust the other. I walked a fine line here. She believed I had been operating under the SIS shield from the beginning and knew nothing of my relationship with the Old Man. Even if I filled her in, I had no idea why Feng wanted Thanos dead. I figured Thanos had screwed him over or interfered in his business somehow. I saw it differently now. There were too many competing interests.

"Jack?" She turned toward me, reached out with one hand. "This is off the record, you know. Just tell me, what were you here for?"

"You know I can't do that. Too much at stake for both of us if I let you in. These men behind the SIS, you don't want to get on their bad side, or any side for that matter. They have power like you wouldn't believe. You know all those channels you have to go through to get something done in the Bureau? That doesn't exist in the SIS. If I need something, I make a phone call. Half the time I'm given instant approval. The other half, he makes a single call and it's done."

"That's the reason, then, isn't it? You were there to kill Thanos."

"You can draw whatever conclusion you like, Lexi. Just don't go bragging about it to the wrong people. You're already in a heap of trouble, and someone wants you dead. Remember that. Rattle too many doors and they'll task the right person to complete the job."

"You mean you."

I shook my head. "I already showed you the pictures. Yeah, someone reached out to me. And I know all the details. I know what you did, the people you were involved with. But I still can't figure out exactly what you're trying to do here, why you care about saving this Thanos guy."

She glanced away, said nothing.

"Christ, we're never gonna get anywhere if you won't let me in on what the hell is going on."

She forced a laugh. "I could say the same."

The girl stepped out into the cold carrying a couple white bags. As she neared the truck, my phone started vibrating. I answered.

"Any luck?" Bear said.

"You could say that," I said, watching Lexi roll down her window again. "What about you?"

"He's back at the house. I ditched the car at that gas station and headed into the neighborhood on foot. Looks like he might be alone inside, hard to tell though. What's the deal with the woman?"

"It's someone I already met."

"Intriguing."

"I'll fill you in shortly." I hung up and grabbed the burger Lexi held out to me.

We ate in silence for the next five minutes. The wind occasionally rattled the truck and found its way inside the cabin. The smell of meat and pickles and fries and bread overtook the musty odor.

Lexi was first to talk. She took a sip of her iced tea and swallowed hard. "I'll set up a meeting for tonight with Kozlov."

"Where?"

She held up a finger to silence me. "One condition, Jack."

"This'll be good."

"We go together. OK? From this point on, we are joined at the hip on this. You're not gonna get all the glory for finishing your mission. We find Thanos, and we take him in and let our bosses figure out what to do with him."

I took another bite of my burger, chewed it slowly, savoring the thick ketchup-drenched patty.

"Is that a yes?"

"I'm thinking about it," I said through a mouthful of food. I took my time swallowing, washed it down with my soda. "All right, we'll do it your way."

She nodded, but the look on her face told me she knew I was lying.

CHAPTER 32

WE MET UP WITH BEAR A SHORT WHILE LATER AT A NEARBY HOTEL. He'd rented a suite with a king bed and two pull out sofas. The wallpaper looked like it hadn't been changed since the seventies. The appliances had been upgraded sometime in the nineties. Bear pulled out two cold beers from the fridge and placed one in front of me, then sat opposite me at the small square table. Our forearms nearly met when we both leaned forward. I caught him up on my conversation with Lexi.

"You trust her?" he asked.

"I haven't known her that long," I said. "But, yeah, I feel like I can trust her."

"Feeling like you can and actually doing so are two very different things." He yanked the pull tab off his can and scratched at his fingernail with it. "She's out there right now, walking around, on the phone. You believe she's calling the guy? Or is she on the phone with someone who'd love to catch us in the act?"

I shrugged. "I don't know about you, but I'm covered by the SIS shield right now."

Bear laughed, tossed the pull tab at my face. I deflected it at the last second. It bounced off the table and landed on the floor.

"You know as well as I do," he said, "that you're only covered as long as Frank says you are. So what, he read you into the SIS again? How far you think that goes with him?"

"Yeah, I know, man. I'm only half-serious. I don't trust him anymore than I trust her. I've known him longer and know what he's capable of."

Bear emptied his can into his mouth, crushed it and tossed it in the sink. "She comes back in, says she's got us a meeting, you're gonna go into that confident we'll walk out?"

"I am," I said. "'Cause if we don't, neither will she. Lexi needs us as much as we need her right now."

"What're you gonna do when we find Thanos?"

"Good question." I'd been thinking about that since we left to meet Bear at the hotel. "I haven't come to a conclusion on that. I guess I want to hear him out, find out what the hell he did to piss off the Old Man enough that he put a contract on Thanos's life."

"So you're gonna play judge, jury, and executioner?" Bear crossed his arms. "Doesn't sound like you, like us. We take the job, do whatever we gotta do, and earn the paycheck. You seriously gonna balk on this one? What happens back in New York when the Old Man finds out? I'm telling you, it won't be good. At the very least the well will dry up. No more work from him, or anyone associated with him. We'll be back on government assistance, dealing with assholes like Frank all the damn time."

I sat silent.

"You never know with the Old Man, Jack. He might set Charles and all his dogs on you. Take you to that compound, into the dungeon and torture all your secrets out of you. And don't you roll your eyes, man. You know as well as I do that it exists, and he's got some creepy frickin' dudes that'll pay you a visit down there. Old spooks from the Cold War days, well-trained in the art of making a man talk against his will."

I said nothing.

"That ain't what I want. Job might not've been assigned to me, but for both our sakes, I might finish it for you if we come across this Thanos guy. To hell with your new girlfriend."

I arched an eyebrow.

"Come on, I know what else her and Frank have in common."

I folded my arms over the table and leaned forward. "Is that right?"

"They've both fucked you, albeit in very different ways."

I cracked a smile. "Look, let's cross the Thanos bridge when we get there. As it stands right now, I'm willing to work with Lexi if it helps her get out of the shithole she's in."

"Just remember she brought her own shovel to that party and apparently kept digging well after the music stopped. And unless you can sit here, look me in the eye, and say you trust her, and truthfully and I mean tuh-ruthfully mean it, I think you oughta off the dude the first chance you get."

I nodded, got up, walked over to the window. It looked out over the parking lot. There were twenty or so cars spread throughout. I figured it would start to fill up around six when all the working stiffs who'd traveled hundreds of miles to be away from their families started piling in from a long day at someone else's office.

Lexi stood on the sidewalk by the main road, talking on a cell phone. Was it Kozlov? Someone else? I thought about why she left me out of the loop regarding the Russian. I was someone worth keeping at arm's distance, maybe a little closer. She had to figure out why I was there. Was that why she slept with me? To get me to let my guard down a little? She had to have known that wouldn't work, not with my background.

She shoved the phone in her coat pocket, turned, looked up at the room. I knew she couldn't see me standing there, but it was as if she were staring right at me. She was too far away to get a solid read on her expression, though I was curious how she felt after her call. She cut across the grass to the side entrance and disappeared from sight.

I sat down at the table and waited with Bear. He'd refreshed our drinks. Neither of us spoke.

Lexi entered the room and went to the fridge. She pulled out a bottle of water, took a drink, leaned against the counter with her right foot crossed over her left.

"All right," she said. "I got us a meeting with Kozlov."

"When?" I said.

"Tonight."

"Where?" Bear said.

"In the city. You'll need to dress up a bit."

CHAPTER 33

WE TOOK A CAB INTO THE CITY FROM THE HOTEL. EASIER THAT way. No dealing with cars that might be tracked or noticed. No worrying about being pulled over and having to deal with local authorities. It wouldn't be the first time I had a mission compromised due to local law enforcement.

We were awash in orange glow from the moment we hit the highway, and it didn't let up once in the city. The streets and buildings were lit up. Like New York, Chicago never slept. At least not the part we were in. I knew just a few miles in either direction a different scene was playing out. Not the upbeat, party class, but the rough life, the millions of inhabitants who had nothing and those among them who were willing to do whatever it took to have just a little bit more.

The cab dropped us off in front of Benny's Chop House. I raised an eyebrow at Bear as my stomach grumbled at the thought of an aged ribeye. Bear patted his stomach.

"Don't get excited, boys," Lexi said as she shoved Bear toward the curb. "This is just where we're getting dropped off."

"We've got a couple hours," I said. "Might as well make the most of it."

We were all standing in front of the restaurant. The cab had pulled away. The line to get in was half a block long. Must've been good if people didn't mind waiting in ten-degree weather.

"Need a reservation for that place," she said. "Or you can wait half the night. And last time I checked, we don't have that kind of time, friends."

"You're the local," I said. "Lead the way."

She moved swiftly through the crowds, finding the smallest seams to pass through, like a striker maneuvering down the field with the ball. Bear and I kept up. If not for her breaking the wave first, we never could have split the groups traveling against us.

Finally, we stopped in front of Ouzo Cafe, which looked to be a Mediterranean restaurant. Unlike many of the other options, there was no menu on the window. The tables were sparsely populated. An old guy with silver wings on the side of his head and no hair on top stood in front of a long grill, arms folded over his stout belly.

"It's good," she said. "Trust me. He's an old family friend."

I pulled the door open for Lexi, then entered with Bear close behind. She shrugged off her coat, hung it on an empty peg on a rack by the front door. The smell of bread and searing meat filled my nose. My stomach tightened in response. Guess it had been a few days since I'd treated it to a decent meal.

"As I live and breathe," the old guy said in a thick Turkish accent.

Lexi smiled, hiked her hand in the air in front of her and waved. "Hiya, Gus."

"My little Lexi, come for a visit." Gus walked out of sight, banged on a door and yelled, "Amelia, Lexi is here."

"Come on." She motioned for us to take a seat at the table closest to the grill.

"And who are your large friends?" he asked, eying Bear. "I'm not sure that I have enough food for that one."

Bear chuckled. "Just throw me a nice size steak and I'll be good."

Gus pointed at him. "Add on a side of scallops, and you have a deal."

"I like this guy," Bear said.

Lexi introduced us all to Gus's daughter, Amelia, then the woman joined us at the table. She and Lexi talked about their home lives. When Amelia asked about Lexi's husband, Lexi said nothing more than she and her husband had split up. Amelia seemed to know enough about the guy's past issues not to press for more details.

Gus served the food, and the family backed off for fifteen minutes so we could eat. Not a word was spoken. None of us knew when we might get another meal like this. I had to assume that the roller coaster would begin the moment we stepped into a room alone with Kozlov.

After we were finished, Gus brought over a bottle of red wine and four glasses. He sat down next to Lexi, reached out and grabbed her hand. His jovial face had turned sour.

"What brings you by, Lexi?" he asked. "I have to assume that these two men are not exactly friends, right? This has something to do with work?"

"Always the astute observer." She raised her glass to the old guy, then took a sip.

He placed both arms on the table and leaned forward. His gaze bounced between Bear and me. "Lexi, she is like a daughter to me. Her and Amelia were practically raised together. You see, in the Turkish Invasion of Cyprus, I worked with Lexi's father."

I felt the expression on my face change against my will.

"Yes," he said. "You didn't think I've been a cook all my life? No, that I inherited from my grandmother. What I was in my previous life was an intelligence agent."

And now I knew why Lexi had brought us here. Wasn't just for a good meal. Gus might have something we could use. He might have some intel. Being that he was located in town, he probably knew a few people. People who might open up to him.

I followed Lexi's gaze around the room, the corners, ceilings, potted plants.

"Anyone been in here recently?" she asked.

Gus laughed. "Come on, you think I would let anyone get away with bugging my restaurant?"

"If they did it right, there'd be nothing to get away with," she said. "You'd never know it was done."

He shrugged. "We check from time to time."

"When was the last time?" I asked.

"Very recently," he said. "Now this must be serious. Spit it out, girl. What do you need?"

CHAPTER 34

LEXI REACHED INTO HER BAG AND PULLED OUT A WHITE envelope. She carefully worked the flap from the edge, pulling back the clear tape covering the seam. There were five or six photos inside. She folded the flap back and set the envelope in front of Gus.

He stared at her for a moment before emptying the contents onto the table in front of him. The photos fell out facedown. One by one he picked them up, flipped them over, and reviewed them, nodding occasionally. He held onto them like he was playing poker. After he had checked all five out, he placed them on the table, face up.

I had expected the photos to be of Thanos, and I wasn't wrong. But the lineup also included a picture of Kozlov and two of the other guys from his detail. A picture of the man I saw run into Thanos's house on the last night Thanos disappeared. There was a photo of Jarred Denton, the politician, wearing a gray suit. And finally one of an older guy I hadn't seen before. He had the look of a powerful man.

Gus placed his calloused fingertip on the picture of the guy in the suit. "Jarred Denton. I'd recognize him anywhere." He looked up at Lexi. "I'd heard he was dirty, but I don't keep up with local politics that much. Guess this confirms it?"

She nodded slightly, said nothing.

"And this guy," he pointed at Kozlov. "He's Russian. And so is this one."

I followed his gaze to the picture of the older man.

"What about him?" Lexi shifted the picture of Thanos to the middle of the pack. "Do you know him?"

Gus took a deep breath, leaned back, crossed his arms over his stomach. He kept his focus on the picture, possibly to avoid looking at any of us while he decided how much information to divulge. It was obvious he recognized Thanos. Why would he hold back?

"Gus, do you know this man?" She paused a beat, leaned her head forward to catch Gus's stare. "This is important. You know I wouldn't be here if it wasn't."

"This man," Gus thumped the photo with his finger. "Why are so many people interested in him? As far as I can tell, he's a businessman. Has his hands in many pots. Nothing too bad, though. Maybe a little intimidation, but to be as powerful as him, you have to have that."

"Do you know his name?" Lexi asked.

Gus remained silent and still for several seconds. The murmur of a crowd of people passing outside filled the void. "Thanos."

"He disappeared," she said. "We received word that a contract was out on him, and he was supposed to come with me. I had a place to keep him safe for a couple of days while I figured out what was going on."

"You're going about this wrong!" Gus slammed his open hand on the table. "You screwed up, Lexi. I don't know why the people around you won't drill this into your thick head. You have to accept the consequences."

"What? Like you? I should get old and run a restaurant instead of doing what I'm compelled to do?" She pushed away from the table, motioned around the room. "And don't act like you aren't still in the game. That's the whole damn reason I'm here tonight. You're as connected as anybody. You've got sources around the globe."

Bear and I sat back and watched the drama play out. Here I thought we were having a quick meal and instead we had a front row seat for tonight's Spy Theater.

Gus's face had turned bright red. He got up, grabbed a fresh bottle of wine and poured a glass for himself. A few gulps later, he'd calmed down.

"This man got involved with the wrong people," he said finally getting to what he knew. "I guess that's putting it lightly. He wound up in possession of something he should have never laid eyes on, and now multiple groups want it. From what I understand, he hid whatever it was, or sent it off for safekeeping." Gus picked up the picture of the older guy. "I don't know who has him, but I can tell you that some very powerful people are all looking for him."

"Who is that?" she pointed at the photo in his hand.

Gus shrugged. "Haven't seen him before."

"What about Kozlov?" she said. "Tell me what you know about him."

"You know him better than I," Gus said. "Former KGB. He has no official ties to anyone I see here."

She leaned her head to the side, opened her eyes wide. "You telling the truth?"

"What reason have I to lie?"

"We're meeting with this man in less than an hour. If he's involved in this mess, I need to know now."

Gus sighed. "He has connections, yes, but he works independently. Now, put a gun to my head and force me to pick his allegiance, and I'll say he doesn't have your best interests at heart. So if you see anyone else in the same room, you better have marked all the exits."

Lexi picked up the photo of the older guy. I leaned in closer to her to study his face. I'd never seen him before, not in person, not on the news, not in a dossier. He hadn't pissed off my bosses enough to draw my attention to him.

But considering the circles we were dealing with, I began to wonder what his affiliation with the Old Man might be. Was this the guy who reached out with the contract on Thanos? Was this guy the Old Man's ally in this tangled spider web of criminal minds?

CHAPTER 35

WHEN WE LEFT THE RESTAURANT AND STEPPED OUTSIDE I WAS AS confused as I was cold. It seemed all my blood had pooled in my stomach, leaving my face and extremities fighting to stay warm.

The time with Gus had been somewhat helpful. We had a few names, a few strings to connect the players together. What we lacked was enough information to make those connections useful. It was too early to assume anyone's involvement in Thanos's disappearance. To do so could cause us to miss an important detail along the way.

The sidewalk was crowded and cabs were few. Lexi tried to hail one, but after three passed her over, she said screw it. Our next stop was less than a mile away. We set out on foot, Lexi bookended by me and Bear. Groups of people split to let us pass. Even the toughest looking guys stepped aside. Looking at Bear's face, it wasn't surprising.

"That's it, up ahead." Lexi pointed toward the soft pink neon glow of an open doorway.

A tall black guy with no jacket wearing some kind of thermal top that wrapped around his over-developed biceps like cellophane sat on a stool in front of the entrance. He didn't pay attention to us until we were within ten feet of the club. His gaze bounced from me, to Bear, and back.

Deep bass resonated underfoot and electronic music filled the air. Muffled chatter rose and fell.

The bouncer held up two fingers, indicating the cover charge of twenty dollars total.

I handed him a fifty. "Keep the change."

He nodded, gestured us in with his chin. We stepped into the softly illuminated tunnel that resembled a birthing canal, meant to deliver us to the club.
A tall slender woman with blue hair stood in a cubby. She held her arm out.

"Take your jacket?" she said.

I shrugged her off. Lexi took off her coat and handed it to the lady. So did
Bear. I didn't see the point. No guarantee we were leaving through the same
door.

The music grew louder with every step forward. I felt the bass in my chest,
my heart pounded in time with the beat. As we moved into the club, I looked
around the room. A long, curved bar started to the right of us, stretched the
length of the building and wrapped around the wall across from us. There
were tables scattered between. Far to the left was a roped off section. I
assumed it was designated for VIPs. Currently it was empty. The dance floor
was aglow in light blue, pink, and silver. There were a couple dozen people
lost in the music, and each other. Their eyes were glazed over. Stares vacant.
They were riding high, and Ecstasy was the vessel that took them there.

We split apart. Bear headed to the bar to get us a couple drinks to help fit
in. Lexi veered off toward the bathroom. I shed my jacket, draped it over my
arm, and walked over to the VIP section, coming way too close to the dance
floor along the way. Two women dressed in clothing that would freeze even
their most private of parts if they were to step outside accosted me. One
planted herself behind me, pressing her chest into my back. Felt like she had
clamps on her nipples. The other danced in front of me, her eyes rolled back
so far in her head I only saw the whites. They draped their arms over my
shoulders, locked me in. I tried to fight them off, unsuccessfully. Couldn't put
up too much of a fight. Might draw the wrong attention.

The woman in front rubbed hard against my leg. She smiled as she worked
up my thigh. She stopped when she felt the hardness of my pistol. Her eyes
came into view. Her grin faded. She took a step back, releasing her grip on my
neck.

"You a cop?" she asked.

The woman behind me took a few steps back.

"Maybe," I said. "Would I have any reason to be suspicious of you?"

She wiped her nose and shook her head, then stepped around me. She and
her friend disappeared to the other side of the dance floor, hand in hand, and
assimilated into a group of six.

Bear showed up, handed me a blue drink. Looked like it was glowing.

"The hell is this?" I said.

He shrugged. "I just named a couple off the board over there."

I held the glass to the light, saw chunks of stuff floating around. "The hell they put in it?"

"Didn't really watch." He pointed across the room. "Was too busy watching them chicks dry hump you."

"They're over there now if you wanna get in on the action. Be careful, though, I'm still not sure one of them's not a guy." I set the drink on a table and pulled out a chair. There was no way I was taking a sip. Bartender could have been told to look out for us, drug our drinks. "What's your feel of this place?"

Bear glanced around. "Not too bad right now. I imagine in an hour or so it'll be packed to the gills. Enough high people to float it to the stratosphere."

I watched the dancers in their trance. "Halfway there already, man."

Lexi crossed the room and sat across from me. She put her phone on the table. "He knows we're here. Said it'll be a couple minutes."

"Great." I kept an eye on the entrance hallway. The faint glow we traveled through on the way in was a hindrance now. I couldn't tell if there was a person there until they passed all the way through. But they could sure as hell see me. I lifted my shirt and slid my hand underneath, resting it on my pistol.

"Easy, cowboy." Lexi directed her gaze up to the ceiling. "They're watching us."

I casually glanced around the room, taking note of ten cameras. Who knew how many more were hidden behind the mirrors and in the lights?

"What do you know about this place?" Bear asked her.

"Not too much," she said. "I know some shady people make even shadier deals in the backrooms here. I know…"

"What is it?" I asked after a few moments.

She stared down at the table. "My ex used to get involved in a backroom game here. High stakes poker."

"Is this the place—"

"No." She took a drink, made a face, spit it back in the cup. "The hell is this?"

I nodded toward Bear. The big man shrugged.

"It's disgusting," she said.

"Never told you to drink it," he said.

"Anyway," she said, "no one here will recognize me. We wouldn't be here if there were any chance they would."

A couple of minutes passed. I spotted a group come through the hallway. One man immediately turned and slipped through a door behind the bar. Three people headed our way. Two muscleheads bookended a short woman with shoulder-length black hair. Her cheeks and eyelids sparkled, reflecting the soft colors of the room. Her eyebrows were drawn in, looking like two big inverted smiles. She had two larger-than-necessary hoops on either side of her nose. Despite that, I found her oddly attractive.

"You are Lexi?" Her Russian accent didn't fit her look. "Come with us."

CHAPTER 36

THE TWO GUYS STEPPED FORWARD TOWARD BEAR. HE HIKED HIS hands halfway. He wasn't surrendering, far from it. Bear was getting ready to react. If one of them so much as put a pinky on him, the big man was gonna throw down.

"They're with me," Lexi said.

"The meeting is for you only," the woman said.

"Then I walk." Lexi turned toward the corridor, grabbed my hand and pulled me with her.

"Wait." The woman had her cell phone in hand, composing a message. She looked up at Lexi. Her eyes flared wide. "Just wait a moment. He is reasonable man, even if you are unreasonable woman."

Lexi's grip on my hand tightened, she pumped it a couple times. Her bluff had worked. Maybe.

The woman lifted her phone and focused on the screen, then she shifted her gaze to her associates and nodded. "He'll see you now."

We were led past the velvet rope into the VIP section, but we didn't stop there. One of the guys pulled back a curtain, the other stopped on the other side.

"Come with me." The woman looked back, motioned with her index finger to follow.

Bear led the way. He'd actually been right behind her since we left the table. She was his type. Fiery and dominant. What a couple that'd make, him at six-six, her barely five-feet tall.

The whole look of the place soon changed. It had gone from champagne dreams to whiskey hangover in the span of a couple feet. The floor and walls were concrete and gray. The ceiling was water-stained. There was no one back here, but it surprised me how easily someone could gain access to this section of the club. Then again, I figured they didn't let just anyone into their VIP area, an area staged to provide quick access to where the *real* action went on around here.

We were alone with the woman now. She led us to the end of the hallway, turned right, and went most of the way down the next corridor. She came to a stop, pivoted on her right foot, stared up at Bear. The music echoed through the hall, but was considerably dampened. It had been louder on the street. I looked at the ceiling and noticed a few vents, and as soon as I saw them, I recognized the fuzzy sound of piped-in white noise. They were masking the club music.

The lady rapped on the wooden door and waited. It opened a few inches a couple of seconds later. She spoke in Russian with a man. We didn't bother to tell them Bear understood every word. The door closed and she spun around to face us.

"Here's the rules," she said.

"Come on," Lexi said. "Let's just get—"

"Here's the rules," she said again, her finger raised in Lexi's face. I began to wonder what this lady did outside of the club. "This meeting is between you and him. He understands you're feeling that you might need protection, so he is allowing your bodyguards to have access. He, however, will be in there alone."

He might be alone, but one move by us, and we'd get mowed down within a few seconds.

"If they cause any problems, you are through. Got it?" She looked each of us in the eye in turn, settling on Bear last.

He started to say something, but the woman rolled her eyes and pushed the door open.

"Rejected." I slapped him on the stomach.

"I'm just getting started," he said.

Kozlov immediately set his sights on me. "Ah, the mystery man from the other day."

"The mysterious Ginger," I said. "Had a hell of a time finding you. Great accent by the way. You a Thespian in college?"

He ignored my comments. "Lexi, I thought we were going to have a brain trust type of meeting, try to figure out what happened to our acquaintance. Instead I see you have brought me the number one suspect."

"It's called a brainstorming session, asshole," I said. "And I'm hardly the suspect in all of this."

Kozlov shook his head, held his hands up. He stared down the woman who remained by the door. "Didn't I make it clear to you to tell these people if they want to be in here with Lexi then they are to keep their damn mouths shut?"

She pulled the door, turned and didn't look back. "What do you expect? You can't follow your own rules and you expect them to?"

Kozlov clenched his jaw. His nostrils flared. His eyes narrowed. He stood that way for several seconds, hands in his pockets. Finally, he broke off his stare and looked down at the ground. "I know this one isn't your bodyguard. What about the big guy?"

"I'm with him," Bear said.

"The question was for her," he said, alternating his icy stare between me and Bear. He had a bit of a mad scientist look to him at the moment.

"He's with him," Lexi said, attempting to control her smirk. "Look, you have to trust me on this. Jack works for a government agency who is interested in finding Thanos. He's on our side."

"Whose side is that?" Kozlov walked over to the bar in his office and pulled down a bottle of vodka and four glasses. He filled each halfway and set them on the table in the middle of the room. "I can tell you, my side is most definitely not aligned with any agency in the United States of America."

"I've got resources," I said. "They can help track down Thanos."

Kozlov took a sip of vodka, swallowed it without any reaction. "Personally, I don't care if I never see Marcus Thanos alive again." He shook his head. "I don't care to see him dead, either. The guy was an asshole, and he did something very stupid. That's why your government is after him. But they aren't the only ones."

"If you don't care, why are we all here right now?" I said.

He waved his hand through the air. "I'm part owner of this club. I can be here whenever I want. Now, all of you drink."

Lexi grabbed her glass and drank the contents in one gulp. She grimaced against the burn, slammed the glass back down on the table. "Cut the act, Kozlov. You told me you had more for me. Well, what is it? Don't tell me we wasted our time coming out here tonight."

Kozlov sat there for a few minutes after finishing his drink. He stared at the empty glass in his right hand. I had the guy wrong from the beginning. He wasn't merely a hired hand performing routine security for a millionaire businessman. And he wasn't the typical KGB thug, either. He ranked somewhere above median level on the power and influence scale, but I couldn't determine how high, and within which organization.

In years past, I'd have used my network of contacts to cobble together a dossier on him. Everything from two seconds ago to twenty years before he was conceived. I wanted to know who his parents were. Who their parents were. The more information I had on hand, the better I could assess and deal with the situation. That was impossible tonight. We were walking around blind here. And it seemed every thirty minutes a new revelation arose that changed everything.

I was only waiting for the next bombshell to drop on my head.

Turned out, I didn't have to wait too long.

"I'm going to take you to meet someone," Kozlov said after several silent minutes. "Let's go."

CHAPTER 37

KOZLOV LED US THROUGH THE NETWORK OF CORRIDORS downstairs to a basement. It was dimly lit with overhead yellow lighting wrapped in small cages that hung from the ceiling. The floor was concrete. There were drains set every ten feet or so. It looked like a great place to kill someone, then go about dismembering and dissolving their bodies. Aside from a hint of mustiness, I didn't pick up the scent of any chemicals or decomposing bodies. Bear glanced over at me, his brow furrowed. He was on high alert. I knew the narrow hallway we were walking through wasn't his favorite place to be. I gave him a quick nod, patted my pistol through my jacket.

Kozlov stopped, turned around. "Coats?"

"Upstairs," Lexi said.

He nodded, held up a finger indicating for us to wait, then he disappeared down the hallway. The echoes of his footsteps dissipated.

"I don't like this," Bear said.

"Relax," I said. "They wouldn't kill us here."

Bear reached through the few inches that separated his head from the ceiling and rapped his knuckles against it. "Concrete. Ain't no one hearing anything through that."

"Nothing's gonna happen, Bear," Lexi said. "At least not here. So save some of that energy for wherever we're going."

Kozlov returned with black tactical jackets draped over his arm. He handed one to Lexi, then Bear. "Sorry, this might be a little tight for you. I don't have bigfoot sizes." Then he held one out to me. "In case you want to fit in with your friends. You might find it useful later."

158 / L.T. RYAN

I grabbed the jacket and folded it up. No point in taking off mine and showing off how easily accessible my piece was.

Kozlov pulled a set of keys from his pocket and turned. "All right, let's go."

We exited the basement and hiked up a narrow set of cracked and rickety stairs. A light set atop a black pole provided enough illumination to keep us from falling over one another as we stepped into the alley. Ice covered the concrete landing, nearly sent Lexi crashing backward. Bear reached out and steadied her.

Kozlov continued toward a black Escalade.

"Man, I really gotta trade my ride in," Bear said. "Maybe get me a big ole' sedan. Cruise in style, you know."

"Let's keep the noise down," Kozlov said. "While my office is safe, I can't possibly know who might be listening out here."

It was a good point, and we knew right then and there the rest of the trip would be taken in silence.

We entered the vehicle, Lexi in front, Bear and me in the middle row captain chairs. There was plenty of room for both of us. Kozlov started the engine, blasted the heat, turned the radio volume up a couple notches. It was some crazy Russian techno song I'd never heard before with too much bass and a simple repeating melody interspersed with vocals I couldn't understand.

I leaned over to ask Bear to translate, but thought better of it. The longer they weren't aware that he understood Russian, the better. It was bound to come in handy at some point.

We drove through the city, away from the lake, and merged onto I-90 west. Kozlov settled in with a line of cars going fifteen over the speed limit in the far left lane. We drifted further west. The concrete jungle gave way to the suburbs and eventually the countryside appeared. Soon we were headed due north, skating along the outskirts of Rockford, Illinois before crossing the border into Wisconsin.

The highway led straight to Madison. What had seemed an innocent attempt to hide two days earlier with Lexi now took on a new possibility. In an hour I'd know.

We pulled off the highway ten minutes after crossing the Wisconsin state line. Kozlov drove into a brightly lit gas station parking lot, pulled up next to a pump. The air that entered the SUV as he exited gave me a jolt of energy. The door slammed shut. Kozlov walked around the back of the vehicle, phone to the side of his head.

"Who you think he's talking to?" Bear said.

"I'd guess whoever we're gonna go see," I said.

Lexi looked back at me. She glanced away as soon as I made eye contact.

"Anything you want to tell me?" I said.

She shook her head, said nothing.

I leaned forward and put my hand on her shoulder. Softly, I said, "Maybe you knew more than you let on the other day."

She looked out Kozlov's window. "We really shouldn't get into that in here. I don't know who's listening. Could be Kozlov himself, pretending to be on a call to see what we'll say while he's gone."

She was right. I was getting antsy, and in my unsettled state had slipped up. I kept my focus on Kozlov from that point on. If he was faking the call he put on quite a performance. He was smart enough to stay out of range of the car. We couldn't even pick up vocal inflections through the windows.

The gas pump handle clanked when the tank reached full. Kozlov stared at it. He nodded a few times, then ended his call. A minute later we were back on the road, waiting in a left turn lane to get on the highway.

"Where're we headed?" I asked.

Kozlov said nothing. He glanced in the rearview and shot me a look as if to say *not another word.*

Not one to let another man ignore me, I persisted. "We've been riding for over an hour. I think it's time to let us in on the big secret."

"You will find out when we get there," he said.

"That who you were on the phone with? The guy at the next stop?" I leaned forward, placed my forearm on the back of Lexi's seat. "You had to update him on the guest list. Right? Tell me, somewhere along the way did you snap a photo or two of me and my associate here?"

He glanced at me twice, quickly, but said nothing. There was a slight uncertainty in his look.

"Anything come back yet? I figure an hour is enough time for whoever you got inside the Bureau or the Agency to do their dirty work. Or perhaps you went back to your old source, and asked an old friend at the KGB to check us out."

Kozlov shook his head. "You don't know what you speak of."

"That's right," I said. "People in the KGB don't have friends. At least not once they defect."

He adjusted his grip on the steering wheel, cracking his knuckles as he did so. "I didn't defect, you arrogant cocksucker."

"Then who was it there that helped you? Saveli Alyosha? Yakim Serafim? Borya Taras?" I paused a beat to let it sink in that I was well versed in my Russian counterparts. "I can keep going, you know."

Kozlov licked his lips, opened his mouth, thought better of responding. "Those names are common in Russia. You're simply bullshitting like all filthy American assholes."

"Talk about true colors," Bear said.

Lexi intervened. "Look, we're all on the same team here."

"My ass," Bear said.

She shot him a look and he backed down. "For right now we are. We have a common goal, and fighting isn't gonna solve anything." She twisted in her seat and looked me in the eye. "Jack, you have to expect they would do their due diligence on you, especially considering I brought you in. They aren't typically in the business of inviting federal agents over for dinner. Know what I mean?"

I took a deep breath, settled back into my seat. "Fair enough. But, Kozlov, I'd love to know what you get back on me."

He smiled for a moment as he looked into the mirror. "I got everything, Mr. Noble."

CHAPTER 38

MY MIND RACED WITH POSSIBILITIES. I HADN'T EXPECTED THAT response from Kozlov. Who had he turned to for information? And what exactly had they told him? My history was long, convoluted, and depending on which file one accessed, full of lies. He might've been misled and told that I was a former Army Ranger, or a CIA operator who'd spent a decade in Africa. Hell, maybe both.

But if he knew I was former SIS, we had a problem. The list of people with access to that information could be counted on one hand. Even among active agents, Frank Skinner was the only one who ever knew my last name. If Kozlov had garnered information related to my time there, that meant someone had betrayed me, or they had hacked one of the most sensitive databases in the US. Either way, it'd be a problem, and I'd have to find a way to alert Frank at once so he could begin damage control and start preparing for a recovery mission.

Being a member of a highly secretive agency put me in a precarious position. I had intelligence that most never had access to, things people couldn't imagine. There were people in a country like Russia who would love to sit me down for a *talk*. Kozlov could demand a million-dollar bounty, and he'd have a dozen foreign agencies engaged in a bidding war.

I felt Bear's stare weigh heavily on me. The same thoughts had to be racing through his mind as well. Though he was never in the SIS, he'd worked alongside me on multiple missions. And since I'd left, we'd contracted with Frank no fewer than a dozen times.

162 / L.T. RYAN

"I see that sweat forming on your forehead." Kozlov had a grin plastered on his face. His grip on the steering wheel was more relaxed now.

I hadn't noticed that I was sweating. Normally I kept my emotions in check, but this time they'd gotten away from me. I had to recover, flip the tables a bit.

"You know a possible last name," I said. "So what? The right facial recognition program could give you that. Probably spit out six or seven others, depending on whose database you queried. I've used plenty of aliases in countries around the globe. At least three in your motherland. Wanna ask me what I was doing there? You'd really get a kick out of it."

Kozlov's smile diminished as his eyes narrowed. He kept them locked on mine. The wheels were turning. He was trying to decide if I was playing a game or not.

One of the benefits of having been associated with an agency like the SIS was that a ton of misinformation had been placed on file. Chances were they had happened upon some of that. The public Jack Noble, which wasn't easy to access, was nothing like the real one. There was some classified material, but nothing too damning.

I had to hope that was all they found.

"So give it to me, man." I leaned forward so we were practically cheek to cheek. "What do you know about me?"

The air in the SUV was thick and heavy. For several moments you only heard the sound of our collective breathing, fast and ragged. Kozlov gripped the wheel and hit the brake. Maybe it was an attempt to rattle me, throw me forward into the dash or something. I was prepared, though, with my feet and arms pressed against the front seats to brace myself.

"That's what I thought," I said. "You ain't got nothing. Next time you want to mess with someone, pick one of your countrymen. They fold under the slightest hint of pressure."

The following thirty minutes were silent and tense. I stared directly at Kozlov in the rearview. Every so often he glanced at me while checking the traffic behind us. I had expected he'd pull over somewhere, make a call. But he never did. He either felt strongly about the intel they'd gathered, or was too much of a coward to tell whoever we were going to see that they might be wrong about me.

The highway signs for Madison appeared more frequently. Thirty miles out, twenty, fifteen, ten. It was no surprise when he exited the highway at the edge of town. We drove through the middle of the city. It was quiet tonight in contrast to when Lexi and I strolled home from dinner, only a few people out.

The clouds stood out bright gray against the night sky. Kozlov lowered his window. I smelled snow on the way.

He eased the SUV to the curb in front of a brick apartment building. A green canopy lined with Christmas lights covered the entrance. Either someone was too lazy to take them down or it was part of the decor.

"Why are we here?" Lexi asked.

Kozlov looked at her, yawned, said, "One of you get in the backseat. We've got a guest coming."

Bear reached for his seatbelt, but I cut him off.

"I got it, man." I threw a quick glance at the back of Kozlov's head. "You stay right where you're at."

I wanted him there in case something went down. Once he wrapped those thick arms around the Russian's neck, the guy wouldn't have a choice but to do whatever we said. As things stood at the moment, there was no reason for Bear to do so. However, the game was always changing. Kozlov was about to introduce someone new to our circle. Who and why were the foremost questions in my mind.

I was surprised when a woman stepped outside. The wind whipped her blonde hair to the side. She reached up and tucked back the strands covering her face. She had on a heavy green jacket with a fur-lined hood. She reached behind her and pulled it over the top of her head. She appeared to be mid-thirties and in pretty good shape.

Kozlov pulled the keys from the ignition, got out and opened the rear passenger door. They were speaking in Russian. They didn't stop to introduce the woman.

She aimed her steel gray eyes at me. Her stare felt like knives penetrating my skull. She had the look of a killer bundled up in a five-foot-four distance runner's body.

We continued through town, turned north, and made our way into the countryside. I slid to the left and watched Lexi in the mirror until there was no light remaining. She stared ahead, no sign of recognition when we passed a street or a house. It was clear that it was no coincidence we ended up in Madison that night. But why had we left? Someone must've fed her false intelligence.

Were we about to meet that someone?

CHAPTER 39

A LONG NARROW DIRT DRIVEWAY CUT THROUGH A FOREST OF TALL thin pines that shaved down the cone of visibility the headlights provided. I leaned forward in between Bear and the unknown woman. She hadn't said a word during the short drive. Neither had Kozlov. I figured we'd learn everyone's role soon enough. No point in getting worked up over it now.

We reached the end of the driveway and stopped in front of a wide red-brick ranch. The windows closest to the front door were lined with heavy drapes. Warm light filtered through the cracks. Every other room appeared darkened.

Kozlov punched a few buttons on his phone, cut the ignition and headlights, and waited. Our breathing soon fogged up the windows. The porch light flicked on, and the front door opened a few seconds later, though no one appeared in the vacated space.

"Let's go." Kozlov hopped down and trekked toward the house. The woman followed. That left the three of us still in the SUV.

"He either trusts us," Bear said. "Or the woods are full of his guys."

"Certainly not the former," I said.

"We're on solid ground here, guys," Lexi said. "Just don't say anything stupid."

"Where are we?" I asked.

She bit her bottom lip for a moment. A slipup perhaps. "I'm not sure, but it has to be someone Kozlov trusts. Come on."

"And just how much do we trust Kozlov?" Bear said.

Lexi didn't respond. She was halfway out of the SUV.

We walked to the front steps. The woman was already inside. Kozlov stood in the opening, holding the screen door for us. Lexi entered first, followed by Bear and then me.

Two lamps adorned end tables next to a long couch. They bathed the room in yellow light. A worn bearskin rug stretched across the floor. A heavy wrought iron and oak coffee table sat on it. On top of the table were a bottle of vodka and a bottle of whiskey and a tray holding six glasses along with a bucket of ice.

"This a social encounter?" I said.

Kozlov shook his head. "With all your experience, you never dealt with Russians? This is how we conduct business."

"What business are we conducting here?" I asked.

"Jack." Lexi shot me a look that said tone it down.

I hadn't even begun.

A toilet flushed, a faucet cut on long enough to run a hand underneath. A door covered in the same wood paneling as the walls set in the back corner of the room opened and a silhouette appeared. He was over six foot tall and lean. His silver hair stood out as he stepped into the light. His face was hard as steel, not so much as a sagging jowl or a hint of double chin. I thought he looked familiar, but then I realized he looked like plenty of old servicemen I'd been introduced to since I was knee high to my dad. A few seconds later I recognized him from the photo at Gus's. This guy had been through the wringer and back and probably advanced on that merit alone until he reached a point where he could make an impact. With which agency, I wondered. Kozlov brought us to him, so it wouldn't be too much of a stretch to assume this guy was former KGB, too. But it could be dangerous to assume that without knowing all the facts.

"Who do we have here?" He stared at Lexi.

"This is the FBI agent I told you about," Kozlov said. "She had an interest in Mr. Thanos, and was at his house the morning it was shot up."

"And these two gentlemen?" he asked.

"I didn't catch your name," I said.

Kozlov stepped forward. "That is not for you—"

The older man cut Kozlov off mid-sentence. "You can call me Yashkin."

It wasn't that he looked like a hundred old men I'd seen before, or even that he was the guy I didn't recognize in the photo. I knew this man. "You sure you don't want me to refer to you as General?"

General Nika Yashkin was an intelligence officer who had risen to prominence during the Soviet-Afghan war. His unorthodox methods brought him notoriety. Ultimately, he was forced to resign for his actions in the early eighties, at least publicly. While his detractors believed he was carrying out an unofficial life sentence in Siberia, in truth he had been promoted to a position of power within the KGB, heading clandestine operations known as active measures from the mid-eighties through the early 2000s, when he went off the radar.

"Have we met?" he asked me.

"I'm fortunate enough to say that we haven't, at least until today. Tell me, though, did you retire from that gig with the KGB? Or you still spreading disinformation throughout the world and aiding terrorists?"

Out of the corner of my eye I could see Kozlov shifting in his stance. I hoped Bear was watching him because I couldn't take my eyes off of Yashkin.

The Russian looked around the room, first at the woman, then at Kozlov. "I'm sorry, I thought these people were brought here to help. Yet I feel as though I am being interrogated."

Lexi cut in. "Sir, please excuse my friend. He is also a member of an agency and is used to leading conversations in such a way. We are here to help, but in order to do so, we need to know a few things."

"Things such as whether I'm retired? What does my past have to do with anything? We need to put our minds together to determine a course of action to find Thanos."

Lexi glared at me for a moment. I knew she had a lot riding on this meeting, though I still wasn't sure what we were about to uncover.

"Mr. Noble," Yashkin said. "Your past deeds in Russia while you were operating under the shield of the SIS did not go entirely unnoticed. I know a number of people from my former life who would very much appreciate the opportunity to meet you in person. You can see how I could make that a reality for them."

I inched my hand toward my pistol.

"That won't be necessary," Yashkin said, gesturing toward my midsection. "You'll have no need for your firearm here, and brandishing it will only get it removed, which will make it difficult for you to protect yourself later, should the need arise, of course."

I lifted my hand a few inches. "What are these threats about then?"

"I simply wanted you to realize that we know all about you. You are not as untouchable as you once were when you were in the SIS."

Lexi looked at me. I could see the confusion on her face and watched it slowly turn to hurt. She'd believed I'd been operating as a government agent this whole time. I decided not to mention that I'd been reinstated. They might clam up if they knew.

Yashkin continued. "And you are not as bulletproof as you believe you are now. There is a mountain of evidence that could implicate you in several dozen crimes, if only one knew where to look."

This wasn't a meeting to determine what each of us knew in order to get Thanos back. It was an elaborate setup.

They wanted me to do a job.

CHAPTER 40

"WHAT'S YOUR ANGLE HERE, YASHKIN?"

Yashkin stared at me, unblinking, for several seconds. Kozlov and the woman were watching him. How much had he told them? Were they simply muscle for the guy, or did he involve them in his decisions?

I wanted to get a read on Lexi, but she was behind me. Turning to look at her would be a mistake at this juncture. I still couldn't get past the fact that we had stayed in a motel only a few minutes away from this guy. She must have known he was here. Why not say anything about him then, and why leave town? If only I knew who was feeding her information.

"I mean, come on," I said. "You wouldn't be pulling out all the stops here, threatening me, if you didn't want something done. So spill. What is it?"

Yashkin took a sip of his vodka. He rose, glass in hand, paced around the back of the couch. It was high-backed, hiding the man from the waist down. He lowered his free hand so it was out of sight, leaving me a little uneasy.

"This Thanos situation," he said, "has grown out of control. It was simple at first, our business with him. A deal here and there, real estate, land development, a way to get a foothold in the States for our company. Over time, Thanos was able to introduce us to new players. People in the government, law enforcement, federal agents."

"People who could turn a blind eye for the right fee," I said.

Yashkin slowly nodded. "You could say that. He also put me in touch with people who operate on the other side of the law."

Out of the corner of my eye I saw Lexi shift her stance. Was this how it all fit together? Had they met during her time in the DCO? For the first time, I began doubting the story of how she blew her cover.

"Thanos was a good ally," Yashkin said.

"Was?" I said.

Yashkin lifted his glass but didn't take a drink. "The problem with a guy who straddles the law is that you never know which side of it he's going to fall on during any given encounter."

It almost felt like he was talking about me. Or Bear. Hell, even Lexi if she was good enough at her job when undercover.

"I love philosophy," I said. "But I'd prefer you get to the point so I can tell you to fuck off."

Bear chuckled. Kozlov took a step forward, hand reaching under his shirt and resting on what I presumed was his pistol. Yashkin lifted his free hand and waved his underling off. He said something in Russian which caused the other man to back off. Through it all the unnamed woman didn't even flinch.

"I've got a better idea," Yashkin said, pacing to the other end of the couch. He continued to the rear corner of the room and stopped in front of a bookcase set next to the bathroom door. One by one, he removed several musty tomes and placed them flat on an empty lower shelf. Then he rose up on his toes and pushed against the back of the case. I heard a pop, then Yashkin's upper body seemed to disappear into the bookcase.

Bear threw a curious glance my way. I had no idea what Yashkin was doing, so I shrugged and went back to watching the now vacated space in front of the bookcase.

A moment later he returned with a black duffel bag with bright yellow handles and lettering across the side. It was written in Russian. He carried the bag over and dropped it on the far right couch cushion then took a seat in the middle. He grabbed the bottle of vodka and filled each glass one at a time, setting them in a line.

"Drink," he said. "Then we'll talk."

"I didn't come here to get drunk," I said. "We need to find this guy so my friend here can clear her name and we can let the authorities deal with him."

A smirk crossed Yashkin's face. I couldn't tell if that meant he knew something I didn't, or he didn't care about my plans. He rose, picked up a glass along the way, extended it toward me.

"Drink."

I took the glass, maintaining eye contact with him the entire time, and threw back the vodka. It burned going down, but I gave no outward sign of it.

Yashkin's posture slackened, his face relaxed. It seemed that the simple act of drinking had appeased him for the time being, which immediately sent me into wondering if the bottle had been laced. I went through a few seconds of false symptoms attributed to anxiety. My heart raced, my mouth went dry, my limbs tingled. I kept my cool outwardly, steadied my breathing. Meanwhile, I clenched all major muscles for a few seconds, then relaxed them.

The symptoms subsided. Well, all except the warmness in my throat and stomach.

"You like?" he asked, eying the fluid in his own glass. "My family started this distillery. One of the finest vodkas ever produced. You see, I always thought I would take over the family business. My father had a different idea once I entered the military and advanced my career. Serving the state was a black mark in his eye. My sister, on the other hand, the subservient wench that she is, was given the keys to the business. You'll notice this bottle is not a recent vintage. You know why?"

I shrugged, said nothing.

"Because she has no passion, and the vodka she produces is manure."

"If you could give it all up," I said, "this whole life you have now, everything you've done to get to this point, to go back forty years and change your path, would you?"

The left side of his mouth turned up in a smile. His eyes had misted slightly. He looked around the room, stopping on the woman and Kozlov, then on the bag at the end of his couch.

"Not a chance."

"The family history is fascinating," I said. "I mean that. But it doesn't have a damn thing to do with what we're doing here. So let's get to the point. What do you want me to do?"

"I am aware of your talents, Noble," Yashkin said.

"Talents? I'm hardheaded and relentless. It gets me into more trouble than it keeps me out of. I can't count how many times that large fella over there has had to bail me out because I won't give in to reason."

"And because of those traits you have a reputation for getting things done."

I couldn't argue with him there. Guess that went along with hardheaded and relentless.

I set my glass down on the table and leaned forward so we were eye to eye. "What do you need me to do that your own people can't figure out?"

He smiled. "Figure out? It's nothing like that. I don't have that many people, for one. And it won't just be you."

"Of course not," I said. "I've got my friends here."

He shook his head. "Unfortunately, they won't be joining you."

A knot formed in my stomach as I noticed movement out of the corner of my eye. Kozlov shifted into position behind Bear. Was Yashkin about to give me an ultimatum?

"Christiana," he said.

The previously unnamed woman approached me.

"Noble, you will be accompanying Christiana to the location we believe Thanos is being held."

"I'm not doing this without these two," I said. "You can try to stop us, but as far as I'm concerned it's three against two. No offense, old man, but you don't concern me."

His face darkened, but his smile held firm. He gestured with his chin toward the bank of windows behind me. "Look out there."

I turned to face the darkness. Saw nothing. "What am I looking for?"

His reflection stood out in the window as he stood. He raised his left arm, hand above his shoulder. Outside a light flicked on and off three times, near where we had parked. Then there was another, maybe ten feet from the first, on the other side of the SUV. Then a third. And a fourth.

"What are those odds again?" Yashkin said. "Think they are still in your favor?"

As I turned, he drew his pistol so fast it didn't register at first. I knew he was carrying, yet his motion was so smooth, so quick, I hardly picked up on it.

"And do you still not consider me a threat?"

The decision I faced had only one realistic choice. If I refused, we were dead. That was the point he was making, and I couldn't put it past him to execute all three of us and bury us in the woods. We might take one of them out, but the men outside had us dead to rights. They were hidden in the darkness, but could see us with no problem. They'd likely been instructed to open fire on Yashkin's signal. Kozlov and Christiana appeared to be well trained operators. I had no doubt the guys outside were as well. Handpicked by Yashkin for whatever his mission was in the US.

"You and Christiana," he said. "The FBI agent and the large one will remain behind in case anything goes wrong."

"Such as what?" I said.

"Such as Christiana not returning. Or Thanos getting away somehow. Or the goddamn mailman coming to the door. The longer I wait, the antsier I get. It's really open to interpretation, Noble. So the sooner you get going and get the information I need, the better for your friends."

"So help me, if you—"

He turned the pistol toward Lexi. Four red dots danced on the far wall, all drawing together in a cluster just over her head.

"You'll do what, exactly?"

What had we gotten ourselves into? The trust Lexi put in Kozlov had been clearly misplaced. But how had she not realized it? Was she working for Yashkin as well? Was all this a show? Or had they strung her along, playing her like a pawn, holding her close until she was needed? I needed a couple minutes alone with her to get the story, learn how he'd portrayed himself over the time they'd known each other.

"Me and her." I pointed at Christiana. "That's it? Kozlov stays behind? Your men outside, they don't go with us?"

Yashkin nodded. "Don't get any ideas. She's deadlier than you are by a factor of a hundred. One of the best close range assassins I have ever had the pleasure to watch. You try anything and she'll have you wrapped up so tight you'll beg her to kill you."

"Sounds fun." This was it, I couldn't stall any longer, and there wasn't much point in doing so. I glanced at Bear.

He gave me a quick nod and that was all it took.

"OK. I'm in. Let's roll."

CHAPTER 41

"SO, HOW DO YOU LIKE WISCONSIN?" I GLANCED SIDEWAYS AT THE woman Yashkin described as being a hundred times deadlier than me.

She sighed, rolled her eyes, directed her attention to the side window.

"Not a fan, I guess. Me either, really. Can't stand their sports teams. I mean, the Packers, after what they did to Favre. Whatever, you can have them."

"Drive," she said. "And shut up."

The Taurus wasn't much to look at. Faded green and rusted in places. It looked like one I drove for a short time in high school until I wrapped it around a tree. An accident that caused me to miss a high school baseball playoff game, which we lost. My father blamed me for both the accident, and the ruined chance at a state championship. Can't recall ever getting credit for a win.

"What's your take on all this?"

"Turn left up ahead." She extended her finger. Her slim hand fed into a thin but muscled forearm.

I scanned the road, didn't see a turn.

"It's about half a kilometer away," she said.

Fifteen seconds later the turn off came into view. I pulled onto a single lane blacktop covered in dead leaves. They kicked up as we drove past, fluttering over the hood and windshield. Another fifty feet and the roadtop cleared. Had someone layered the leaves at the turnoff to make it look as though it was deserted?

"How much further?" I asked.

"Keep driving."

I wasn't sure what to expect of our adventure, but the further we went into the woods, the more I grew concerned their plan wasn't for me to return to the house. What was the point of that, though? As far as I knew, Yashkin had no beef with me. I hadn't pissed in his corn flakes. Never took a job that affected him directly. Of course, indirectly was another story. I had no way of knowing the organizations he was connected to these days. Every person he knew twenty years ago had gone in their own direction. Any of them could have reeled him into who knows what kind of business dealings.

"This Thanos guy," I said. "What do you know about him?"

"I'm not paid to know about him," Christiana said, finally offering a response. "My job is to escort you and for us to gather information from him. I do not care about where he came from, or where he is going. I'd be happy strangling him after we are done with him, but my understanding is that he is to live."

"Your understanding? You weren't told beforehand?"

"We are to call in the moment we have what we need, and at that time—"

"What is it we need?"

Her head swiveled toward me. "And at that time we will be told what to do with Mr. Thanos."

"What is it we are trying to get out of him?"

She looked away without replying.

"Christiana," I said.

"Do not address me by that name."

"Then what should I call you?"

"Nothing. Do not address me at all. You do what I say, when I say it. Do you understand this situation? You are not in control, Noble. I am not in control. Yashkin is. Yashkin has given me instructions, and part of those instructions are to tell you what to do. So shut up, and drive."

I backed off her for a bit and continued on the road. My initial thoughts proved incorrect as we pulled up to a stop sign and Christiana directed me to turn left. We headed due north on an empty two-lane road, passing through Wyocena, Pardeeville, and Belle Fountain. I recognized the area as being close to the Wisconsin Dells. We'd vacationed there when I was a kid, fished the deep fjords in search of catfish the size of Buicks. Mostly caught a bunch of blue gill. These days the small towns had little to draw my attention, but I remained vigilant on the chance someone was waiting for us.

After forty-five minutes, we reached the town of Montello.

"Pull over," Christiana said.

I eased the car to a stop under the population sign, which indicated the town had swollen to almost fifteen hundred people. I thought about the inhabitants of Montello. How many had grown up here and stayed? Returned in their older age? Where did they work? That one always crossed my mind in places like this. Sure, there were positions for some here, but I figured a good portion had to travel to Madison or Green Bay each day to earn their living.

Christiana unlocked her door, stepped out into the cold. A light snow had started falling a couple minutes prior and already dusted the sidewalk. As she walked away, I wondered how much of what Yashkin had said about her was true. She was medium height, slim but strong, judging by her muscle tone. Her stature would work for her in certain situations, but against some opponents, she would have less of a chance of survival. Was she used as a black widow to draw her target in sexually, and kill them when they had their guard down?

She returned to the car, brushed the flakes off her coat as she sat down.

"Yashkin sending his men?" I asked.

"Why would he do that?" she said.

"I dunno, either way, you tell me."

"Tell you what?"

"Why do you need me?"

"What do you mean?"

I was growing weary of questions answering questions. "He's got plenty of men. He's got you, and you seem more than capable of handling this alone. If there were more than a couple possible men to deal with at our destination, he'd have sent more than just us. So why me, Christiana? Is there something in store for me wherever we're going? I just want to know ahead of time."

"Of course I could do this alone." Her lips curled. She seemed offended I even mentioned it. "They know the others' faces, and can link them to Yashkin."

"They who?"

She ignored my query. "They can't link you to him. If anything, they'll recognize who you are. That'll cause a problem for your government, which is an added bonus. I'm sure there are certain individuals and committees who would love to find out what an agent for a secret intelligence service is doing in Wisconsin."

"What anyone does, I guess. I'm here for the beer and cheese."

The joke was lost on her. She shook her head. "Drive."

We didn't have far to go. A couple of turns later she focused her attention on a long, corrugated steel warehouse. The sliding doors on the end were large enough for a semi to fit through. Behind the building four silos of varying heights stood out against the snowy sky. Pastureland spread out to the east. Woods to the north and west.

"What's this place?" I asked.

"Our destination," she said. "But don't pull in here. Go past and park on the shoulder when I tell you to."

I spotted a guy seated near an entry door on the side. He had his arms folded over his chest and appeared to be sleeping. At the very least, the car passing by did little to concern him.

A wide ditch ran alongside the road, leaving little room to park. I pulled a couple feet onto the grassy shoulder, leaving enough room for Christiana to get out without falling into the ditch. The car stuck out in the road. I figured there wasn't much traffic this time of night, and anyone who happened by the old car would assume it had broken down.

Christiana hopped over the ditch and stepped into the woods. I followed a few seconds behind. We trekked toward the building and remained hidden inside the tree line with the road to our right. She aimed a red tinted flashlight at the ground. It cast enough light for us to see a few feet ahead, yet was dim enough to be invisible from beyond the woods.

"So what is this place?" I said. "Secret KGB headquarters?"

She shrugged. "A warehouse I guess you call it in the States?"

"Warehouse, yeah."

"Doesn't matter. Thanos is what we are concerned with, and I believe he is in there."

"How do you know?"

She looked over at me. In the still night, with only a slight trace of moonlight illuminating her face, she looked soft and attractive. I found it hard to believe I stood next to a killer.

"Let's just say I coerced the information using a special set of skills I possess."

"You're a temptress."

"Why do we put these names to such things, especially when women are involved?" Her expression changed, and the hardened killer appeared. "We don't do this for men, do we?"

"Who's the we you're talking about? I don't care how you achieve your goals. You do what it takes. You kill without conscience. I get it."

"I had a list of suspects, and found one of them. It was easy from there." She paused a beat. "I don't exactly enjoy that part of my job. I have a husband, two daughters. You think I want them to know what I do? They think I am a global business strategist, and that is why I travel so much. It hurts to lie to them, even more to leave them behind for weeks at a time. But I know that my actions make life better for a lot of people, and I can lay down next to my husband with a clear conscience because of that."

For a second, I thought I saw a trace of watering in her eyes, but a thick crop of tree cover blocked the reflection off the snow clouds and cast us into darkness before I could tell. In a group with the others, she was hard as stone. But out here, alone with me, the two of us kindred spirits in this crazy covert world, I was seeing a different side of her. Maybe it was the night and conditions, but somehow a bond existed between us.

She switched the flashlight off and stopped. Her voice dropped to a whisper. "We're almost there."

The settling snow mixed with our soft footsteps. We walked along the edge of the woods, traveling east, investigating the perimeter of the building. We started back toward the road again. When we were three-quarters of the way there, Christiana stopped.

"Move quickly and quietly straight ahead until you are up against the building. Do not deviate one foot from my path. Understand?"

I nodded, but she had already taken off. I secured my pistol and sprinted after her.

Halfway there I was blinded by a spotlight aimed right at me.

CHAPTER 42

DESPITE WHAT SOME PEOPLE SAY, THE FIRST INSTINCT IS OFTEN incorrect, which is why I resisted stopping dead in my tracks while mired in a cone of white light. To do so would have guaranteed my capture or death, possibly both and I wasn't keen on seeing either any time soon. I pushed forward, cutting left, then right, like I was making my way to the end zone dodging linebackers and defensive backs.

Christiana waited a dozen yards ahead of me, her back against the steel wall. She had her pistol out and raised. Her head whipped side to side as she searched for oncoming danger.

I'd sprinted the last twenty feet so hard I left myself no room to stop. It took everything in my power to avoid slamming into the wall. Pain seared through my left knee as I jammed my foot into the soft ground. Might've been worse had it been concrete.

I rested with my hands on my knees, catching my breath.

"I don't see anyone," she said. "You?"

With my hands on my knees, I looked up and down the length of the building, then out at the field we'd crossed. "Nobody. And the light's not moving."

She twisted at the waist and craned her head back. I followed her gaze toward the small light fixture. She shone her light on it.

"Motion detector." I shook my head. "Nearly blew my damn ACL over a motion sensing light. The hell are we doing here? I thought you had this place scoped out."

"I didn't walk it." She took a few steps away from the building and turned to face me. "I know how we can get in, so follow me."

Our pace slowed considerably as we pushed through a heavy wave of snowfall. It pelted us head on now. Felt like icy daggers on my face. The wind had picked up. That, or the sweat that had coated my body made me more sensitive to the breeze. I noted it wasn't as bad as a couple of days ago. Always amazed me how a few days exposed to the elements made me more resilient. I had a feeling it'd come in handy as the night progressed.

The rumble of a diesel engine grew louder with each passing second until it seemed to vibrate through the building. Brakes squealed high and tense. The engine roar grew deep and steady. Through the snow, I spotted a cone of light stretching out past the building.

Christiana stopped without warning. I didn't notice and bumped into her. In a flash, she spun and had my right arm locked, one of her legs wrapped around mine throwing off my balance, and her pistol under my chin.

Our mouths were inches from each other's and I felt her breath hot on my lips. Her eyes were wide with hatred and anger.

"Relax, it was an accident."

"So help me," she said. "You touch me again and I will scatter your brains all over the side of this building."

I regained my balance and let go as she untangled her body from mine. I had figured she moved quickly, but that sequence of events caught me by surprise. She was as lethal as they came. How much would it cost to get her off Yashkin's payroll and onto mine?

"Were they expecting a delivery?" I said.

"I wouldn't know." She was back to business. "But I don't think so. This place isn't operational during these months."

"They might not be producing, but maybe they have storage. This building, those silos back there."

"Come on." She crept forward until we were near the end of the building, where her pace slowed even more.

Despite her earlier warning, I remained right behind her with my left hand grazing her back. We remained out of sight at the edge of the building. Two distinct voices rose and fell. It was difficult to make out what they were saying over the hum of the diesel. I picked up a word here and there, but couldn't manage to string a sentence together.

I tugged on her jacket. She leaned back, turned her head toward me so my mouth was next to her left ear. It left her positioned to keep an eye on the area in front of us.

"Let me take point," I said.

She turned her head further toward me. "Why?"

"I want to survey the area."

"Too risky. Let's wait."

"Waiting is against my nature." I pulled her back. Her posture left her off balance, making it simple to slip past her and get to the edge of the building. I heard the men louder here, but still couldn't determine what they were talking about. Then I got a break.

"No shipments, man," one of them said.

I placed my face against the freezing metal siding and inched my head toward the corner. Snow continued to slap my face. I was clad in black, but would be easily spotted against the white field in the background. The light-washed area in front of the rig came into view. A man dressed in a plaid flannel jacket faced away from me. His arms were outstretched, he held papers in one hand. They flapped in the wind. He had to be the truck driver. The other guy walked away from him, toward the other end of the building. Was that the guy I saw perched on a stool in front of the side door? I had to assume it was someone else, at least until I had a visual.

The truck driver lowered his arms, shook his head. He cursed a couple times, referring to the other guy as a type of donkey. The man turned ninety degrees, faced the truck. I pulled away from the corner and pressed against the building.

"What's going on?" Christiana asked.

"Not entirely sure, but it looks like the driver was trying to drop something off and was refused." I peeked around the edge again. The guy trod toward his rig. "Looks like he's leaving."

We waited there for several seconds. The truck door opened with a groan, slammed shut with the force of a hurricane-strength gust of wind. The engine idled for another minute.

Christiana kept watch over our six, monitoring the other end of the building and the field. I stood with my back against the steel wall, flat as I could. I kept my focus straight ahead and listened for changes in the environment.

The transmission grated as the driver shifted his rig into reverse. The rumble deepened. I looked over, saw the white container backing onto the snow-covered blacktop. He squeezed the cab onto the road without sliding into the ditch. The constant roar diminished, leaving a void in the air with nothing to fill the vacuum. Ringing persisted in my ears for several seconds. It wound down to a high-pitched hum before fading completely.

At least an inch of snow had accumulated on the ground already and it showed no signs of stopping.

"We're good now," I said.

Christiana grabbed my wrist. "Let me lead now."

"I got it."

"No," she said. "I do. You stay back at least twenty feet. And do not come with me around the next corner."

Our next step was the riskiest. There was nothing between us and the road. If another person pulled in front of the large building, they'd have us dead to rights.

I nodded and signaled for her to wait a minute. I hadn't been able to get a good look at the layout with the truck out front. Easing around the building, I sucked in a whiff of diesel fumes. It didn't make sense. The truck had left five minutes ago. Any remaining smell wouldn't have only lingered in that spot.

I pressed my hand against the side of the building and felt a slight vibration. Looking up, I spotted a vent. They were using a generator inside, and it vented out to that spot, angled down and away from the building. A gust of wind must've directed it at me at that moment.

The area from here to the other side of the building was flat and covered in gravel. The two large doors remained stationary, even when the wind gusted. I spotted no cameras. The lights across the top of the rail that held the doors were off, and didn't look to be motion sensing. I couldn't guarantee the same on the other side of the building, though.

"All right," I said. "Get going. I'll move once you clear the bay doors."

Christiana nodded and brushed past. Her left arm and shoulder dragged against me.

It was difficult to put this much trust into the woman. What lay waiting on the other side of the building could be a trap, or worse. She could be in on it. It seemed an elaborate setup, if that's what this was. What was the point in putting both of us through all this? Yashkin had to realize her life was in danger from the moment we left, regardless of what he threatened to do with my friends. If he wanted me dead, best to have done it at the house.

I cast all doubts aside. The operation was legit. No way around it. That still didn't mean I was in the clear. Once the job was done, everything changed. I would no longer be needed. And neither would Bear and Lexi.

Christiana turned and gave me a thumbs up, and as she did, a man appeared at the other end of the building.

CHAPTER 43

I KNEW MY NECK WOULD BE SORE THE NEXT MORNING WITH HOW fast I jerked my head back around the corner of the building. I saw enough of the man to know he carried a rifle, and he held it loosely in Christiana's direction. My pulse pounded in my ears with each passing second. Five had passed and I hadn't heard a sound.

The cold air blasted me through my unzipped jacket. My hand gripped the pistol in my waistband. I steadied my breath, counted down from three, pulled the firearm and stepped out from cover.

They were gone.

I couldn't call out her name. The guy could have her kneeling on the other side of the building, hands wrapped around the back of her head. I stepped forward with my left foot, brought my right up next to it. I did this half the length of the building with the pistol at the ready.

A hint of her voice rose. She sounded calm, in control. But a second after I had heard it, it was gone. There was no time to waste. If it blew our mission, fine, but I had to get to the other side.

I hurried forward, careful not to step too hard on the gravel. Still my footsteps crunched, alerting anyone waiting of my advance. I held the pistol at arm's length, gripped with both hands. If anyone but her appeared, they were getting six shots center mass. Questions could wait for the afterlife.

A slamming sound against the building reverberated through the steel. Christiana grunted and exclaimed in Russian.

To hell with my footsteps. I sprinted the remaining distance, drove my shoulder into the corner of the building to slow me down as I rounded it.

She was on the guy's back, one arm wrapped around his throat, the other acting as a counter lever, sealing the hold and cutting off his air supply. Her face was tucked tight to his back. He waved his arms frantically, weakly beating her on the back of the head. She didn't let go. Somehow the guy managed to drive himself upward off his knees, sending his body, and hers, into the side of the building. It was the same sound I had heard a moment ago. It hadn't been effective then. But this time, the move resulted in Christiana losing her grip and sliding down. The guy dove forward. At first, I thought he was doing so out of panic and in an attempt to pull some oxygen into his pained lungs.

But then I saw the rifle on the ground a few feet in front of him.

I rushed forward to kick the weapon out of his reach. It was too risky to shoot, or yell even. I had no idea who else was waiting inside. They must have heard the struggle and would be waiting for us. Before I made it three steps, Christiana was on his back again. She controlled his legs with hers, and barred one of his arms as she resumed her choke hold. Using her momentum, she twisted his torso off the ground. His free arm was pinned beneath their combined bodyweight.

"You OK?" I called out, wiping sweat off my face with my palm. It felt like a sheet of ice had formed over my skin.

She grunted in return, then leaned in for a second before twisting her entire body away from the guy. His neck popped halfway through the move, his body went limp. Christiana released him from her grip and rolled away. I knelt next to the guy and felt for a pulse. There was none. She'd snapped his neck like it was nothing.

I rose, walked over to her, extended my hand. She grabbed it and hopped up.

"What?" she said, meeting my stare with her own.

"You might actually be deadlier than me."

"Impressed?"

I shrugged. "Maybe."

She moved to the door, placed her hand on the knob and turned. "It's open. I'm going first again. Cover me."

I picked the rifle off the ground and waited until she cleared the doorway, then followed her inside. Heat blew down from a unit mounted above the door. I tugged off my hat and the warm air heated the sweaty mop on my head while Christiana continued down the hallway. Lights mounted to the ceiling dimly lit the space. The walls were framed but only drywalled in some places.

I moved down the hall, clearing the open areas as I went. There was enough distance between Christiana and me that anyone watching her move past might come out before I got there. It was still better to make sure than suffer a surprise attack.

The corridor angled away twice. Both times I lost visual of her, but managed to hear her light footsteps as she proceeded forward. But then they stopped before I reached the next corner. I didn't know what to expect when I turned. She might have another guy wrapped up, or maybe already disposed of.

When I had her in sight again, she was standing in an opening roughly eight feet wide. Her hands were up near her shoulders. She had her head cocked, and her body leaned to the right a bit. She was trying to look less threatening as she spoke in Russian.

A man responded in kind.

Was it Thanos? Was this the big secret? He was actually Russian? Nothing Yashkin had said led me to believe this, but at that moment, it seemed plausible.

Christiana took two steps forward.

The guy yelled something, and it sounded as though something crashed on the floor. I heard a gagging sound, almost like a muffled scream.

Christiana seemed to stop herself from looking in my direction. She lowered her chin to her chest, spoke softly. It was all in Russian.

Not knowing what was being said, I knew I had to cover some ground. I put my shoulder against the wall and moved forward. The pistol in my coat pocket bumped against my hip with every step. I had the rifle in hand with a round chambered.

As I moved toward her, Christiana kept going forward, matching me step for step. Smart move. It covered any sound I made on the concrete floor.

The guy yelled again. She froze in place, said something calming.

Opposite the opening there was a large window. It didn't provide the best reflection of the room, but as I drew near I could make out Christiana and two figures beyond her. One stood tall, arm outstretched toward someone on the floor. The guy was on his side, one knee drawn to his chest. He covered his head with his right arm. I leaned in as close as I could without placing myself in view. The guy on the floor had something wrapped around his head tucked in his mouth. Was he Thanos?

Christiana spoke louder.

The guy swung his arm toward her. The firearm glinted in the light. He aimed it at her for a few seconds before redirecting it back to the man on the floor.

I made a single clucking sound with my tongue. Nothing that would sound too out of place in the environment. I didn't want to make the guy with the gun even more frantic.

Christiana picked up on my signal. She took a deep breath, exhaled loudly. Said something to the guy, and then started toward him.

He stiffened, swung his arm around.

I raised the rifle high and tight to my body, lurched around the corner. The guy froze in place, his pistol halfway between his prisoner and Christiana. His stare locked in on me. His arm followed suit. If he was any faster I'd have three holes in my chest. I lowered the rifle, aimed. His left hand caught his right. He lifted his firearm.

I squeezed the trigger. The explosion rocked the room, bounced off the four walls, making the room louder than a collie-town rave. Every muscle in my chest and core tightened. I had sensations of burning, freezing, panic, and rage.

Across the room, the other guy stood tall, chest out. His eyes were wide. His arms hanging oddly at his side, elbows back, bent, arms out. He took a step forward, dropped to a knee, and fell over.

CHAPTER 44

THE MAN TWITCHED AS LIFE LEFT HIS BODY. HE CLUNG TO HIS firearm. Blood pooled from the wound to his chest. My ears rang with the rifle blast still fresh. I patted my stomach, chest, and head making sure I hadn't been wounded.

Christiana twisted at the waist and stared at me. She held a pistol in her right hand, aimed at the floor.

"Are you OK?" I said.

"I think so," she said. "You?"

I nodded, then we both turned our attention toward the other guy on the floor, curled up in a fetal position.

"That's Thanos?"

"Yeah. Looks like he made it, too."

We met in the center of the large room. Thanos rolled over onto his back, and laid there in a bridge-like position, with his bound hands supporting his lower back. His face was bruised heavily on the left. A gash lined the top of his head. His eyes danced wildly between us. He kept talking even though the blood-stained gag prevented him from saying much.

"You want me to do the honors?" I said.

She nodded and took a step back.

I leaned over the man. My pistol pulled the right side of my jacket down further than the left. I could do it now. Take him out, and then have a staring contest with Christiana. We weren't partners. I was forced to come here with her. What happened to Thanos after this moment was out of my control if I pulled off that gag and let him talk. Yashkin wanted this guy, and that meant the FBI, SIS, CIA, and anyone else who wanted to hear what Thanos had to say could take a walk. They'd all be out of luck.

Frankly, I didn't care if any of them saw Thanos alive again.

I grabbed the gag with my left hand, reached into my pocket with my right. I'd been leaning over too long. Blood rushed to my head and caused the outer edges of my vision to darken.

"What are you doing, Noble?" Christiana said.

I held the pistol grip tight, threaded my finger between the trigger and guard. I didn't even have to pull it from my pocket. The shot was lined up perfectly. One bullet, one kill. Then spin around and hold Christiana at bay, see if she'd listen to reason.

"Don't make me do this, Jack."

I turned my head enough to see that she had taken a step back and took a strong stance. Her hands met two feet in front of her. She aimed her firearm at me.

"If you shoot him, I'll have no choice but to take your life." Her voice cracked. "Please don't do this."

I knew she cared more about the information he held than my life, but it felt like she didn't want to kill me. I took a deep breath, had trouble believing the situation I found myself in. I should've shot everyone outside Thanos's house that night I hid in the woods. Would've saved everyone a lot of trouble.

Thanos pleaded with me through the gag. His eyes were wet, tears fell down the sides of his cheeks.

What did his life mean to me? Nothing. But completing this job for the Old Man wasn't worth the value I placed on my own head.

I tightened my hand around the pistol, took my finger off the trigger. Then I yanked the gag down past his chin, revealing his battered mouth. He was missing his two top front teeth, and two more on the bottom. They were raw and jagged, and blood spilled out of the corner of his mouth. He rolled onto his stomach and tried to get to his knees.

"Let me help you." I grabbed him under his arm and jerked him upward. "Come on, work with me."

He let out a loud groan and finally made it to his knees.

"Thank you." He looked at me, then her. "Thank you both."

"Don't thank us yet," I said. "We're not saving you, just collecting you."

He narrowed his eyes and shook his head. "Who are you?"

"That's not important," Christiana said. Then she turned her attention to me. "Search the men for the keys to the handcuffs."

"Let's just leave them on. Safer that way."

"I agree, but at some point we'll need to get them off and I'd rather not saw through them, or his arms."

Thanos took a deep breath and choked back a sob.

"Was it something she said?"

He looked away, shaking his head. A difficult situation had come to an end for him, but he wasn't in the clear, and he realized it. As I searched the dead guy on the floor, I started the process of questioning Thanos. I knew that was part of what Yashkin wanted me there for, and the Old Man had been interested in the information I could extract.

I decided to attack his ego first. "You must've done something incredibly stupid to get your ass dragged all the way out here and beaten like that."

Thanos pursed his lips, grimaced, then spat blood on the floor between us.

I hopped to my feet, stepped up to him. He was a big guy, but on his knees, he only came up to my waist.

"So tough all of a sudden. You know what I could do to you right now?"

"Bite me," he said.

I swung my heel back, then drove my foot forward into his groin.

Christiana stood to my side, wincing as she watched Thanos collapse face first onto the ground, landing in his own bloody puddle of spit. Whatever information Thanos held onto was now gone, and she knew it.

"No key," I said. "Gonna check the guy outside."

The cold hit me like a Zamboni rolling over me. The adrenaline from the shootout had fueled my internal furnace. The snowstorm was about to provide a correction.

I walked past the guy Christiana had dispatched, he wasn't going anywhere, and headed out to the street. The snow had covered the asphalt. A nice undisturbed white layer stretched in both directions. No one had come by during our time inside. I worried that a concerned neighbor might swing by, check out the disturbance. Then again, we were out in the country. Rifle shots were common and ignored by locals.

Glancing above the large sliding doors that dominated the front of the warehouse, I noticed a square cutout aglow around the edges with light. It led to the warehouse loft providing an easy way to load or unload items stored up there. The wind kicked up and rattled the door. It came out a few inches, then slammed shut again.

I pulled my coat close to my body and tucked my arms over it until I reached the dead guard. Thankfully he hadn't moved. Would've created a whole new set of problems if he had. I wasn't prepared to test my readiness for the apocalypse. I unzipped his jacket and rifled through his pockets. Found a pack of cigarettes and lighter, which I pocketed, as well as his wallet and a spare pistol. I took the cash from his wallet, and put the pistol in my other pocket. He had no ID or cell phone on him.

In his pants pocket, I found a keyring with at least a dozen keys on it. It only took a second to weed out the house and car keys, leaving me with three possibilities for the handcuffs.

I rose and stepped back inside, letting my jacket fall open. I stood there under the heater for a few seconds. Tense muscles relaxed for a couple moments. One more step complete. It was almost over. Soon I'd go home to New York and sleep this nightmare of a job off.

And then every muscle in my body tensed when I heard the round discharged.

CHAPTER 45

THE GUNSHOT SOUNDED LIKE A CANNON TRAVELING DOWN THE narrow hallway. The echo and reverberation left me slightly disoriented and confused. The next few seconds seemed to take an hour as I gathered my thoughts and bearings.

What the hell had just happened? Was Thanos armed, and we missed it? Hell, the guy was half naked on the floor when I left a few minutes ago. There weren't many places he could've been hiding a firearm. And he was handcuffed, making retrieving let alone firing a gun almost impossible.

Several more shots were fired in rapid succession. Christiana's scream rose and fell between the sound of a 9mm discharging in rapid succession.

I armed myself with my pistol and the sidearm I'd looted off the guard, and raced down the makeshift hallway. The sight lines were awful. I feared I'd come face to face with an assailant at each turn.

Stopping in front of the window like I had earlier, I took in the reflection of the room. The light hanging from the ceiling swayed, possibly it had been hit by a round. The long shadows it cast danced across the floor. Thanos was lying on his stomach, a dark pool around him.

Where was Christiana? Had she found a way outside?

What about the shooter?

I had no idea what she armed herself with. Thinking back to the first shot, it could've been a .45. She could've used that on Thanos, then emptied her nine, then fled the warehouse. Did that even make sense, though? Five minutes ago I was prepared to finish Thanos and she stopped me.

Movement caught my attention. It was Christiana. She hadn't fled after all.

In her attempt to secure a better position, she knocked over a stack of boxes. I kept my stare focused on the window, looking for the shooter to reveal himself.

Christiana tucked herself in between the pallet of boxes and the wall. It wasn't the best place if the assailant spotted her. Cardboard boxes weren't going to stop much. Crouched low, she managed to keep herself out of most sight lines unless the guy was on the other side of the wall from me. I wanted her to know I was there, that I had her back, so I took a few steps forward, partially revealing myself to half the room. I tapped on the wall, hoping to draw her attention, *and* the shooter's.

It worked.

No sooner than she caught sight of me, the cannon erupted again and a hole blew through the drywall above my head. A cloud of building material rained down on me.

I withdrew a few feet and turned toward the window again. My heart pounded against my chest and my lungs worked overtime. I forced myself to slow my breathing down. In the event a clear shot opened up, I couldn't ruin it with shaky hands.

A quick glimmer caught my eye. The shooter had revealed himself as he shifted his sights from me to Christiana. The swinging light in the middle of the room reflected off the rifle scope.

Was this guy there the whole time? Why had he waited so long to take action?

Then it hit me. The square door to the loft above the large doors out front. He'd scaled the wall and entered through there. Had we been tracked? Was it one of Yashkin's men? Maybe he wanted Thanos, Christiana, and me dead. That could explain why he'd sent me along with her.

I played the shot in my mind. It wouldn't be easy, not with a handgun. Unfortunately, the rifle I had used earlier lay on the ground a few feet from Thanos. I had no chance at retrieving it. If anything, I could unload enough on the guy that he'd retreat and Christiana would have time to reach my position, then we could flee the warehouse.

I took a deep breath. Closed my eyes. Counted back from five. Then I swung around the edge and opened fire.

Only nothing happened. My sidearm had jammed. I tossed it and reached for the backup.

Christiana rose slightly. It wasn't much. A few inches. But it was all the shooter needed.

I rushed toward her.

The guy stiffened as he lined up his shot. The rifle exploded in a violent eruption that sent me skidding to my knees, falling back over my ankles. Christiana's head snapped sideways as her torso slammed back into the wall. She stood there for a moment, then slid down, leaving behind a thick crimson trail.

I lifted my left hand and fired six rounds at the loft. No clue if I came anywhere near the guy as my eyes were fixed on the ceiling. I flung my feet out in front of me and caught a glimpse of the shooter as he turned and retreated deep into the loft. He wasn't hiding. The loft door slammed against the frame. The guy had jumped outside.

I hurried past Thanos to Christiana. She lay motionless on the floor, her hand covering a blossoming stain on her dark jacket. I knelt down, grabbed her wrist. Her eyelids fluttered open. She looked around, settled on me for a moment.

"Oh, Christ, you're still with us," I said.

She opened her mouth in an attempt to speak, but said nothing. Her eyes clenched shut, mouth twisted into a pained grimace. I moved her hand to the side and unzipped the jacket. She'd been hit close enough to the heart that it didn't make sense she was still alive. I worked the fabric of her shirt open and tore a large chunk off, folded it, placed her hand on top of the wound.

"You hang in there. You hear me?"

She blinked her eyes open, licked her lips, and managed a few words. "Don't...don't let them...find me...here. I-I-I...can't be...found...like...this. Please, Jack." Her eyes closed for a few moments. She swallowed hard. "My husband and children can't know."

I squeezed her left hand. "They won't. You be strong for a few more minutes. I'm gonna go take care of this asshole."

Her chances of making it out of that warehouse alive were slim, whether I stayed or not. It wasn't in my nature to sit by while an asshole made an escape. I zipped my jacket, pulled my hood tight. On the way to the exit I cleared my pistol of its jam, then holstered it and armed myself with the rifle.

The heavy snow reduced visibility to a few feet. Seemed that way, at least. All I could see was white upon white. It had accumulated four inches or so already. The air was thick with woodsmoke. Maybe there was a house closer than I thought.

Halfway across the front of the warehouse, I spotted the first tracks. Footprints, a handprint, and two divots where his knees had hit after jumping from the loft. They led toward the woods Christiana and I had trekked through.

A strong gust of wind hit me from the behind. The overhead door whipped

196 / L.T. RYAN

back and cracked against the steel facade. A dim cone of light cast down on the ground illuminating me.

I felt naked and exposed out there with a shooter nearby. Had he taken off running, or was he lurking nearby? I darted out of the light and toward the corner of the building.

I didn't make it there in time.

The muzzle blast caught my eye before I heard the thunderous gunshot and felt the searing pain in my side.

CHAPTER 46

THE IMPACT OF THE SHOT SPUN ME BACK TO THE LEFT UNTIL I collided with the front of the building. The impact jarred the rifle loose from my left hand. It thudded when it hit the ground a few feet away. The swirling snow and constant drone of the wind left me trying to figure out which way was which. I had to move, but my first step sent me careening face first into the snowfall.

Get up!

The voice of my father yelled out in my head. I was ten years old again, on the mat, trying to manage a breath into my crippled lungs after he'd laid me out.

I looked up at the building. The loft door danced back and forth throwing light and shadows all around.

The woods.

I turned my attention back to the thick trees where the shooter had fled. Was he still there? And where was the rifle? I couldn't see it, so I felt around the snow. No luck.

I had to get to my feet and move. I drew my left knee up. Waves of pain rode up and down my side, causing me to call out.

Across the distance I heard him chamber another round. My outburst had led him right to my position.

Grimacing against the pain, I tightened every muscle and flung myself upward, driving my right foot forward. My left hand instinctively went to my side at the site of the wound. I worked my fingers around to figure out where I'd been hit. The pain centralized on the outside of my hip near the waistline. I pushed in hard to gauge whether the bone had been fractured or shattered. It hurt like hell, but nothing moved or crunched. And I had mobility. Must've just grazed me.

The building offered the best cover, so I made my move.

He fired again. Missed.

I kept going until my right shoulder plowed into the steel. What now? I could retreat back into the building and figure out a way to reach out to Yashkin. Christiana had to have some way to communicate with him. There were only a couple of ways to get inside, and I could cover them from one location while doing my best to keep her alive.

Rage built inside me. I could taste it like acid-coated steel forced into my gut. No way I let this guy go without a fight.

I pulled my pistol. The magazine still held fourteen rounds. I aimed toward the woods and fired one every few seconds while sprinting across the field. The snow bit at my face. My hip burned, feeling as though it tore with every step. I plowed forward, unable to see much at all, just white and the shadow of the looming woods in the distance. The pistol ratcheted my wrist up and back with every shot. Gunpowder overpowered my senses.

With the first line of trees in sight, I stuck out my left arm and prepared to stop myself. Not the best move. My hip slammed into the tree trunk, sending a bolt of fire and lightning through my side. I slammed my mouth shut, grunted through my teeth, choking a scream in my throat. I couldn't give away my location again.

Another rifle shot ricocheted through the woods. The round thudded against a nearby tree. Chunks of bark and wood flew at me. I took cover facing the warehouse. Through the storm the light from the loft grew brighter and then dimmer.

Was Christiana still alive? Had I made a mistake leaving so quickly? What of the items Thanos had brought with him? I could've left something important in there. Once the police secured the area, there'd be no chance of recovering it. I realized though that if Thanos had something of value to negotiate with, he wouldn't have been held in such a precarious position.

The night grew silent again except for the soft sound of falling snow. I stepped out from behind my cover and moved deeper into the woods. Each step was placed slow and deliberate to avoid making too much noise. I stopped every ten feet, listened through the howling wind for signs of the shooter.

I wondered if he was there for us, or if he'd happened upon us. The unexpected delivery truck suddenly made sense. This guy was probably in back.

While the guard was distracted, he hid across the street. Once inside, he took Thanos out first, so it made sense to assume that had been his primary target. Everyone else was collateral damage.

Everything went still. I froze in place when he racked the rifle. Where the hell was the guy? Where would the shot come from? There were a half-dozen options for cover and I couldn't decide on a single one.

"You coulda lived, asshole."

I turned toward the sound of his voice, but a cracking sound further to the right caught my attention. I dropped into a squatting stance, pistol extended, attempting to see through the night. The snow still fell, but not as intensely in the forest. Still, it was thick with shadows and trees and impossible to tell what was happening beyond ten feet.

He said, "Put your hands up, discard your weapon, and I might let you live."

I didn't respond. He wasn't sure where I was now.

"Unless you'd like to end up like that traitor and the bitch back there."

He was trying to goad me into a response, but I wouldn't give him the satisfaction. The more he talked, the more he gave himself away.

"You're a real dumbass, Noble."

He knew me?

The words played over and over as I closed my eyes and let my instincts guide me in the right direction. Get this wrong, and I'd give myself away. All he had to do was have his eyes open and he'd know where to shoot.

I took a deep breath, swung my outstretched arm left, then fired.

He grunted, yelled, "God dammit!"

Something hit the ground. It was solid but too light to have been him. I rose and took off in the direction I'd fired. It didn't take long to find him. He was crouched over, one arm tight to his stomach, the other reaching for something on the ground.

He grabbed the buttstock and lifted his rifle. I'd managed to shoot it out of his hand. Had I taken a digit or two along with it?

I could easily dispatch the guy right then and there. But he had information that would die with him. I held on tight to the pistol and closed the gap between us with a sprint. He looked up at me when I was a couple of feet away, brought the rifle up in defense like he wielded a staff.

I turned into him with my injured side, wrapped my left arm around the rifle. He struck out with his good hand, landed a blow to my cheek. My head snapped back to the left. I stared up at the treetops and falling snow for a moment.

The blow had slowed my momentum, but I was close enough to hit back. I gripped the pistol by the hot barrel, swung my right arm out like I was swinging a mallet, and drove the handle into his face. Cartilage crunched. He choked on tears and saliva and blood.

I pulled him in close, lifted my right leg, drove my foot into the side of his knee. It buckled, and he tumbled forward, relinquishing his grasp on the rifle.

"Who the hell are you?" I grabbed a handful of his hair and yanked his head. My right arm was cocked, ready to deliver another blow to the bloody mess of a face. But I stopped.

I knew the son of a bitch.

CHAPTER 47

THE GUY WHO CHARLES HAD INTRODUCED TO ME AS MATT STARED
up at me. Blood lined his lips, dripped off his chin like a leaky goatee.

"The hell are you doing here?" I yanked his head back as though that
would get him to speak up.

His eyes rolled back, he licked his lips.

"Who sent you? How long have you been tracking me?"

He raised his left hand, index finger pointed upward.

"What're you saying? God sent you?" I drove my knee into his chest.

His eyes clenched shut, face twisted. His limp bodyweight threatened to
pull his scalp free from the hair I had a grip on. And then he moved faster
than a man that injured should. It felt like a snake bit my right calf. The pain
was sharp and confined at first, then spread clear down through my Achilles
into my foot.

Matt then drove his shoulder into my legs. I planted my right foot to brace
myself, but my knee gave out and I toppled over. Instinctively, my left arm
went up to shield my face, my right arm out to cover my chest and core. But
there were no additional blows. The guy had clawed his way up and was
trudging through the woods.

"Not today," I yelled.

I pulled myself up and started toward him. Pain flashed through my leg
and I stumbled forward. I reached down and grabbed the wound. The gash
was wide and felt deep. Blood dripped from my fingers onto the fresh snow. I
took off my coat, tore the sleeve from my shirt and wrapped it tight around
my leg. It'd have to do.

I grabbed his rifle off the ground and got to my feet. The long firearm made a decent cane to support the injured leg. With every second that passed, Matt slipped further away. I'd lost sight of him shortly after falling. Now I wondered if I'd encounter him again. He was too wounded to stand and fight, so fleeing was his only course of action. Where would he go? Did he have a vehicle waiting? Did he know about the Taurus parked on the side of the road? I took a course directly toward the street rather than the car.

Each step sent a wave of pain through my body. Shot on one side. Stabbed on the other. Next time I got my hands on the guy I wouldn't give him a chance to talk. I'd FedEx his head to Charles and wait for an explanation.

As I neared the wood's edge, I heard an engine crank. It whined high a couple times, then went silent before finally turning over.

"Come this way," I muttered, leaning into a tree and lifting the rifle. I waited there for several seconds as the Taurus idled in the distance. No point in moving any closer. I'd make myself vulnerable, and miss the shot if the chance arose.

Headlights washed over the road. They came from the wrong direction though. The sound of another vehicle overtook the Taurus. A white truck rolled past, leaving thick impressions on the snow-covered road. Its loud V-8 subsided as its taillights faded into the distance. The area grew quiet except for the sound of the snow tapping the ground.

How had I let Matt get away? This wasn't the first time in my life I'd been surprised to come across somebody I knew while working. The community was a small one, and chance encounters were bound to happen. I let it get the best of me. If Matt had had a little more strength, he could have gone for my femoral artery instead of my calf. It must have taken everything he had to attack me, then run off.

I waited a few more minutes to see if he'd ducked and covered upon hearing the approaching truck. But I never heard the sound of the Taurus again. I wanted to wait there, see if he appeared. But the warehouse had to be dealt with before anyone arrived and notified the authorities.

I skirted the edge of the woods until I reached the clearing in front of the building. It stood out like a steel giant in the snowfall. Light leaked along the roof line in a few places. The loft seemed secured. I realized then that the wind had died down. It made the trek across the field a little easier, but not by much. I left a spotted trail of blood in my wake. I wasn't sure how much longer I could stand on my feet before addressing my wounds.

Once inside the building, I shed my coat and went about looking for supplies in the offices off the hallway. There had to be some kind of first aid kit in there. A yellow tinted box was mounted to a wall in a room with a conference table and seven chairs. Looked like it had been handed down over a couple generations. I pulled it free from its mount and hurried to Christiana. I glanced at my calf, grimaced at the thought of what it looked like under the red-stained makeshift bandage.

Even before I reached her, I knew Christiana had passed. I dropped the kit next to her legs and took my time kneeling down at her side. Her neck revealed no pulse. Her skin had already started to cool. I rested my elbows on my knees and buried my head in my hands. Her loss tore at my soul. Why did I feel this way over someone I hardly knew? Someone who, if Yashkin had given the order, would have aimed at me and pulled the trigger without a second thought, no regrets on her part.

Why did I have them?

Maybe she was my counterpart in this crazy life of a killer and I felt drawn to her for that reason. Maybe part of me longed for what she had back home. A family. And it hurt to know they'd never see her again. And this prompted my own realization that loved ones weren't something I could have in my life.

I rocked forward onto my knees and began searching her body for anything useful. I found a phone wrapped in a wallet case in her back pocket, as well as a pocket knife. Both could come in handy.

The first aid kit contained a roll of tape, gauze, peroxide, ointment, some bandages, and a few other items. I used the pocket knife to cut away my pants leg. The wound was deep and smooth. It'd picked up some debris from outside. I poured the bottle of peroxide over the gash. Intense stinging lasted for a solid thirty seconds, and offered a perfect opportunity to seal the wound. I gripped my calf and pressed it together, mashed some gauze over the wound, then wrapped the medical tape up and down my lower leg going a couple inches past either end of the gash.

It hurt like hell standing up, but I made it. Maybe I'd luck out and there'd be no muscle or nerve damage. I had little confidence in that after the first step.

I limped over to Thanos. The guy was spread out on the floor the same as I'd left him.

"What the hell did you do?"

I looked around for the rest of his clothing. Had they stashed his belongings somewhere in the room? Stacks of boxes offered plenty of places to hide an item or two. I walked the perimeter of the space, stopping to investigate the little cubbies randomly placed along the way. Nothing. With the pain in my calf increasing to the point I no longer felt the flesh wound on my hip, I was ready to call it a night. I pulled my phone out and started to dial Frank.

Then I spotted it. A blue sport coat hanging on the wall next to where I'd entered and exited the room each time. I made my way over. Blood trickled through the bandage, over the tape, and down my leg. I ignored it. There'd be time to patch it up again soon enough.

I pulled the sport coat off the hanger and flipped it around. Zegna. Expensive, coming in around two grand, maybe more. The kind of thing Thanos might wear. He was laid out in his boxers and socks now. Where were his pants and shoes? I slipped my hands into the chest pockets, came up empty. The front pockets were sewn shut. I bunched the jacket up in my fists and felt all around. Something had been sewn into a small compartment at the lower back.

Another use for Christiana's pocket knife.

"You're still doing a good job," I told her. Maybe she heard me, maybe she was already gone. Either way, she was helping out.

I cut a slit wide enough to slide two fingers into the lining. It was out of the way, not too obvious if someone else inspected the jacket. I worked through the compartment and locked down a folded piece of paper between my index and middle fingers.

But before I could open it and take a look, I heard a banging against the side of the building.

"Door's open over here. Come on!"

CHAPTER 48

I SHOVED THE PAPER INTO MY POCKET AND BRACED FOR THE attack, knowing I couldn't withstand another physical assault. The door slamming shut reverberated through the drywall. There were at least two sets of feet pounding the floor, moving fast. I couldn't brace myself well enough to use the rifle, so I stood there with the pistol held out, aimed at the spot where they'd enter the room.

A deep voice bellowed, "Jack?"

The ground beneath me turned to Jell-o. My right leg slid out from under me and I dropped to my left knee, gripping the wall with my fingertips.

"In here, Bear."

Lexi sprinted into the room, head turning side to side. She nearly tripped over her feet when she spotted me and tried to stop too quickly. Her gaze traveled around the room, stopping for a moment on the lifeless bodies.

"Christ, Jack," she said. "What happened?"

"Did you find him?" I said.

Bear rushed over and began a medical assessment on me. "Find who?"

"Matt." I tried to lift myself off the ground.

Bear put his hand on my shoulder and pressed me down. "Who's Matt? He the one that did this?"

I eased down to the floor and leaned back against the wall. "Yeah, he did all this." I gestured around the room, then to myself. "The guards were our handiwork."

"What about Christiana?" Bear asked. "She turn against you?"

"Just the opposite, man. We formed into a team pretty damn easily." I lowered my shaking head into my hand. "He hit her from the loft after nailing Thanos."

"How'd he miss you?" Bear had his hand on my calf.

I winced in pain as he felt for muscle damage. "I was outside checking the guard for a key. I unloaded when I came back in, but it was too late. He'd already done the damage."

Bear nodded. "What about your leg?"

"Matt went out the door up there and I followed. We got into it in the woods. I made a mistake, underestimated him. Thought I had it all under control and the bastard pulled a knife and sliced my leg." This was the first chance I'd had to reflect on what went wrong. "The Taurus, you find it?"

"Find what?" Bear said.

"The car, man. The one we came out here in."

Lexi walked toward us. "We followed a phone signal out here. Found it on the ground maybe a quarter mile from here."

"The white truck." I recalled waiting with the rifle, hoping Matt would come my way, when they drove past my position.

"Yeah, that was us," Bear said. "All we found was the phone, no car."

"Wasn't there a blank spot in the snow where the car had covered the ground?" I said.

"It was laying in the middle of the road." Lexi pulled the phone from her pocket and showed it to me. "No car."

"He got away." I clenched my fist and slammed it back against the wall. "Wait, how'd you two get out?" I hadn't considered how the two of them had managed to get here.

The right side of Bear's upper lip twisted into a smile. "They got lack-adaisical."

"That's putting it lightly," Lexi said. "I don't know if they thought three against two put things in their favor, or what, but one of those guys walked right past Bear with his MP5 dangling from his harness."

Bear mimed his movements. "One lunge forward, snatched it and put two rounds through his ribcage at heart level. Turned him around, then got the guy across the room. Lexi finished off the third guy with a choke hold."

"Ginger?" I said.

"Kozlov?" Bear said. "Yeah, he left shortly after you did. Half-expected to find him here."

I wondered if he and Matt were connected. Had Kozlov dropped Matt off here to take us out? Was the semi that pulled up a coincidence?

"What bout Yashkin?" I said.

Bear lowered his chin to his chest and shook his head. "He'd gone into a backroom maybe five minutes before it went down. Guess at the sound of the first shot he bolted out a window. By the time I made it outside, he was gone."

"All wasn't lost, though." Lexi held up a device that looked like an early nineties cell phone. "They were tracking Christiana's phone with this. That's how we were able to find you."

She'd brought two phones, it seemed. The one I pulled off her body was her personal cell, the other she'd left in the car. When Matt stole the vehicle, he tossed the phone. Maybe he knew they were tracking it.

Bear hopped up to his feet. "You're in pretty bad shape, partner. Don't know what would've happened to you if we hadn't shown up."

"This?" I gestured toward my hip and calf. "Flesh wounds. I'm good to go."

He held out his hand. "Prove it."

I grunted as I pulled myself up. Bear offered no assistance other than allowing me to yank on his arm.

"Good as new." I turned toward Lexi. "You got a burner on you?"

She nodded, pulled the phone out and tossed it to me. "Who are you calling?"

"No one." I limped across the room until I stood over Thanos. The folded paper I'd taken from his coat felt like a brick in my pocket. "Give me a hand turning this asshole over."

Bear put his gloves back on and flipped Thanos over like he was nothing more than a human-sized pancake. I snapped four photos of the guy, then sent them off to a secure number owned by the Old Man. On the final picture, I added a note that said, "Done. Send Payment."

I tossed the phone back to Lexi, who proceeded to reset it to factory settings and then dismantle it.

"All right," Bear said. "Let's get outta here."

"One more thing." I pulled Frank's phone out. There were two numbers stored in the contact list. One went to Bear, the other I assumed to Frank. I selected it, pressed send, and waited.

"Jack?" he answered. "Christ, I've been waiting to hear from you. What's going on?

"I'm gonna be brief, so listen up. I'm standing in a warehouse in Wisconsin with two dead bodies on the floor. The man is Thanos. He was shot with a high powered rifle from twenty yards out. I don't know the identity of the shooter. I had him and he got away. The second body is female, belongs to a woman named Christiana Zhenya. Killed by the same shooter with the same rifle. This is what you are gonna do. You're taking her body, and you're gonna set it in one of those cheap planes you keep on hand when we need an accident. You'll fly that thing over some remote corner of western Pennsylvania, and you'll crash it into the woods. When it comes time for her family to find out what happened, she was taking a flight to another meeting and the small craft lost signal and went down, leaving no survivors. Her family is not to find out what she was doing here. Got it?"

"Yeah, Jack, sure. I can do that." He paused to clear his throat. "What the hell happened there?"

"You prove to me you had nothing to do with this, and I'll fill you in. Until then, I don't trust your ass."

"Look, stay put where you're at—"

I hung up the phone and tossed it onto Thanos's chest. Bear did the same with his cell. He looked over at me, nodded.

"On our own again," he said.

"Seems to be a recurring theme," I said.

"Is there usually a female lead on these missions?" Lexi said.

"No," I said. "But we'll make an exception this time."

"Good choice," she said. "Now let's get somewhere we can make an ID on that shooter."

CHAPTER 49

LEXI LINGERED A FEW STEPS BEHIND US WHILE ON THE PHONE. All I picked up from her conversation was someone would meet us in a couple hours. I was leery of trusting her, but given what had happened that night, there was no other choice. She was as deep into this as us now. Whoever Yashkin was, if we hadn't pissed him off before, he had surely crossed the line between dislike and hate by now. Was he the type of man to stick around and fight, or would he regroup and come after us later?

I stretched out on the rear bench seat of the pickup truck. Bear took the wheel. Lexi ended her call, pocketed her phone and hopped in the passenger seat. She leaned back and looked at me.

"Get you anything?"

"Got some water up there?"

"We'll stop and get some," Bear said. "Almost outta gas anyway."

"Great."

Seemed every time we stopped at a gas station, something went down. Not only that, having to stop meant a chance we'd get caught on camera. The damn things were everywhere now, and all linked together. If an analyst had the right credentials, they could get access to multiple feeds, and using special software, locate a license plate. From there, LPRs, license plate readers, would spot us on any major highway we traveled on. It came down to how much pull Yashkin had, and who he worked with. If he had a friend or two in the right places, and I had no doubt he did, all he had to do was give them the license plate of the pickup Bear and Lexi had stolen. We had to hope he didn't have it memorized. A guy like that, though? He probably did.

Bear stopped at the first open gas station he spotted. While he filled up, Lexi ran inside, paid for the fuel, some water, and snacks. She returned to the car with a stockpile of beef jerky and almonds, which she split evenly between the three of us.

"Not quite a steak dinner," she said.

"It'll do." I peeled back the plastic and took a bite. It was tough and salty and spicy and hit the spot. I washed it down my scratchy throat with half a bottle of water, then ate another piece while the afterburn of the first lingered.

Bear fired up the engine, shifted into drive, rolled to the exit. He glanced over at Lexi. "Where're we headed?"

"Someplace safe." She pointed left and said, "That way, all the way to Oshkosh, then hop on 41 North."

"Green Bay?" he asked.

"Little bit past there." She drummed her fingers on the console between them.

"Nervous?" I said.

She shook her head. "No, just ready to get this all figured out."

"You and me both. Actually, I'm ready to visit Bear on his vacation and crash on the beach for a week. You can roll me up and down with the tide."

"Vacation's over, baby," Bear said. "I'm ready to work now. Don't think I'm gonna let you slack 'cause you're a little cut up."

I covered my eyes with my hand and leaned my head back. A rough estimate put us an hour away from our destination. I could sit there anticipating what was to come, or I could trust Lexi had it under control and grab a nap. I opted for sleep, but even with the swaying of the truck and the steady hum of the engine I couldn't quite make it there. Instead, I cleared my head and stared out into the darkness.

The truck rolled along for an hour. Pain had set in as my muscles stiffened due to lack of movement. Fire ran up my left side, down my right leg. The aches spread as I sat up and moved my legs in an effort to stifle cramped muscles. I glanced at the clock to gauge how long I'd been out. Almost an hour had passed. While I hoped there was more sleep in store, I didn't plan on it anytime soon. If Lexi's contact turned up any leads on Matt, we had to act fast. The guy was probably planning his escape into Canada, if he wasn't there already.

"How you doing back there?" Bear glanced at me in the rear-view.

"Hanging in there. Little stiff, but I'll manage."

"Get off here," Lexi said, pointing at the exit. "We're gonna get you patched up in a few minutes, Jack."

Over the next ten minutes, Lexi guided us away from the highway through a network of unmarked country roads. There was nothing but woods as far as I could tell. No streetlights. No houselights. No cars. I spotted a couple deer and other critters, that was it.

"Slow down," she said. "It's going to be up here on the left. And there it is."

Bear eased into the turn.

"OK," she said. "You're gonna have to cut your headlights."

"How the hell are—"

She opened the glove box and pulled out a flashlight. "Only as we need it, though. Go slow and you should be able to make it through here."

Bear sighed, cut the headlights, and moved forward with his foot on the brake. We bounced along the dirt road with Lexi shining the flashlight for a second or two every so often.

"Why no lights?" I asked.

She pointed up. "Never know who's watching."

"Where the hell are we?" Bear said.

"Stop the truck." Lexi smiled, rolled down her window, stuck her arm out and aimed the flashlight straight ahead. "We're here."

CHAPTER 50

I THREW MY ARM OVER BEAR'S SHOULDER AND USED HIM AS A crutch. My calf didn't respond to the stretching, leaving my foot dangling at an awkward angle. I'd heard of drop foot before, but thought it was a symptom of significant nerve damage. The wound hurt like hell, but didn't seem that severe.

"You two wait here." Lexi placed her hand on my chest, patted it, then turned and jogged up to the side of the building. A soft glow appeared next to her, partially blocked by her hand. Looked like a keypad.

"Government facility?" Bear asked.

"Guess it's an FBI location. Kinda odd spot for it, though."

"Not the oddest we've seen."

"Definitely not."

We'd been all around the world, inside safe houses hiding in plain sight, and others buried deep in a mountain. Nothing surprised us anymore.

A door opened in front of Lexi. A tall, skinny man stood there, silhouetted by the light behind him. He reached out and placed his hands on Lexi's shoulders. She leaned in and hugged him, then turned and waved for us to join her.

The guy looked to be in his fifties, with salt and pepper hair, dark eyebrows, and a mostly white mustache. His face was narrow and angled. He wore thick black-rimmed glasses that reflected the overhead lights

"Fun night?" he said, looking at me with a hint of curiosity in his eyes.

"David, we can't get into what's going on, OK?" Lexi said. "I told you that on the phone, so don't prod us."

"It's in my nature to ask questions," he said. He tapped Bear on the arm to get his attention. "Take him into that room at the end of the hallway."

I was surprised to see a young, attractive, dark-haired woman dressed in scrubs waiting for us in a sterile room. I glanced at Bear. He concurred.

The lady turned away from us and grabbed a chart and said, "Get out of those clothes and put them in that bag over there."

Bear piped up. "Ma'am, I had my physical a couple of months ago, but if you wanna check—"

"I suggest that if you don't have any bullet holes, lacerations, puncture wounds, or bite marks, and you don't want any in the next few minutes, get out of my room."

"About the bite marks," Bear said.

The woman stopped fixating on the end of her pen and raised her gaze up to Bear. "I can arrange that, if you wish. It won't be from me, though. And you can trust me, it won't be somewhere you'll enjoy."

"You'd be surprised—"

"Bear," I said. "Come on, she's here to patch me up. Let's cut her a break. Go see if you can help Lexi."

He shrugged us off, kicked the stop holding the door open, and left the room. The door closed with a clank behind him.

"Your friend has quite the sense of humor," she said while writing on the chart.

"He's just making up for me," I said. "Little beat up at the moment, can't find much to crack jokes at."

"I often find it a sign of insecurity in men when they have to act in such a way in these situations. I mean, can't you just man up, or grin and bear it, or, my favorite, rub some dirt on it."

I removed the paper I'd pulled from Thanos's jacket, then stuffed my clothes in the bag like she had requested. She tossed me a pair of gym shorts then patted the metal table and waited for me to hop on. The table was colder than the snow-covered ground outside. I was thankful for the shorts.

Her face scrunched up as she investigated my calf. "When was your last tetanus shot?"

"Little cold out to be worried about that, isn't it?"

"It's your life. We can take all the chances you want with it."

"I'd prefer to live," I said. "At least for a little bit longer. My last one was within the last four years."

She opened a cabinet and pulled out a syringe and small bottle. "I'm gonna give you a shot just in case. Have you ever had an adverse reaction to this before?"

I shook my head. She proceeded with the shot, then went about cleaning the flesh wound on my hip and suturing it. She then turned her attention back to my calf.

After cleaning and sterilizing the laceration, she said, "Pretty clean cut. You lucked out and avoided any major damage. It'll be sore for a few days, but overall it should heal up nicely." She pulled off her gloves and tossed them into the trash. "So, you tried jumping a fence and landed on a sword? Am I close?"

I laughed. "Something like that."

Her expression soured. "How'd the other guy wind up?"

"He should be deceased." I looked up at her, found her dark eyes locked on mine. "I had him dead to rights. I don't know what happened, why I let up. I guess I thought he was done and the rest would be up to me. Then he pulled a knife from God knows where, sliced the back of my leg. Maybe he was sandbagging the whole time. Perhaps the fear of dying gave him one last jolt of adrenaline which he used to get away from me."

"Jesus," she said. "I forget sometimes, you know, working in here. When I was in the military—"

"Which branch?"

"Army. You a vet?"

I nodded. "Mostly. Marines."

"Ahh, oorah, and all that." She nodded. "Anyway, I was in Afghanistan working out of a makeshift medical facility. Had to amputate limbs, trying to perform miracles on guys who were basically dead before they hit the ground. I was tuned in then. But you don't think about these things happening on our soil."

I understood where she was coming from. She, like most people, hadn't been exposed to the underbelly of our country. Most wouldn't be able to handle it if they knew what really went on.

"What's your name?" I asked her.

"Kate," she said.

"Well, Kate, if I had to take a guess, you'd be doing a lot more work on the other guy if he were in here. Although, if he shows up, give him a shot that'll finish the job for me."

She winked. "You got it."

CHAPTER 51

.

I FOUND BEAR AND LEXI TALKING WITH DAVID IN A ROOM DOWN the hall. The woman who had patched me up followed me in, carrying the bag of clothes. She set them on a stainless counter and gave everyone a report on my condition.

"There's no way you'll keep him off it," Bear said.

I agreed. "Not with these guys still out there. I can rest after this is done. Until then, I have to keep moving. Sitting still is a recipe for death."

"I can only offer you advice. It's up to you to listen." She turned toward David. "It looks like there's enough on the clothes to do a workup."

He walked over to the bag, looked inside, nodded. "Go ahead and get it started. Don't waste any time with it, either. We need to get the results as fast as possible."

"What're you doing with them?" I asked.

"DNA," he said. "If you beat your attacker as badly as I imagine you did, there should be some of his blood on your clothing. Maybe some from the man inside the warehouse, too."

"Thanos," I said.

He glanced at Lexi. "That's who we know him as."

"What reason would he have to lie about his name?" I said. "Ninety percent of what he did was legit, right?"

"He did a lot, Jack," Lexi said. "So that extra ten percent is a pretty big deal. Look, I'm not saying his name isn't Marcus Hamilton Thanos, from Chicago, Illinois, but if there's any of his DNA on you, we'll be able to match it in the database."

"You're not FBI," I said to David.

He laughed, shook his head. "Most definitely not. I'm, well, let's just say I'm not classified these days. At least officially."

"Not my place to ask questions." I looked to Bear for his opinion. The big guy gave a quick and simple nod. His nose kind of scrunched up as he did so. His way of telling me it checks out in his book. "So how long do we gotta wait for the results?"

David puffed his cheeks and sighed as he glanced up at the ceiling. "It's pretty fresh, though not ideally preserved. Best would be to collect the samples straight from the donors. But given the tech I have in this facility, we should have it all split and fed through the system within twelve hours, often sooner."

A surge of panic raced through me. "I can't be here, we can't be here, for that long."

Lexi placed her hand on my chest. "We're safe here, Jack. We brought nothing with us."

"Hell we didn't," I said. "The truck's sitting out there. You know they can trace it with telematics."

"First off, who is gonna trace it?" she said. "Yashkin? You think he's sticking around here looking for a damn truck? And second, this facility is scrambled."

I looked to David for assurance.

He nodded, extended an arm in a swooping motion. "The entire place and a quarter-mile surrounding it. Even if you had a cell phone with you, you wouldn't be able to make a call. Nothing can penetrate the zone, not even satellite imagery picks us up. Looks like nothing but woods."

I took a deep breath, shook my head. "Just doesn't feel right to me."

David lifted a finger as he left the room. The rest of us waited, the sound of our breathing rising and falling filling the void.

"I'll get started on this." Kate grabbed the bag of clothing, stopped at the exit, looked at me. "Let me know if you have any issues with pain."

I waited until the sound of her footsteps dissipated, then held out my hand, revealing the paper I'd taken from the warehouse.

"What's that?" Bear said.

"Not sure yet," I said. "Got this out of the lining of Thanos's coat. Haven't had a chance to look at it yet. Hell, for all I know, it could be something that fell onto the jacket while it was being sewn."

"Or it could be something he was hiding," Lexi said, leaning forward to take a closer look. "Open it up."

"OK," David said from some feet away. "Maybe this'll calm your nerves."

Bear and Lexi stepped away from me as I tucked the paper into my waistband. We all stared at the doorway as David re-entered the room carrying three firearm cases.

"Top of the line gear, here." He set them on the counter and unsnapped each case. "I assume you're familiar with the MP7. You won't find them any more tricked out than here. The scopes switch between infrared, laser, dot, and magnified sights. You've got single semi-auto and three-round burst options. Two standard thirty-round mags, and one extra capacity that'll get you sixty rounds. I've got tactical gear in all sizes, too. Guarantee you'll leave here well-equipped for wherever this assignment takes you."

Assignment?

What had Lexi told him? I shot her a look. She averted her eyes. I guess it didn't matter at that moment, she'd fill me in whenever it was safe to do so. If it had to wait until we left, so be it.

"You all are free to arm yourselves now," David said. "I've got some chow cooking and it should be ready in fifteen minutes. Go back to the foyer and take the east hall to the end. We'll get you filled up, then you can rest while the DNA is brewing."

CHAPTER 52

WE ATE BEFORE RETREATING TO A BUNK ROOM SUITABLE FOR sleeping up to eight people. Bear and I took one side, Lexi the other. We met in the middle a few minutes later.

"Keep in mind this room is most likely monitored," I said. "Talk in generalizations, nothing specific."

Bear and Lexi agreed as I unfolded the paper. I'd considered what we might find on it. A name or an address. Maybe someone or someplace where we could get to the bottom of why Thanos had been taken, revealing his secret. Lexi seemed unsure of the reason, and I trusted her on that, though I still wondered if she was holding back. Perhaps now was the time when I'd find out.

I stopped with one fold left, looked Lexi in the eye. "I need to know if you're withholding on us."

It looked as though I had slapped her across the face. Hard. Her head snapped back, lip curled up, eyes closed hard. She shook her head and then locked eyes with mine. "You think I'd lead us through all of this if that were the case? Christ, don't you think we would've avoided the meeting with Kozlov if I knew enough to get us on the right track? I'm as blind in this as you, Jack. And, I mean, if you can't trust me by now…"

"That's not what I'm saying."

"You sure about that?" She licked her lips, looked away from me. "Why are you even asking then?"

"All right," I said. "You're either one hell of an actress, or you're one-hundred percent on board."

"Maybe not for long."

"Come on, you telling me you're confident in everything I've told you?" I paused and waited for a response, but there was none. "That's what I thought, Lexi."

"I'm up for a good fight as much as anybody," Bear said. "But how about we get on with this before someone comes to whisk us away again?"

He was right. We were wasting time and creating bad blood between us by offering up messages of distrust. I apologized to Lexi, blamed my injuries and the pain meds Kate had given me. A reasonable excuse. I flipped the folded paper over and placed it on the middle of the table.

We all stared at the number for several seconds. Twelve digits, starting with five-five. Lexi mouthed it. Bear tipped his head as he read it silently.

"A phone number?" Lexi said. "Five-five, where's that?"

"Brazil," Bear said.

Lexi and I stared at him.

"What?" he said. "I was there not long ago."

"So we've got a country code," I said. "How long are the numbers there?"

Bear exhaled, flapping his lips like a motorboat. He held up his hands, one mimicking cradling a phone, the other punching buttons. "City code is two, then the rest of the number, uh, eight."

"So ten plus the two-digit country code and we've got twelve," Lexi said.

"Sounds about right," Bear said.

"We need a phone," I said.

"Won't make a difference here," Lexi said. "Not gonna get a call out unless you're on David's secure line. And it's probably not a good idea for us to use that."

"Both of you commit it to memory. Lexi, how well do you trust this guy here? Can he get us to Brazil?"

"He's got the connections to do so. How quickly? That I can't tell you without talking to him. As far as trust, I trust him with my life. He'd likely do anything for me, no questions asked."

"Why?" Bear said. "Why would he do that?"

"He owes me," she said, leaving it at that.

"OK," I said. "We can't do anything about this right now. Let's get some shuteye and attack it in the morning."

As I lay there, I considered the probability we'd find an answer at the other end of the phone number. It seemed like we had a shot. Yet, there was something about it that felt all wrong.

CHAPTER 53

"THIS HAS GOTTA BE IT."

I opened my eyes and looked around the room. Bear was seated at the table with a mug of coffee and a plate of food. He held the fork mid-air, stared at Lexi. She stood in between the two of us, holding a piece of paper. Her smile and the vigor with which she spoke indicated she had news to share.

"Jack, come on," she said. "Get up."

My right leg had stiffened from the knee down. I stretched over the edge of the bed, waiting for gravity to do its work. Slowly it lowered toward the ground. Pain flared throughout my calf, centered on the patched up laceration.

"How you doing there, partner?" Bear said through a mouthful of food.

I winced in pain. "Hanging in there. The hell you eating?"

He stared at the clump of food on the end of his fork. "Pancakes. I think. This place ain't no Waffle House, but the food's serviceable."

"You're gonna feel like garbage in a couple hours after all those carbs."

He shrugged, pointed at my bandaged leg. "I'll still feel better than you will."

I turned my attention to Lexi. She had managed to find a change of clothes. Fresh black pants, a black long sleeve shirt, and black tactical boots.

"What's this all about?"

"The number checks out," she said.

I swung my other leg over the bed and sat on the edge. "How so? How do you know?"

"I had David run it—"

"We talked about this, Lexi," I said. "I don't know how comfortable I—"

"Look, I saw an opening, and I took it. We could sit around all day, or you could call into SIS, but as far as I'm concerned all the resources we need are right here. Might as well take advantage of them." She folded the paper and shoved it in her pocket, turned away from me and headed toward the door.

There are times when it's hard to let go. I preferred to be in control whenever possible, but I was confronted with a situation where my normal channels weren't accessible to me. I couldn't trust the Old Man considering I'd met Matt on his watch, and then the guy showed up a thousand miles from New York, ready to kill me. And Frank, well he was Frank. At this point I had no clue whether he was friend or foe. If I let him in on any of this, we were sure to see him, or his guys, at our next destination.

"Lexi, stop."

She had her hand on the doorknob. "Why should I?"

"What'd you find out?"

"You don't have to do this, Jack. Neither of you do. You can leave. I can take it from here. Thanos was my case anyway. All of this is my mess to deal with. Why don't you guys just go home?" She stepped through the doorway, let the door fall shut behind her.

I shot Bear a look. He shrugged, took a bite of food.

I hopped off the bed. "Too friggin early for this, man. I need some coffee."

"For what it's worth," Bear said. "I'm willing to see this through to the end."

I pulled the door open and stepped into the hall, my head swiveling from left to right. I flinched back at the sight of Lexi standing a few feet away. She had her arms folded over her chest, and one foot pressed against the wall behind her.

"Leaving?" she asked.

"What is going on here?" I said. "One minute you're excited to show me something, the next you're trying to send us packing. Makes no sense. We're in, Lexi. OK? We're with you until the final whistle on this one."

She nodded, lowered her chin to her chest, reached into her pocket. The black clothing looked good on her, accentuated her curves. She unfolded the paper and handed it to me.

I studied it for a moment. A wave of possibilities washed over me. "You're kidding me, right?"

She looked up. "That's what he found."

"Fernando Sousa?"

She nodded.

"Fernando Sousa as in leader of the Brazilian Senate? What did he have to do with Thanos?"

"Working on that. In the meantime, I say we hop on the Gulfstream David has been so kind to lend us and go interrogate Sousa today."

"We haven't talked about this much, but do the men you were dealing with while undercover have something to do with this? You think Denton might be involved here? Did he have dealings with Sousa?"

She turned and leaned against the wall with her shoulder. "I only saw the basics of his finances. That's what I did while undercover, fixed money for them. But he wasn't totally on board with letting me in on his dealings yet. Another week and I would have had it all. Maybe this wouldn't have happened if I hadn't screwed up."

"You can't know that. What about McGrath? What'd he have to do with Brazil?"

She shrugged. "As far as McGrath goes, I never saw anything connecting him to South America. He preferred his European contacts in the drug industry. He had someone on the inside here in the States for weapons."

I paused a moment before my next question. "And Thanos? What about him?"

She took a deep breath, nodded. "He's got connections there."

"Had."

"Yeah, I suppose so. But they don't know he's dead. Look, you don't know everything I do about Thanos. This could get tricky if we cross the wrong people."

"You can fill me in on the flight, yeah?"

She nodded. "Glad to have you with me, Jack."

CHAPTER 54

I SAW KATE TO CHECK ON MY WOUNDS AND RE-BANDAGE AND WRAP my calf. She said everything looked good and I should be back to normal within a couple weeks. Didn't feel that way, but then again, it didn't matter. I had to make it work starting today. I met Bear in the kitchen, grabbed a mug of coffee, and filled my stomach with eggs and bacon. He helped himself to another serving of pancakes, while Lexi and David reviewed the flight plan. I'd reached the point where I was comfortable with him assisting us. He had every opportunity to turn us in last night and he didn't. And I had to admit, I was curious about the guy. He seemed to be a master of many trades.

The Gulfstream could get us to Rio inside of eight hours. That'd be plenty of time for David to dig up anything and everything related to our target and his connections. We had to know every link between Sousa and Thanos. I was curious to see how it tied in with Yashkin and the people in Chicago Lexi was working to bring down while undercover, because right now everything was one big cluster in my mind.

By this point, Frank had to be nearby. There was little doubt as to his involvement with Thanos, though in what capacity still eluded me. Frank didn't care about unethical businessmen. He didn't deal in finance. If Thanos had been diverting five million a year to support a terrorist, Frank wouldn't give a damn. His focus would be on the terrorist. He'd let someone else deal with Thanos to get the names Frank had to chase. By this line of thinking, it wasn't a stretch to assume that Thanos was involved in some sort of terrorist activities beyond donating money. Lexi shot this down immediately.

We'd ditched the car, phones, and anything we had on us the last time we saw Frank. Unless he'd implanted something in one of the three of us, he'd never come near this facility.

I still couldn't shake the feeling we'd see him soon. My mind needed calming.

"Any news on the warehouse?" I said.

Lexi looked up from the chart she and David were leaning over, shook her head. "If it makes you feel better, David can try and ping SIS activities to see if they've got someone here yet."

I considered the option for a moment. "Frank would be watching for that. I don't want to drag David into the middle of that mess." I pushed my plate to the center of the table and leaned back in the chair, arms behind my head. "I suppose it doesn't matter too much if someone else gets there first. News on Thanos will break eventually. We'll be out of the country either way."

"Speaking of which." Lexi tapped her fingers on the table. "How closely does Frank monitor air traffic?"

I shrugged. "Guess that depends on whether he feels he needs to. He's got the resources to know what's going on at any moment."

David looked up from the map. "You all might as well be flying in an invisible jet today. He won't find you. No one will. You can slip in and out of any country as long as I have twenty minutes warning."

"Who the hell are you?" I said to him.

He smiled, shrugged. "I could tell you, but..."

"Don't even go there, pal." I laughed. "I like you, man. You might hear from me again one day."

"Oh, Jesus," he said. "I don't know if I can handle any more drive-bys. Lexi is one thing, but I gotta draw a line somewhere." He smiled as he traced his finger across the center of the table. "Besides, it appears that I'm doing you a favor here today. Not the other way around. So you should be prepared for me to come calling on you when I need a, uh, problem dealt with."

"Anytime," I said.

Bear echoed my sentiment.

Kate hurried into the room. All eyes fell on her. "I've got some results if you all are interested."

It was DNA test result time. The first test would be matching my DNA. I was curious about their database access. Certain aliases were planted for different agencies. So if they came back with alias A, I'd know who was helping him. Or who he had hacked. The SIS and other agencies used the tactic to narrow down who was muddling around in our business.

I limped down the hallway with Bear on one side, Lexi on the other. They kept pace with me in case I needed someone to lean on. I told them not to worry, but they remained with me, stride for stride. We entered a small meeting room at the other end of the facility. A rectangular table with three chairs on either side filled the space. I took the one closest to the door, leaving my back exposed. It was uncomfortable, but I didn't expect anyone to sneak up on me inside the building.

Kate dimmed the lights, then took her seat. She connected her laptop to a projector. A few keystrokes later, a chart appeared on the wall. She gave us an overview of what we were looking at and then proceeded with more detail.

"Four different results were returned. All four came from blood samples found on the clothing we collected last night." She pecked at the keys and the chart was replaced with my photograph. "Here, obviously, we have you, Jack Noble, from Crystal River, Florida."

I slowly turned my head toward David. He met my gaze, a slight smile on his face. Who the hell was this guy? The only way to access the information Kate just spouted was to have the highest level of security clearance available, the kind only three people in the most restricted area of the Pentagon had. Not even the best hackers in the nation, guys like my top asset Brandon, could gain access to that database.

On the one hand, I felt violated. In thirty seconds these people could have my life story.

On the other, I knew we'd know for sure who was who in that warehouse.

"I don't think we need to go any further there," David said, looking at me and nodding.

Kate's fingers worked the keyboard once again. After my image disappeared, we were staring at Thanos. My chest and abdomen tightened as I waited for the reveal.

"Marcus Hamilton Thanos," she said. "US-born, but parents immigrated from Greece in the late fifties. His father was rumored to have ties to individuals in Russia, which it is believed help fund his fledgling business and grow it into the quasi-empire that Marcus took over and turned into a money producing machine. The CIA has long believed that Marcus Thanos kept close ties with his father's contacts in eastern Europe after his father's passing."

I glanced at Lexi to see if she looked surprised by the information. Her expression was solid and steady, not revealing anything.

Kate leaned over to the side, out of sight. She returned with a manila envelope from which she pulled a stack of papers. She tossed four or five sheets stapled together toward our side of the table.

"That's more on Thanos you can read up on while in flight."

The image changed again.

"Christiana," I said.

"Sort of," she said. "This is Christiana Zhenya. A former member of the KGB who was expelled from the agency due to a refusal to carry out an order. Apparently she developed a sense of morality and wouldn't terminate a target because the mark's children were present. When pressed by her handler to complete the job and leave no witnesses, she ripped out her comm gear and fled. No one could tell if the bullet she took was shot by the man she was sent to kill, or another agent nearby. Common practice in that agency is to have any agent they deem a risk tailed by another agent. After all that, the target still ended up dying, as did the children."

I stared into her pale eyes once again. Christiana wanted her family to know nothing of her dealings in our world. It made sense she'd balk in such a situation. And whoever her handler was knew it. That's why they had someone waiting in the ready to complete the job and take her out. They didn't deem her a risk. They wanted her out of the picture. Perhaps she was close to Yashkin, and after he left, they wanted none of his liabilities around.

"Apparently the bullet was a strong enough punishment, because she was released from her position, then she dropped off the radar for five years. Showed up about twenty-four months ago, working for a former General and high ranking KGB official named Nika Yashkin." She flipped to another image, this time of the General. "That's Yashkin right there. We had intel that he was in the country as recently as a day ago. All chatter along that front has stopped and we're not sure where he is now."

Our side of the table remained silent. Whose intel were they working off of regarding Yashkin's whereabouts?

"Last one." She shifted in her seat, straightened her back, put up an image of Matt. "Vasiley Rudin. Former military intelligence officer who served under none other than one General Yashkin. Followed him to the KGB. Shortly after Yashkin's, um, retirement, Rudin joined him in his new enterprise."

Bear leaned forward and looked past Lexi at me. "Weren't you calling him Matt?"

I nodded. "What aliases do you have on file for Rudin?"

Her fingers danced on the laptop keyboard for several seconds. She tapped her mouse and the screen changed again, displaying a rudimentary dossier of Rudin. Among the names and information, Matt Henschel stood out. There was a police record attached. I pointed it out. Kate opened the file and read off a laundry list of crimes. Breaking and entering, assault, assault with a deadly weapon, resisting arrest, and so on.

"I have trouble believing those charges are legit," she said.

"Most likely an attempt to give him some 'street cred,'" David said. "Tell me, where'd you learn his name, or alias, I should say?"

I changed the subject. "What about his other aliases? Do we know who he's associated with based on name?"

She sighed as she hunched over the laptop and began pecking at the keys again. I noticed she only used her index and middle fingers to type. "It's sending me on a roundabout. It'll take some time, but I think I can map everything about him by the time you land in Brazil."

I leaned back in my chair and stared up at the ceiling for several seconds. We had all the info they could provide. And I was more confused than ever.

CHAPTER 55

THE RISKIEST PART OF OUR DAY WAS THE TWENTY-MINUTE DRIVE north to the private and deserted airstrip in the middle of the woods. The trip had been one long line of evergreen. We were a stone's throw from Canada and I had half a mind to sprint off in that direction with every intention of getting lost. Only thing holding me back was that I could barely walk, let alone run.

Before we boarded, Kate gave me a bottle of pills with instructions to take no more than two every six hours. I popped one on the stairs, and another once I was seated and had a glass of water in hand. I was tempted to chase it with a shot of whiskey, but decided against it. The meds were bound to get me loopy, and I needed as much of my wits about me as possible.

Bear opted for a drink or three. From the moment the car stopped in front of the jet I noted his anxiety building. The big man was scared of nothing. But flying twisted his nerves into a bundle that left him more vulnerable than any other time. It was painful to watch. He made it through every flight we'd been on without too much of a scene, managing to internalize his living hell at thirty-six-thousand feet. He was aware there were other chemical options available, but alcohol was the only one he knew he wouldn't grow dependent on outside of an aircraft.

Bear and I settled into plush executive seats opposite each other. Lexi plopped down next to me, leaning her shoulder into mine.

"You don't mind, do you?" she said.

I leaned back against her, turned my face toward hers. "You could use a shower, but I think I can manage."

She reached over and backhanded my gut with enough force to make me cough.

"That'll teach you," she said.

"Caught me unaware," I said. "Try again and—"

She landed another blow, though this time I was prepared.

"Maybe you should sit next to him." I gestured toward Bear.

She lurched forward toward the big man.

He immediately threw up his free hand while guzzling his drink down. After swallowing hard, he said, "Not a chance. Can't go into Brazil with both of us all banged up."

Lexi stood in the aisle between us, looking down at Bear. "I suppose you're right. Better if I beat up on Jack only for this flight."

She fit right in with us. How would she feel about the kind of work we did? Once an FBI agent, always an agent? Could she look past the gray areas we spent most of our time in? Doubtful. Besides, it was enough keeping tabs on Bear. It'd be hell to add the responsibility of another life to watch over.

Bear was staring past me, held his glass up, pointed over my shoulder. "What do you suppose they're talking about out there?"

I looked out the window and saw David and the pilot standing close to one another, having a conversation. Kate was standing off in the distance next to the car.

"Hopefully not about which prison to drop us off at," I said.

"Or which country that prison is," Bear said. "We'll be flying past some places we weren't exactly authorized to operate in."

"Allegedly," I said. "And, yeah. A few of those prisons in Central America are nothing to laugh at. Inmates run the show. Those places take on a life of their own."

"You two have worked together for a long time," Lexi said.

"You could say that," Bear said.

"You were in the SIS as well?" She lifted an eyebrow.

Bear shook his head. "I have had no desire to follow someone else's orders since the day I retired from the Marines."

"Is that where you met?" she asked.

"Recruit training," Bear said.

"I hated that asshole right there," I said.

"Feeling was mutual, partner."

"How'd you two become friends?" she asked.

"If I recall correctly," Bear said. "I beat the ever-living hell outta him and basically made him my bitch."

I almost fell out of my seat laughing. "Is that right?"

Bear had a huge grin plastered on his face. "Something like that."

"Fact of the matter is they didn't give us much choice. We were shipped off mid-way through Recruit Training to a new program the CIA had recently started. They wanted guys that weren't completely molded in the Marine way. Guys like me and Bear who stood out as complete and total hardheads, but fit to serve. They'd have broken us sooner or later, but since we were holding out, they had another option for us."

"So we ended up doing time with a bunch of Agency jackwagons." Bear stretched his legs and folded his arms over his chest. "Spent a number of years all over Europe, Asia, Africa. Good number of them with Jack, until he left and went to work with Frank."

"When was that?" she asked.

"Round about oh-two," I said.

Bear looked down, shook his head. "What a shit storm that was."

Lexi leaned forward, elbows on her knees, like a little kid hanging on every word. "What happened?"

"Unfortunately, there were some very powerful people involved and now it's so classified we can't talk about it." I looked out the window. "At least not until we're over Brazil."

"You guys had any fallout over the years?" she asked.

"You grilling us for a reason?" Bear smiled, but only out of charm. It was a legitimate question.

She leaned back and shrugged it off. "Just curious."

At that point the pilot stepped on board and our conversation dropped off. He smiled and introduced himself and told us we were cleared to depart and to let him know if we needed anything at all during the flight. He joined his co-pilot at the front of the plane, pulling the door shut behind him.

"Well, that's my cue." Bear put on a pair of headphones and closed his eyes. His massive arm muscles rippled. His pecs clenched and unclenched. It was a technique he used to release anxiety. I'd adopted it over the years whenever stress hit me hard.

There was no long lead up to us taking off. The plane spun a hundred-eighty degrees, then lurched forward as though we'd been shot out of a cannon. Seconds later we were in the air gaining altitude rapidly. A couple thousand feet up, we banked hard to the left. Lexi flinched forward, grabbed my thigh.

"Feel free," I said over the roaring engines.

She leaned in and said, "Sorry." Her breath was hot against my neck.

A few minutes later, the noise level dropped and the plane leveled out. Bear remained hooked up to his headphones, eyes shut. He'd remain that way for a little bit longer, but soon enough the anxiety would subside and he'd rejoin us.

I got up and excused myself, found a fridge and grabbed a couple drinks. The pain meds had done a number on my leg. Almost felt like I could run on it. Downside was it felt as though a cloud had descended upon my head. When I returned to my seat, Lexi had a magazine draped over her lap. I looked around in an attempt to figure out where she found it. Eight hours was a long time, might as well fill it with some reading. She didn't look up when I handed her a bottle of water.

Soon after I slipped into a codeine-induced sleep. When I awoke, four hours had passed. Lexi was reading a Clancy novel now. Still wasn't sure where she'd found it. I leaned against her, brushing shoulders with her. She lifted her head, looked over at me.

"What're you gonna do when this is all over?" I asked her.

She folded the corner of the page she was reading and closed the book. "I hadn't thought much about it. I guess I've kinda figured everything would just work out, you know."

"Come on, don't feed me that garbage. We're the kind of people who are thinking not only five moves ahead on our current op, but ten moves ahead in life. I know you've got some sort of plan in mind."

She sighed, dropped her head back against the rest and closed her eyes. "I've been pursuing this for so long, Jack. I'm just hoping that whatever we find from this guy in Brazil, that I can use it against the men who screwed my life up."

"Your husband?"

Shaking her head, she said, "No, not him. For one, I have no idea where they placed him. And I don't want to know. I'm talking about those bastards I was working to bring down."

"You think they're all connected?"

"Thanos is the link in all of this." She unscrewed the cap off the water bottle, held it close to her mouth without taking a sip. "We just have to hope that this ties it all together, because I'm having a hard time putting a couple of puzzle pieces in place."

"David's working on that, too, right?"

She nodded as she sipped her drink. "Yes, he's cross checking every database, every briefing that hasn't been redacted to the point of being worthless, and every contact he can trust who won't ask him twenty questions in order to figure out the link between this cast of characters. And like I said, Thanos is in the middle."

I glanced at my watch. "He's got four hours left to figure it out."

The cockpit door opened up and the pilot strode out. He smiled at us as he passed. Did he have any clue who his passengers were and what they were doing? I assumed he did, based on the private conversation he had with David. This guy had to be David's go-to pilot. Hell, he might even have the pilot on some sort of payroll or retainer. A *when I call, you come,* type of thing.

He grabbed a couple waters out of the fridge and headed back to the cockpit, humming an old Cole Porter tune. He stopped a few feet past us, turned back. "Fun fact, we're getting ready to head over the equator. That means we'll be at zero latitude. If we crossed the Atlantic, about three hundred miles off the coast of Africa we'd be at zero squared, as I like to call it. Zero lat and longitude."

Lexi bit her lip as the guy walked away. After the cockpit door closed, she let out a laugh.

"What was that all about?" she said. "Here we are about to infiltrate some Brazilian politician's office, possibly setting off an international scandal, and he's telling us about zero squared?"

"Coordinates," Bear said.

"Nice of you to join us," she said.

"I've been up for a while, waiting for you two to start making out."

"Better go back to sleep then," she said. "'Cause in your dreams is the only place that's happening."

"The spot he's talking about is the Gulf of Guinea, three hundred or so miles south of Ghana." Bear removed his headphones and rubbed his eyes. "Sorry, I'm just an old trekhead. Always enjoyed that stuff. But, every place has coordinates, and that spot is zero-zero-zero-zero-zero-zero, zero-zero-zero-zero-zero-zero."

I straightened up. "Wait a minute, say that again?"

He spouted the string of zeros once again.

"You gotta be kidding me." I jumped out of my seat. My right leg buckled and I nearly collapsed. Bear extended his arm to steady me.

"What is it?" Lexi asked.

"We're going the wrong way. We need to turn this plane around."

CHAPTER 56

"YOU CAN'T BE UP HERE." THE PILOT STOOD AND SHOVED HIS hand into my chest. Behind him, we plowed through a floating field of white. "I'm authorized to use deadly force, you know."

The co-pilot gripped the controls tightly. Maybe this was their first flight with our kind of clientele.

"Go back to your seat and I'll come see you before we land." The pilot dropped his hand and lowered himself into his seat.

"Relax," I said. "I just need to know if you can plug in some coordinates and tell me where in the world they point to."

He glanced over at the co-pilot and nodded. The younger man punched a couple of buttons, changing the look on the dashboard computer, then glanced back at me.

"What are the coords, sir?"

I read them off a quarter-note at a time, starting with five-five. As he entered them, the imagery changed from our present location over the Caribbean. When it settled, we were looking at eastern Europe.

"Moscow," he said.

We'd almost made the biggest, and likely last, mistake of our careers. If we'd have busted that politician in Brazil, who knows what kind of international scandal would have arisen from it. The location of the coordinates made perfect sense given who we'd been dealing with the past few days. How had I not thought of it before?

I ran my hand through my hair. "Change your course to Moscow, then."

"You've gotta be kidding," the pilot said. "One, we're already chartered for a destination. You can't just change things like that. Two, getting into Russia is going to be a hell of a lot different than Brazil."

He had the look of a teenage boy about to get his butt whooped by three bullies.

"I don't care," I said. "Call David and make it happen."

David had told me he could get us anywhere as long as he had twenty minutes notice.

The pilot pulled a phone from the wall beside him and punched in a series of numbers. The pause while the phone rang seemed to go on for hours. The pilot nodded at his co-pilot, cleared his throat and began talking.

"Sir, we've got a situation here. Our passengers are telling us that we're going to the wrong destination." He paused a few beats. "Yessir, here's one of them."

"Noble," I said.

"This is David," he said.

"I figured."

David said nothing.

"Well, what?" I said.

"I was waiting for you to explain yourself."

"Nothing much to explain. We were wrong about Brazil. The real destination is Moscow."

"Moscow?"

"Punch those numbers into your search bar, two groups of six."

"You're kidding me," he muttered before he ever hit the keyboard. "Coordinates?"

"You got it."

"Five-five, uh, three-seven, that sounds about right for Moscow."

"Damn right it does. And you were there with me this morning. You saw who that DNA matched up to."

"All right, all right," he said. "Put the pilot back on, then contact me on this line when you land. I'll work on gathering whatever intel I can on that location."

"Appreciate it." I handed the phone to the pilot. "Suggest you turn left right about now."

The door slammed closed. The plane banked left. I steadied myself with both hands against the wall, then returned to my seat.

"What's the deal?" Bear said. "Why're we changing course?"

"Going to Moscow," I said. "Those numbers we got off that paper from Thanos's jacket, that wasn't a phone number to a politician's office in Brazil."

Bear's gaze danced along the ceiling. I saw the moment of clarity hit him. "Coordinates. Fifty-five and thirty-seven, guess what would put us near the damn Kremlin, huh?"

"Something like that." I turned to Lexi. "This isn't the same as stopping off in Brazil. You get that, right?"

She nodded. "I'm aware."

"Plenty of people think things are all hunky-dory between our countries. They're not. A lot of the same stuff going on in the early eighties is still happening. They're constantly trying to plant people amid our intelligence community, and we're doing the same. The spying that goes on between the two countries is higher than ever, and if I had to predict it, it'll continue to get worse. You see what I'm getting at here?"

She sighed. "Of course. We need to watch every step, be invisible."

I lowered my head, took a breath, looked back up at her. "I need to know what kind of man David is."

"He's a good man, Jack. We can trust him."

"If I didn't feel that way, I never would have stepped onto this jet. That's not what I'm asking. I need to know if this goes horribly wrong and we end up in custody, can he get us out? 'Cause if he can't, I'm gonna to place a call to Frank and brief him on what we're about to do."

Bear groaned. "And if he doesn't like it, we're guaranteed to be picked up."

"I still don't know exactly what's going on here," I said. "I'm inclined to believe Frank knows a lot more than he let on. Those gaps you have in this story, Lexi, my bet is Frank can fill them in." I stopped, looked out the window right of Bear's head. "I can't believe I'm gonna say this. Somehow I just convinced myself that I should call him."

"David started his career as a code-rigger for the NSA," Lexi said. "The guy's a genius. Unchartered territory is how they described his mind. They pulled him out of school when he was fifteen years old and put him to work in a think tank. It was fun and games to him, but the work wasn't challenging, for the most part. Then one day, he sees the results of a task he completed. Pictures most of the world never sees. A village bombed. Women, children, innocent, dead on the streets."

Bear and I nodded slowly. We'd seen the harsh realities of war up close. Those images flashed in my mind fresh as the day they were imprinted in my memory.

"So he decides that he wants to stop. Problem is, now he's twenty-one and spent his teenage years in a box. He has absolutely no social skills with people his age, not that they were great before the NSA snatched him up. He has no family. There's nowhere for him to go, except someplace within the intelligence community. He moves into a role as an analyst and again excelled at his job. Over the course of the next thirty years or so he advanced. Moved laterally to the CIA for a while, deputy director of SOG."

"Special Ops guy," I said. "Wonder how much he knows about that program I was in?"

"I'd assume a lot. He probably didn't need any database to gain access to your files. With a mind like his, that information was probably locked in his mental vault. Anyway, that was his last stop, but retirement was only a formality, as you can see. He's still very much active, very much supported by certain people in the Pentagon."

David's background intrigued me, and eased some of my concerns. I didn't get the feeling that he knew me from the past, or had any ill will toward me. Hell, we'd been up in the air more than four hours. I only had a few options once the plane touched ground. So if the guy wanted me hauled in, it wouldn't take much to do it.

"OK," I said. "I'm all in with him. Frank can wait, for now. At some point he'll need to be notified of what's going on."

"David's got our backs, Jack. I wouldn't be doing this if he didn't. We can't say the same for Frank."

I settled back in my seat. We had a long flight ahead, with no idea what was going to happen when we landed.

CHAPTER 57

WE LANDED ON A PITCH BLACK RUNWAY A HUNDRED MILES NORTH of Moscow. I couldn't see a thing out of the window and nearly broke my seat-belt when the plane surprisingly lurched upon touchdown. We had stopped in Gibraltar to refuel, but none of us got off there. It'd been a solid fourteen hours since I'd placed my foot on the ground. I stood behind the co-pilot as he opened the door and dropped the stairs, taking in my first look at our surroundings. If anyone was watching, the Gulfstream would've stood out like a Christmas tree amid the blackness of night.

We were at David's mercy here, having traveled with limited documentation and supplies, with an original destination of Brazil, a friendly country. Russia wouldn't take so kindly to the three of us on their soil. David had arranged for an asset to meet us at the airstrip to provide us with everything we'd need.

I descended the stairs quickly and scanned the area after my eyes adjusted. There was a feeling of naked helplessness that went along with standing exposed in every direction. A lone assassin could take each of us out with a rifle and we'd never know where they were positioned.

At the far end of the airstrip a set of headlights flashed on and off three times, and then remained on. The vehicle drew nearer, though I couldn't hear it over the whining of the jet's turbines. Instinct kicked in, pleading with me to head back up the stairs. I fought off the urge and stood my ground.

The pilot thumped down the steps, leaned over the rail next to me. "I'm armed. You know, in case something goes wrong."

"You'd be better off giving that pea-shooter to me," I said.

He pushed off the rail. His right hand traveled to his poorly concealed pistol.

"You're gonna get yourself shot." I gave him a look that said back away from me. "Get back on the plane so the others can come down here."

The pilot retreated to the cabin. Bear took his place.

"What's going on out here?" he said.

"That car, that's what. Been sitting there for about thirty seconds, idling."

He scratched his beard. "Maybe we should head over."

I looked out into the black of night. "I'd prefer to stay right here for now."

"You afraid of the boogeyman, Jack?"

"I'm afraid of being detained in Russia while here on an SIS badge. Let's just hang tight and see what happens."

Lexi slipped past Bear and stood next to me. She was holding the satellite phone David had given her before we boarded. "Want me to give him a ring and find out what's going on?"

A stream of red arced through the air from the driver's side of the car and hit the ground with a mini fireworks display. The driver flashed his high-beams then pulled forward. The black sedan rolled to a stop ten feet from us. The windows were tinted. A whiff of cigar smoke streamed past as the front door opened.

The man that stepped out was about my height and probably ten years older. He wore all black and made no effort to conceal the pistol strapped to his leg. He stripped off the glove on his right hand and extended it toward Lexi.

"I am Artur. I assume you are Lexi, yes?"

She nodded, pulled away from his grip. He grabbed my hand, and I saw why she reacted the way she did. His skin was colder than death.

"Jack," I said. "That's Riley up there. He's got a fear of Russia, so he's hesitant to come down off the stairs."

Artur stepped back, arms out, and turned at the waist. "Nothing to fear here. This is the Motherland. You are welcome and safe while under my protection."

"How much did David tell you?" I asked.

He shrugged. "More than enough."

"Why should we trust you?"

He reached into his pocket and pulled out a coin, tossed it to me. "Know what that is?"

I knew what it was as I'd received one from the President as well. I handed it back to him. "Aside from David, who else do you work with? Feed intel to?"

He sliced his hand in front of his throat. "Only him. He can deal with all those other, ah, dicks. Those bastards left a bad taste in my mouth."

"Then why help out at all?"

"I love my country. Hate the direction it is going. Maybe you help? Yeah? Isn't that enough?"

I knew there was far more to the story than that, but didn't get the feeling that pushing him would result in any more background info being divulged. The running theme for the past day had been *In David We Trust*. That now extended to Russia.

"Before we get in the vehicle, I have things for you." He reached into his pocket and a few moments later the trunk lid popped open.

We followed him around the back of the sedan. There were three duffel bags arranged in a line. Artur reached for the first one, handed it to Lexi. The next one went to Bear. And the final one he tossed in my direction.

"Keep you sharp. Yeah?" he said, grinning.

"Yeah, whatever, man." I unzipped the bag and pulled the flaps back. Inside were clothes, probably two changes, a hardshell Hechler and Koch case, a box of ammunition, a knife, a cell phone, a wallet, money clip, and passport holder.

"These clean?" Bear held his passport up.

"Crystal," Artur said.

"Close enough," Bear said. "But let me warn you, I get any trouble at all with this—"

"Riley," Lexi said. "We can verify with David. If there's any issues, any flags raised, he'll get it resolved without us even having to swap out creds."

I popped open the firearm case. A .40 caliber USP Tactical pistol with a threaded barrel greeted me, along with two extra magazines and a black suppressor. It was a larger handgun, and that didn't bother me one bit. Bear was outfitted with the same. Lexi was issued a Glock 19.

"Happy?" Artur asked.

We all nodded. I was impressed a phone had been included, though we were better off buying burners at the first opportunity in order to minimize the risk of being tracked. Nothing was untraceable. If they had video footage of us entering a drug store and making the purchase, all they needed was the store's receipt, then they could get the number and track it from there. The chance of that happening was minuscule, and a risk I'd take a hundred times out of a hundred.

Bear and I took the backseat while Lexi and Artur climbed in front. Artur fiddled with the console, pulling up a map. I studied the pink navigation line that zigzagged across a span of a hundred miles.

"That our coordinates at the end?" I asked.

"Yes," Artur said. "Supplied by David."

"You mind if Lexi re-enters that information?"

The car fell silent for a few moments. Artur's ever-present smile diminished while he stared at me in the rearview. Trust was a fickle beast, and it didn't take much to ruin it between two people who hardly knew each other, but who could probably figure out everything about each other because of similar experiences.

He nodded a couple times. The smile returned to his face. "I don't see that as a problem. I can understand your, how you say, apprehension. In fact, Lexi, while you do that, I'll place a phone call."

Lexi fingered the GPS buttons and worked the coordinates into the machine. Over the vehicle's speakers a phone started ringing.

"Yeah, Artur, what's up?" David said.

"Just trying to ease our more experienced passenger's mind."

David laughed. "Jack, believe me, you can trust Artur with your life."

"A lot of trust being asked here," I said. "Can you tell me what we're gonna find at the other end of this drive?"

"I've pinpointed it exactly, Jack. Brought it up using a long-forgotten-about spy satellite. We're looking at a small building north side of the city. Been monitoring it for the past four hours, almost ever since you gave me those coords. Tell you, I haven't seen a single person come or go. You hit it fast, and you hit it hard, and there shouldn't be any issues."

"Shouldn't," I muttered.

"What's that?"

"Nothing. Keep your eyes on it and let us know if anything changes."

"Will do," he said.

"What about our friends? Any word on them?" I caught Artur looking at me in the mirror again.

"They've gone dark," David said. "Can't stay that way forever, though. I'll find them."

Artur was still staring at me after we ended the call. His smile had faded again.

"Help you?" I said.

"What friends?" he said.

I shrugged. "Better not be anybody you know, cause then that means we'd have a problem."

He turned at the waist in order to face me. "A friend of mine, a woman, she—"

"OK, we're all set," Lexi said. "He had us programmed for the right location."

Artur broke his stare off and turned his head toward Lexi. "See, good news. Let's go."

I played his words over in my head. *A friend...a woman.*

Was he talking about Christiana?

CHAPTER 58

ARTUR DROPPED US OFF A HALF-MILE EAST OF OUR DESTINATION. The wind whipped hard from the northwest, blowing fat, wet snow in our faces. The smell of the sedan's exhaust lingered for a minute. I couldn't tell if the wind blew it away, or if my nose had frozen to the point that I could no longer smell. The taillights faded into the white blur and the gusts overtook the engine.

Artur hadn't elaborated on his comment about his female friend. I thought he'd be present for the rest of the mission, so I didn't push him on it. I had to fend off the curiosity for now. Chances are we'd see him again once we were finished. I could ask then.

We trudged through eight inches of fresh powder that sat on top of a winter's worth of packed snow and ice. The boots I had on did a fine job of keeping my feet dry. The rest of the gear kept most of the cold out. Artur had supplied us well. Bear led the way, navigating from memory. Lexi stuck to the middle, while I watched our six. The streets were deserted, making my job relatively easy. I scanned each building, every window, looking for peering eyes or any other sign of a lookout. Few windows were lit with shades drawn open. It wasn't the poorest area in Moscow, but to call it affluent would be a lie.

The sound of voices rose as we neared the first intersection. All three of us reached for our concealed weapons. Call it training, or instinct, or whatever. My gloved hand tightened around the pistol grip. The usual sense of security that provided me wasn't there. Even though I had inspected the pistol and noted that it had been freshly oiled, this was the first time I'd handled it, and I found it difficult to trust a firearm I'd never shot.

I moved ahead, crossed the threshold first with Bear a step or two behind. The alley was lit up, fire bellowing from an oil drum. Rising smoke looked black against the oncoming snow. I counted seven people huddled around the blaze, bare hands dancing with the fire.

"Homeless," Bear said. "Keep moving."

I watched the group as we passed. All but one paid no attention to us. The one that did, however, stuck out. He was young and clean-shaven. The flame colored his face red. He watched me through narrowed eyes with his hands stretched out toward the can. I kept my hand on the pistol. Less than twenty yards separated us and he was lit up like a Christmas tree. If this guy made a move, I'd fire a round into his chest without hesitating.

We cleared the alley and pushed forward another block. I watched the street and buildings less, kept glancing back toward the alley. We turned right, traveled another block, then went left. A loud pop rang out. Streetlights in every direction began blinking on and off before fading into darkness like a long line of dominoes falling.

"That's convenient," Bear said.

I nodded as a similar thought crossed my mind.

"Could just be the storm," Lexi said. "We're in Moscow, not New York or Chicago. The infrastructure here is horrible."

The hum of generators began to fill the air. I caught whiffs of diesel and pulled my scarf over my nose to filter it out.

Clinging to the shadows, we kept moving until our destination was in sight. Bear climbed a wide stairway and ducked into an alcove in front of an entry door. From there he and Lexi watched over the entrance of the building across the street, while I backtracked half a block. I walked up the closest cross-street and stepped into a back alley. Surveillance showed that it ran directly behind the target building. There appeared to be one exit square in the middle of the building and fire escapes up to the roof on either side of that.

I moved slowly through the undisturbed snow. Tucked between four and five story buildings, the sounds of generators and wind gusts were blocked out. It was serene back here. Might as well have been hiking in the mountains. Flakes hitting the ground sounded like cockroaches crawling around. My eyes adjusted over the next few minutes to the contrast between white and black. There were people tucked into overhangs and exits, wrapped in tattered blankets and newspaper, just trying to make it through the night. I tuned in to their coughs, sniffles, cries. They shifted as I passed, retreating behind their makeshift homes rather than attacking.

The exit came into view. I retrieved the pistol and, with no fear of local authorities spotting me, held it out in the open. I pulled out the phone Artur provided from my pack, navigated to the speed dial and made the call.

"You in position?" Bear asked.

"Good to go back here," I said.

"All right. Lexi contacted David and he said nothing's changed and no one has come or gone since the blackout."

"He have any ideas on that issue?"

"Yeah, he said a transformer blew about a quarter-mile from here. Already determined that it's due to the storm. Nothing nefarious going on."

"I can live with that." I took a few steps out of the shadows, stood in front of the door. "What else did he say?"

"Call got dropped. She tried reaching him again, but there's nothing happening. Must be something with the satellite. Too much interference. Again, storm related."

"Sounds like we're good to go. Let's not waste any more time. Count me down, partner."

Bear started at ten and worked down to five. The call ended. They were almost in position. I moved forward, continuing where he left off.

Four...three...two...one.

I reached for the handle and turned it. It gave without hesitation. The hallway was aglow with red emergency lights along the baseboards. Warm air thick with propane coated me as I moved through the corridor. A baby's cries slipped through the cracks of the first apartment I passed. His mother sang softly to him. I couldn't make out the words, but the tune was one hummed around the world.

It wasn't a shotgun hallway offering me a view straight through to the front door. Instead, the wall stuck out in places, forcing me to move left, then right, and finally left once again before I reached the front of the building. A spike of cold air raced past as the door hung open a couple inches. Lexi stood next to it, pistol out, aimed upward. She held a single finger to her mouth. I slowed my pace, leaning close to each apartment I passed, listening for movement within. Since the first one, I hadn't heard another sound. I glanced at my watch and calculated that the time was after ten at night. Most people would've been in bed by now. Or maybe the place was deserted. I wouldn't put it past certain people coming in and taking over a building like this.

The howling wind through the corridor ceased when the front door sucked shut. Lexi remained focused on the stairwell in front of her. She nodded a few times, then shifted her gaze toward me while waving me forward. Once I was clear of the hallway, she ascended two steps at a time. I followed close behind, throwing a glance back at the front entrance every few seconds.

We stood with Bear on the second-floor landing, each of us watching a section of the hall or stairwell.

"What do you think?" Bear said.

"We're in the right place according to the coords," Lexi said. "But now... I'm not sure."

"I don't think any of us are." I took my eyes off the front door and looked up the next set of stairs. "There has to be some connection to Thanos here. You think there's a mail room here? Something with names?"

Bear pointed to the closest apartment with the barrel of his weapon. Next to the door was a black mailbox mounted to the wall.

"I guess we can start waking people up," he said. "With no power, it'd be thirty minutes, maybe more before the cops show up if someone calls."

I shook my head. "What're we gonna do? Go in and tell them Thanos was assassinated, where's his grandma? There's gotta be something else here."

"It'd help if we knew what we're here for," Bear said.

"Someone's gotta know," I said. "Why else kill Thanos? They wanted the secret to die with him. They sure as hell didn't count on us getting this close. The coordinates got us here. But there's gotta be something more to the code."

Lexi swung her head left to right. "Look at the numbers."

The stickers affixed to the doors looked like they were painted in blood amid the emergency lights.

"What about them?" I asked.

She pointed at the four closest apartments. "Every one begins with two-two."

I ran through the first floor hall in my memory. "It was the same downstairs." I thought I knew where she was going with this. The coordinates started with five-five. "This building's only four stories tall, though."

"What were the last two digits of the latitude?" Her eyes widened as she waited for me to answer.

"Four-four," I said.

"And zero-five were the last two of the longitude." Bear lifted his hands over his head, held his pistol in the air. "What are the chances?"

He led the way to the fourth floor. Gusts of wind rattled the exterior windows, whistling through the cracks. The bitter cold hadn't set into the building yet, but there were more drafts the higher we climbed.

We stopped three steps shy of the fourth floor landing and waited. I listened over the sounds of our rising and falling breaths. A floor creak disturbed the quiet. Bear looked to me to see if I'd heard it, too. There was another creak, then the sound of footsteps.

Someone was in the hallway walking toward us.

CHAPTER 59

I GESTURED FOR LEXI TO FALL BACK. HER EYES BURNED AT ME, but she did as requested, retreating to the mid-floor landing and keeping an eye on the stairwell.

Bear pressed his back against the wall, flattening himself as much as possible. I moved past him, stopped at the corner of the wall, took a deep breath. The steps were only feet away. They came to a halt. It sounded as though someone dragged a broom on the ground. The person was walking away.

I stepped out from behind the wall and took in the surroundings. The hallway was lit up red like the others. A man dressed in fatigues and carrying a rifle moved toward the other end of the hallway. He stopped, slowly turned his head to the right.

Grimacing against the pain in my calf, I pulled the knife from my belt, rushed forward, wrapped my left arm around his neck. He raised his rifle, but I quickly threaded my right arm through his, torquing it at an unnatural angle at the elbow. He lost control of the rifle. It hit the floor with a thud. The guy tried to stomp his heel on my foot. I pushed my left hip into him, withdrew my right leg, and plunged the knife into his neck. His body stiffened for a moment, then he started flailing his arms. I leaned back, drawing him off his feet, over my hip. My wounds ached, but with every passing second the pain dulled. Warm blood spilled onto my cheek. I bit down hard, clamped my eyes and lips shut.

A few seconds later his body went limp. It was over. I eased myself upright, letting the guy slide to the floor. Bear scooped up the rifle and found a cell phone as he rummaged through the guy's pockets. He handed the firearm to me while he worked the phone's lock screen. He knelt down, grabbed the dead guy's arm, and placed his thumb on the home button. A lit up blank screen appeared. Bear accessed the phone's apps, but it looked like a stock setup, and chances were it was not the man's personal device, rather a work phone. Maybe someone else could get some intel off of it. Bear pocketed the device.

"Guess she was right," he said softly, pointing toward the only door with soft light flowing from underneath. "Four-four-zero-five."

"What do you suppose is in there?"

"Gotta be something valuable after claiming all these lives."

"I don't know if we'll even recognize it if we find it."

He shrugged. "I'm gonna call Lexi up."

I split my attention between the door and watching Bear as he motioned for Lexi to join us.

She scanned the hallway in both directions, her eyes settled on the man on the floor. "Who's the dead guy?"

"Friend of Bear's," I said.

Bear chuckled. "Looks like you figured out the cipher. Good job. We're taking bets on what's inside now."

"I wish I knew." She wiped her forehead and exhaled deeply. "Thanos was supposed to tell me everything that morning at his house."

"We need to get in there," I said. "I'd rather surprise whoever's in that room than have them aware we're coming."

Bear took point on the door. I stood to his left, pressed against the wall. Lexi was on the right, pistol aimed at the hunk of wood separating us from inside. Bear backed up, bounced on the balls of his feet a couple times, then in a fluid motion lunged forward, driving his size sixteens through the door near the handle. The door cracked in half, busted off the hinges. The deadbolt snapped.

Lexi moved into position, covering Bear. I moved in front of her and went in low. She placed her hand on my right shoulder as she squeezed past the doorway and positioned herself against the wall. I scanned the apartment. The same emergency lights lit the space. To the right was an eating area. To the left a sitting area with a blank television. The kitchen was empty. A hallway stretched into the darkness directly in front of us. Voices called out from the back room.

I took a few steps inside, aimed the rifle down the hallway with a flashlight clamped between my left palm and the barrel, bright enough to temporarily blind anyone who stepped in its path.

Bear moved past me, posted up at the refrigerator, a few feet from the hallway opening.

The door at the end of the corridor flung open. A barrel poked through, then turned toward me. I stepped out the way. The round ripped through the wall. By the time I moved back into position, the shooter had retreated. The open doorway behind me felt unsafe. There could be others in the same building, making their way up. Also, the shot would not go unnoticed. Someone would place a call to the authorities. A gunshot would have to take priority over most calls during a blackout.

I slowly moved toward the hallway, nodded at Bear as I walked past. He glanced toward Lexi and held up a finger. I knew he had my back. The shooter had emerged from the open door at the end on the left. If only he'd pop out now. I'd tag him before he knew I was there. I stopped short of the door, waited against the opposite wall with the rifle aimed a foot above the latch.

Two male voices spoke hurriedly in hushed tones. Closing my eyes, I tried to picture where they were in the room. Chances are someplace with cover, so first thing to look for would be an overturned dresser or other piece of furniture. Considering the part of town we were in, I didn't think anything they'd be hiding behind would have much stopping power.

Bear stood close behind me now. His deep inhalations were slightly raspy. The cold did that to him. A clock ticked down in my mind and with every passing second we drew closer to an inescapable situation. The men in the room weren't coming out.

Which meant we had to go in.

CHAPTER 60

BEAR DID THE HONORS, SLAMMING HIS FOOT INTO THE DOOR. IT whipped open. The men cursed us as they dove out of sight.

I leveled the rifle and stepped through the opening. The flashlight lit up all corners of the room. As I suspected, a dresser had been knocked over, but it appeared heavier than I had thought. I placed three rounds two feet off the ground, and a foot and a half apart from each other. They tore through the furniture. The second shot earned a pained scream. Seconds later the guy popped up clutching his stomach. I adjusted my sights, fired, blew a hole in his forehead.

"Get back!"

Bear's words came just in time. I saw the barrel extend over the dresser and switched off the flashlight. Muzzle flash lit up the room like a strobe light as I dropped to a knee, then flopped flat on my stomach up against the dresser. The guy sprayed the room and hallway with automatic fire, punching through plaster. It rained down, crashing on the floor. Within seconds the assault ended.

I rolled away from the dresser and got to a knee. Bear popped back in the room, hovered behind me, unloaded on the guy. Every shot hit him damn near dead center. His body jerked, head snapped, weapon swung from the strap around his neck. He collapsed to the ground.

My ears rang. The air stunk of gunpowder. I swept the flashlight across the smoky room.

Lexi called out from the hallway. "Everyone OK?"

"We're good," Bear said. "These other two guys, not so much. Keep us covered while we search the room."

Bear picked up the dresser and pulled each drawer out. They were filled with shirts and pants and socks and underwear, but nothing more. He went around behind it, stepping over the dead men on the floor, and smashed the back panel until he could wedge his fingers behind it.

"Anything?" I asked after he had it removed.

He shook his head, pulled out a flashlight, turned his attention to the men. I dismantled a nightstand while Bear searched the guys.

"No phones," he said. "Not even a wallet or money clip."

"Think they knew we were coming?"

"Guess it's possible." He aimed a beam of light in my direction. "Anything in there?"

"Nada."

"Let's check there." He zigzagged the light over a louvered closet or bathroom door.

"I'll do the honors." I pulled myself off the ground using the rifle as a crutch, took a step forward.

The doors flung open and a small framed man holding a revolver as long as his forearm opened fire. I dropped to the side, bringing the rifle up as I went down, and pulled the trigger without taking aim.

The man fired every round his gun held, and continued pulling the trigger for several seconds after he ran out of ammunition. His mouth hung open, eyes bugged out, staring straight out as though he were looking at a ghost. He held his firearm close to his chest. The barrel drooped toward the floor, then the gun slid out of his hand. Blood spread from a hole in his chest, spilled from his mouth.

I glanced back at Bear. He stood in a defensive stance, pistol aimed at the guy.

"Good work," I said.

Nodding, he lowered his piece. "Thanks, man."

I shuffled toward the closet. The guy's mouth worked open and closed like a fish out of water. He tried to talk, but only managed a couple gurgling sounds. I felt nothing watching him collapse and die. After all, he tried to kill us. But we would have preferred to take one of them alive. These bastards didn't give us much of an opportunity for that, though.

"What's that?" Bear aimed a thin beam to the side of the guy. "A briefcase?"

I grabbed the metal case. The guy's arm lifted with it, attached with hand-cuffs. Under the handle was a ten-digit combination lock built into the case.

"What are the chances that's related to Thanos?" Bear said.

I searched the guy's pockets but couldn't find a key for the handcuffs. "I'd say pretty damn good. No way to unlock the cuffs, though."

Bear held up a finger, left the room. He and Lexi exchanged a few words, but I could only make out the sound of their voices. A few seconds later, he returned with a cleaver.

"You up for this?" he said.

"All you, man." I got to my feet and took a few steps back, searching the room for a hiding place where someone might've stashed the key. It wouldn't be in the room, or the apartment. Someone on the outside had the key to the handcuffs, and the combination to the briefcase. I had a couple suspects in mind. Thanos was an obvious choice, but I didn't believe it was him. I think he knew of this place, but that's all. What about the people trying to kill him? Again, that was possible. Yashkin's fingerprints were all over this, but if I had to guess, I think he wanted to know the location rather than protect it. He wanted the briefcase.

Of course, I could have it all wrong.

It took six good whacks with the cleaver to sever the man's arm at the wrist. Bear discarded the hand like a bad cut of meat.

"Gonna clean this off," he said, holding the briefcase up and stepping into the hallway.

I took one last glance at the carnage and then exited the room. Bear opened a door in the middle of the hall, shone his light inside, then stepped into the darkness. The water cut on, splashed over his hands and the briefcase.

Lexi stood by the front doorway. She looked exhausted, but smiled when she spotted me.

"How're you holding up?" she asked.

The ringing in my ears from all the gunfire made it so I barely heard her. And there was something else distracting me.

Shadows blocked the dull red glow in the hallway.

CHAPTER 61

"LEXI!"

The figure stepped into the doorway before she could react. A pistol appeared momentarily, slid behind Lexi. Her eyes narrowed as she took in the expression on my face. She turned to face the shadowy assailant.

I'd left the rifle in the bedroom. I pulled the HK, but there was no shot available. She was in the way. The attacker opened fire on Lexi as she lashed out at him. Her body jerked back, then she caved in as another shot sent her to the floor.

The guy was in my sights. I pulled the HK's trigger. Nothing happened. I squeezed again. The slide was jammed. Before I could attempt to fix it, the man turned his firearm on me. I dropped where I stood and rolled toward the wall. Several shots were fired within a few seconds. The sounds bounced off the walls and ceiling of the narrow corridor behind me, sounded like shots were being fired from both ends. I racked the slide multiple times and cleared the jam, then chambered a fresh round. Everything went silent except for the ringing in my ears. That only grew louder.

I rolled over my right leg, onto my stomach, aimed at the doorway. Empty. Where had he gone?

Bear hopped over me, said, "Are you all right?" He had his sidearm pointed at the front of the apartment as he reached down to help me up.

I grabbed his hand and got to one knee. "Yeah, I think so." Looking around the room, I spotted two bodies on the floor. "You got him?"

"Think we both did." He turned away, pulling me up as he started toward Lexi's body.

We both knelt down next to her.

"Help me turn her," I said, already hooking her arm and pulling her torso off the ground. It was the wrong thing to do, but I could tell by the exit wounds that she didn't have much time left. Maybe if we were inside Grady, one of the top trauma hospitals in the US, at the moment she was shot, she'd have a chance. But here in Moscow? Forget it. Even if they could help, they'd only patch her up enough for the KGB to go to work on her.

Lexi stared up at us, but it looked as though she saw past us. Her fingers extended, moving back and forth slightly. I pressed my palm into hers. She gripped my hand tightly for a moment. Then her grip went slack. She worked her mouth, trying to talk. I leaned in so our faces were almost touching.

She let go of me. Her hand fell to her chest, where she fished a chain from under her tight shirt. There was a locket on the end in the shape of a heart. "My-my-my..." She closed her eyes hard, grimaced in an effort to beckon death to wait a few more seconds. After swallowing hard, she continued. "Give this to my father." Her eyes locked on mine and I saw the moment life left her body.

"Fuck!" I screamed, yanking the locket from the chain. Rage built like lava, climbing my throat, filling my body with fire. I wanted to kill someone, yet I had no idea who was responsible.

Bear walked over to the window, parted the blinds with his thumb and forefinger. "We gotta get going, Jack. I hear sirens, and I'd say ninety-nine percent chance they're coming for us."

I got to my feet, leaned over, pulled Lexi up. "Help me, man. We can't leave her here. Can't let her be found like this."

Bear pushed me out of the way and heaved Lexi over his shoulder. Her hair spilled down past his waist. "Take the briefcase." He extended his arm toward me. I grabbed it from him, and he pulled his pistol from his waistband and started toward the hallway.

I reached out, said, "Wait a sec." I reached in her pocket and retrieved the satellite phone. She'd programmed the driver's number in it before he had dropped us off. Heading down the stairs behind Bear, I called Artur and told him to meet us at the end of the alley.

Bear stepped into the hallway. I stopped and stood over the man who'd killed Lexi. A ski mask covered his face. Bending over, I tugged it off his head.

"Christ."

Bear stopped in the middle of the hallway, looked back at me. "What?"

"It's Matt." I recalled his real name. "Or Vasiley Rudin, I should say.

Yashkin's guy, the same one that killed Thanos and Christiana. How the hell did he track us here?"

"Let's figure it out when we're away from here." Bear hustled down the hall. "Come on, Jack. Let's go."

I snapped a photo of Rudin, then left the apartment. We hurried down the stairs and through the main level hallway to the rear of the building. A woman holding a baby leaned out of her open doorway. Her eyes got wide when she saw us and she slammed her door shut. The baby's cries pierced the silence.

Bear stopped at the exit. "That piece of shit cleared and good to go now?"

I held the pistol up, aimed at the ceiling. "Yeah, I'll take the lead."

As he backed up to the wall, Lexi's body started to roll off his shoulder. He dipped down, then up, repositioning her. For a moment, she looked alive, as though she hadn't been shot just a few minutes earlier.

"Come on, man," Bear said. "Let's do this."

I leaned into the door, cracked it open. Frigid air sliced through the opening. Felt like my sweat froze into a thin sheet of ice. I shook off the cold and opened the door far enough to get a good look at the alley. A long stretch of white folded out past the last building.

"Let's move." I led the way with little regard for my exposed firearm. Any of the bums that moved as we approached found themselves staring down the barrel. If one dared come a step closer to us, I'd have no problem ending their life.

We were halfway down the alley when the sedan pulled up. Artur stepped out, looking over his shoulder at the way he had come. He placed one hand on his forehead, blocking the falling snow. A few seconds later, he motioned with his other hand for us to hurry, then he turned and opened the rear door.

Bear double-timed it, moving past me. He stepped out from the cover of the buildings and managed to fit both himself and Lexi's corpse into the back of the car.

Artur met me at the edge of the alley. I nearly collapsed as I stepped into the open area. He threaded an arm under mine and helped me into the passenger seat, then ran to the other side of the car and got in. A half-block down the road he said, "What happened in there?"

I leveled the pistol at his chest. "You tell me."

He glanced between the pistol and the snow-covered road, keeping the sedan within the tracks left behind by other cars. The orange lights lining the road turned on. Windows along the apartment-lined street flickered with light.

"What are you doing?" he yelled.

"You tell me what happened back there, Artur, because as far as I know, only a few people are aware we're in Russia, and you're the only one on the ground with that information." I lifted the pistol so it was aimed at his head. "Who the hell did you tell?"

CHAPTER 62

ARTUR KEPT THE WHEEL STEADY AND REMAINED FOCUSED ON THE road. Apparently seeing the pistol aimed at him once was enough. I got the feeling that he wasn't like me or Bear. That his job consisted mostly of what he was doing right now, ferrying around the people in the middle of the action, rather than being a part of it. He choked on his replies to my questions, furthering my belief.

I changed tracks with him. "You mentioned something about a friend, a woman. Who were you talking about?"

He licked his lips, glanced sideways at me. His eyes widened as he stared down the barrel. Poor guy couldn't take his sights off it now. I flicked the tip toward the road in an attempt to redirect his gaze. It worked. He started to speak.

"My wife," he said slowly, taking a deep inhalation between words. "Her name is Christiana Zehnya. I thought she was to return with you, but..." He looked toward me, this time ignoring the firearm making eye contact.

What was true and what wasn't? Why had she fed me a story about a family who thought she was away on business?

"Christiana was your wife?" I said.

His head tilted to the left. "Not officially." He slowed at the intersection and turned left, pushing us further away from the scene of the gunfight. "We've been together four years now, but she has a family. There's no love there, not between her and her husband. She loves her little girls, that's it. We thought that after this op, we'd be able to take them and flee."

The sting of her partial truths only lasted a few seconds. She had to protect those she loved, including Artur. I'd done the same, and had no doubt I would again.

"Sorry to break it to you, Artie, but she's dead." I lowered the pistol away from him.

Other than his eyes misting over, Artur showed no signs of distress over the news.

"I know this is tough, but I need to ask you a few more questions."

Nodding, he wiped his eye with his sleeve. "What could I possibly know?"

"Vasiley Rudin," I said. "That name mean anything to you?"

"Of course. He and Christiana were partners at times, and were working on this operation together."

"Under Yashkin's orders?"

"Yashkin?" He looked at me with a furrowed brow. "The deposed General? No, for the American."

"The American?" I stole a glance at Bear and saw he was as confused as I was.

Artur slowed the vehicle to a crawl and pulled over. "Yes. The American. I guess you wouldn't call him that, but that's how we refer to David."

I pulled Lexi's phone out and pushed the entry for David. Through a haze of static, the call connected after a several second delay. The line rang several times then disconnected with a click. I glanced back at Bear again. He shook his head as though he was thinking along the same lines as me now. The implications of what Artur had told us moments ago raced through my mind. Did this mean Yashkin and David were working together? Or were Yashkin's men working behind his back? If both Christiana and Rudin worked for David, why did Rudin kill her in the warehouse? Was he seeking the information solely for his own gain and she threatened his chances? He showed up at the apartment in Moscow. Either David sent him, or he already knew of its existence.

"Artur," I said. "Did Christiana ever mention Yashkin?"

He shook his head. "Not that I can ever recall." He straightened in his seat. "We met four years ago and never once had I heard her mention him."

"All right." I put my hand over my eyes and rubbed my temples. "Just... just get us out of the city, someplace quiet."

"Preferably near a running body of water," Bear said.

I looked back at him and nodded. We'd reached a point where we couldn't count on anyone to get us out of the country. We had to dispose of Lexi's body somewhere no one would ever find it.

Two hours later we were over a hundred miles from Moscow, deep in the thick forest. Bear finished digging a four-foot deep grave. The frozen ground hadn't made it an easy task. I stripped Lexi's clothes and wrapped her in a blanket from the back of Artur's car. The clothing we tore into shreds and planned to throw into a river on the way out.

"Will that be deep enough?" Artur asked gesturing to the hole in the ground.

I could see that the grave was symbolic for him. He wasn't burying Lexi, a woman he hardly knew. Wrapped in the blanket was Christiana and he was saying his goodbyes.

"It's good," Bear said. "Always a chance someone might dig her up, but who's gonna find her out here? Even if they do, how much are they gonna care?"

They left me alone at the gravesite after we placed her body and covered it with dirt. I squeezed the locket tight, wondering how I'd break it to her father that his little girl was gone. I said my goodbyes to Lexi, recounting a few of the personal moments we had shared. I wondered what could have been if this had gone differently. And I realized that her dedication to clearing her name would mean anything between the two of us would never have worked. I stomped the ground around her grave and covered it with leaves and pine needles and sticks. Finally, I grabbed a heavy white rock and worked it a few inches into the ground to mark her resting site.

We worked our way west, close to the Latvian border. This wasn't an area of the world where Bear and I had many contacts. I'd tried a few more times to reach David with no luck. The line rang, then disconnected in the same manner as earlier. After a while, I figured it wasn't a good idea to hang onto the phone, as he likely used it to track our movements. I left it under a rest stop toilet, connected to a server in China.

It was close to five a.m. when Artur pulled off the highway and stopped the car outside of a small town.

"I'm afraid this is where we must part," he said, keeping his eyes straight ahead. "I can tell you two are resourceful enough to figure things out from here. Now, I need to determine my next steps. After what you've told me, I think I need to reconsider my current arrangements." He took his hands off the wheel and looked at me. "I propose a gentleman's agreement. You never saw me, and I never saw you."

"Fair enough," I said.

Artur reached down along the door and popped the trunk. "Take the bags, leave the pistols. I'll dispose of them. The passports should be enough to get you across the border, but I wouldn't count on them getting you much further than that."

I shook his hand before exiting the sedan. Bear waited at the trunk. He retrieved his creds from his bag, but left everything else behind. Seemed like a good idea, so I followed his lead. The bags could've had tracking tags sewn into them. He stood there with his arm stretched out over the trunk, pistol in hand.

"Think it's a good idea to leave it?" he asked.

I closed the lid, faced him. "No, I don't."

Artur shifted the car into drive and pulled away, making a large loop in the middle of the road. He didn't look our way as he passed. Instead, he had his hand up to his eyes. Grief over the loss of Christiana, and his life as he knew it, had set in.

"Come on, man," Bear said, ejecting the magazine from his pistol, then shoving the sidearm in his waistband. "Let's go find a phone. I think it's time to call Frank."

CHAPTER 63

THE WARM, SALTY AIR COMING OFF THE MEDITERRANEAN lingered in my mouth and soothed my sunburned nose. A month had passed since that tragic night in Moscow. There wasn't an hour that went by since that I didn't think about Lexi. I tapped my pocket, feeling for the locket I'd kept close since she passed.

A call to Frank that night got us a ride out of Russia in the back of a semi filled with cleaning supplies. A twelve-hour drive through Latvia and Lithuania culminated in me and Bear being discarded like used dishrags outside of Warsaw, Poland. A man I knew from my past in the SIS delivered us to a safe house. It took two days to recover from the smell in the trailer, and another five before we were allowed to leave the location. I maintained contact with Frank throughout the stay. He was pissed with how things went down, but managed to get over it. And he stressed that he wasn't behind any of it. He had no idea why interest in Thanos was so heavy. If the man who had taken us to the safe house had mentioned anything about the briefcase, Frank must've overlooked it, as he never brought it up with me. Through the course of our conversations he confirmed what I had believed about Yashkin. He orchestrated the whole thing, playing sides against one another. The reason for killing Christiana remained unclear. Frank was also unable to confirm any suspicions about David, refusing to even recognize the man existed. Hard to believe, considering there wasn't much that didn't filter through Skinner these days. It told me everything I needed to know, yet I still didn't know everything.

My last contact with Frank was the day we left the safe house. He had fresh credentials delivered so we could work our way through Europe. He wanted us to stay put for a few weeks, keep our heads down until he knew it was safe to re-enter the States. I told him I'd do him one better. All I needed was a way to contact Yashkin. Frank had been reluctant at first, but soon realized that a world without the Russian psychopath was probably a good thing. He came through for me a few days ago after managing to track down a working number for Kozlov.

The Russian was highly suspicious when I called. I told him there was no ill will, I simply wanted to make a business deal. I had located what they were looking for, had it in my possession, and would exchange it for five million US dollars. He balked until I agreed to make the exchange in public. That was what I wanted anyway.

The waitress stopped in front of the table, blocking my view of the sea. She placed a carafe of wine and a glass down in front of me. "Are you ready to order?"

I raised my coffee mug, swirling the mud on the bottom. After she left, I checked my watch. Less than five minutes until the meeting. The briefcase rested in the chair next to me, covered with a tan linen jacket. Next to it was a Beretta. I had another holstered under my shirt. I prayed Yashkin gave me an excuse to use it. I didn't care if we were out on a busy street. At the same time, I wanted to walk away from the meeting unscathed, five million dollars richer.

Kozlov emerged from a group of American tourists a block from the restaurant. His hair and beard were trimmed short. He had on a loose shirt and baggy pants, no doubt to conceal his weapon of choice. He stood on the corner waiting for the line of cars to come to a halt at the traffic light. Reaching for his ear, he nodded. I glanced up at the buildings, searching for a face in the windows. They had to be in my line of sight somewhere. I redirected my attention to the Russian as he crossed the street. The guy was sloppy, frequently patting his sidearm through his clothing. How had he managed to last as long as he had?

He lifted his glasses and made eye contact with me. I gave him a slight nod as I pulled the chair with the briefcase closer. Kozlov scanned the faces on the patio, then glanced across the street. I followed his gaze and finally spotted the silhouette I'd been searching for.

"He gonna join us?" I said, pointing directly at the other man.

The boutique door opened, bells dangling from the handle ringing out, the door catching in the breeze and hanging there for a few seconds before Yashkin appeared. He had on dark sunglasses, cargo pants, and a purple shirt.

Not sure what he was hoping to achieve, but if standing out was it, he'd accomplished his goal.

"Sit." I gestured to the seat across from me.

Kozlov slid his backpack off and set it on the ground next to the chair, then plopped down. He adjusted his pistol.

I smiled and shook my head at him.

"What?" he asked, straightening his shirt.

"Nothing." I kicked the chair to my left out a few inches and gestured toward it when Yashkin reached the patio.

He grabbed the wrought iron frame and pulled it out. The legs grated against the concrete, causing a few nearby patrons to cast scolding looks in our direction.

"You have it?" he asked, getting straight down to business.

Nodding, I said, "I do. And I'm guessing your end is in the backpack?"

Yashkin reached over the side of his chair and retrieved the bag, unzipping it as he lifted it toward the table. He set it in the middle, tipped it toward me.

"Good?" Yashkin asked.

"Yeah, looks good," I said without bothering to inspect the money inside.

He eased back in his chair, smiling. "You surprise me, Mr. Noble."

I held up a hand. "No names, Yashkin."

His lips drew tight at the mention of his name. There was no telling who else might be in the vicinity, watching the meeting from afar. And neither of us had a guarantee that the other wasn't wired, working for some agency or another. If so, I felt confident I had the upper hand in this situation.

"Anyway," I said. "What surprises you about me?"

"Everything that happened, and here you are, ready to move on for a nice sum of money."

"Can't change the past."

"Only learn from it, right?"

"Something like that."

"No one ever does, though." His smile faded as he leaned in, gesturing for me to come closer. I obliged him. Our faces were inches from one another. He lowered his sunglasses and looked me right in the eye. "Artur never figured that out. Hopefully you can carry the lesson for him instead."

"When did you do it?"

"That night." His smile faded as his cheeks darkened three shades of red. "After you bested my man and took what was rightfully mine." He took a deep breath, the color drained from his face. "That's OK, though. I know that we took something important from you as well. Anyway, we caught up to Artur sometime after he'd dropped you off. To his credit, he never revealed how you got away, even as we lopped off his fingers. He kept babbling on about Christiana." Yashkin rolled his eyes and waved his hand. "She never should have involved herself with that man. You see, she was going to take what you have, sell it on the open market, and run off with Artur. Can you believe that?"

I held his gaze for several seconds, staring into his blue eyes. "I guess they both got what they deserved then."

He pounded his fist on the table. "Yes. I knew you were like me. I can see the coldness in your heart through your dead eyes."

"Not so sure about that." I drained the rest of my coffee. "What about David?"

He pushed his bottom lip out and shrugged. "I'm sure I don't know anything about any David."

"Right. Of course you don't." I dropped a twenty on the table and placed the coffee mug on top to hold it in place. The breeze continued to blow steadily at us. A dark cloud covered the sun. I reached over and slid my jacket off the briefcase. "What's so important in there that so many people had to die? That you'd be willing to part with so much?"

Yashkin's smile returned. He leaned back, folded his hands and placed them on the table in front of him. "Don't be a damn fool. Take your money and disappear and forget you ever had anything to do with this."

CHAPTER 64

I WALKED AMID A CROWD OF STRANGERS KEEPING THE SEA TO MY left, stealing glances at the blue water while thinking I had enough cash on hand to buy a hell of a boat. I could sail out of the Med to the Atlantic, kick around the coast of Africa, make my way to Australia and New Zealand for a while.

Maybe for a lifetime.

Had to be parts down under where I'd never be found.

By this time the two Russians should've lost sight of me. Yashkin would have wanted to check the contents of the briefcase. I pictured him setting it down on the table, turning it so the combination lock stared back at him. Anticipation built as he worked the numbers, rewarded with a satisfying click, his treasure now inches from his fingertips.

"He's opened it." Bear piped in through the wireless ear piece tucked in my left ear canal. "And you've got a tail."

I resisted the urge to look back to locate the man following me. *Trust in Bear.* He'd get the wannabee assailant in time.

I imagined Yashkin's face as he peeled back the lid of the briefcase and rifled through the papers, which were nothing more than a class of second graders' homework we'd found stashed in a folder on a bench in Geneva, Switzerland. It was a stroke of luck finding them the same day we were in the city to conceal the actual documents. See, we'd cracked the briefcase's lock in Germany, after we had left the safe house. The documents Yashkin desired so greatly that he was willing to part with five million dollars were hundreds of miles away, safe and secure in one of my numbered accounts. I figured if the coded information they contained was worth more than all the lives that had been lost, plus millions of dollars, maybe it was better I held onto them for a while.

"Oh man, you should see this, Jack." Bear cackled in the earpiece. "They're furious. He showed the stack of homework to Kozlov, then threw it up in the air. Papers are drifting down on the patio like the snow in Moscow." Bear kept the line open, filling it with deep, concentrated breaths. "They're on the move now, headed your way. Stay the course, bro. Don't panic."

My jacket, which was folded over my arm slid down my forearm, concealing my hand as I freed the Beretta from its holster. The screaming crowd behind me indicated I might not need to discharge the sidearm.

"Kozlov's down."

A twinge of disappointment raced through me. Part of me wanted to take the man out myself. I pushed forward to the next intersection, turned right, away from the sea. I waited there for confirmation. Another collective gasp arose from the people on the street.

"Tail's about a half-block from you. Be ready, but note that there's a wave of people coming your way."

The crowd's collective anxiety preceded them in the form of panicked yells and the excited shuffling of feet on the pavement.

Another crack tore through the air.

"And there goes Yashkin." Bear whistled a maddened tune, sounded like a Bluejay on acid. He sucked in a sharp breath, held it. Another shot. "Don't worry about the tail. His brains are plastered on a store window. Gonna see if any other roaches come scrambling out before I break down."

The crowd reached the intersection behind me, some in a dead heat, knocking others over. The rest scrambled past, with some turning in my direction with no regard for oncoming traffic. Tires squealed on the asphalt as drivers attempted to avoid taking out the wave of frantic pedestrians.

"All right," Bear said. "We're good. I'm out. Weapon is clean and broken down. Gonna dispose of it right here. Meet you in an hour."

CHAPTER 65

WE MET ON A DESERTED COUNTRY ROAD OUTSIDE OF GRENOBLE, France. Rolling hills and farmland stretched out as far as I could see. A warm breeze blew from the southwest. In less than ten minutes I had acclimated to the smell of manure.

I had arrived in my rental car fifteen minutes before Bear. During that time, not so much as a stray dog had wandered past. This was the kind of place I could hide for a couple months and no one would ever know, as long as I had an accommodating host. Bear and I had a few friends in France, but none knew we were there. I hoped it would remain that way. Soon the story would be all over the news, and neither of us needed someone connecting the dots.

Bear parked his rental ahead of mine. Exhaust lingered for a few seconds before the wind disposed of it. I spit the aftertaste out of my mouth. A few seconds after cutting the engine, he exited his vehicle, slamming the door shut behind him. The sound was lost in the void. He walked around the back of my car, where I waited, seated on the trunk lid, the Beretta next to me.

He ran his hand through his shaggy hair, folded his arms over his chest, nodded a couple times while looking around.

"Nice spot," he said.

"I thought so," I said.

"You contacted anyone yet?"

"No. You?"

"Who the hell am I gonna call?" He shook his head. "You're the talker, not me."

The sun was high in the clear sky, nothing to block its path. It beat down on my forehead. Almost felt like it was July.

"I suppose," I said. "Anyway, I'll reach out to Frank soon, give him an update and make sure we're clear to re-enter the States."

Bear took a deep breath and glanced around. "Thinking I'm gonna find a place out here for a while."

"Two-and-a-half million should set you up decently."

He chuckled. "I'd say so. Maybe even enough to buy me one of them girls like you get all the time."

"They won't come as cheaply for you."

"At least they'll leave satisfied." His smile faded after a few seconds. "You headed back to Geneva still?"

"Yeah, gotta get the account set up for Christiana's daughters."

"How much are you donating here?"

"One and a quarter."

"And the other half of your cut?"

"Going to Lexi's dad."

"You're a saint, Mr. Noble. You truly are."

I lifted the pistol. "I tend to think those folks on the other end of Mr. Beretta here would disagree with that sentiment."

He held up a finger. "Oh, almost forgot." He jogged back to his car, clouds of dirt rising with each of his footfalls. He opened the back door, reached in, and returned a moment later with a six-pack.

"You do still love me," I said. "For a minute there, I thought you might bail on me after this mess. But now…" I grabbed a bottle and cracked open the top with my teeth and took a long pull. It was hoppy and bitter and hit my palate just right. I wiped my mouth with the back of my hand. "You did good, big man."

Shaking his head, Bear chuckled to himself, then drained half the bottle in a couple gulps. We remained at that spot, me seated on the trunk, him leaning against the fender, until all six beers had been consumed. Afterward we said our goodbyes with plans to meet up in another couple months, perhaps sooner if either of us got into any more trouble, of which we both agreed there was a good chance.

I stood there after he left until the plumes of dust had settled and the land was peaceful once again.

CHAPTER 66

THREE WEEKS LATER I WAS BACK IN THE US. MY FIRST VISIT HAD been to Northern Virginia where I met with an acquaintance I shared with Frank Skinner. Frank had convinced me the documents could be a matter of national security. Though my path had led me away from his line of work, there was still a part of me that agreed with him the best thing to do was turn the information over and let the right people go to work on it. He assured me after they were through, the docs would be destroyed so they would not wind up in the wrong hands. The difficulty I experienced turning them over was quickly erased by the extra million dollars Frank slid into my account.

He'd also taken it upon himself to open up Lexi's last investigation in Chicago and found enough evidence to bring McGrath and Denton down under a number of charges ranging from racketeering to attempted murder. There was a chance none of it would stick, but at least her work hadn't died in vain.

I hopped a train to Indianapolis for no reason other than a flight would have taken me there too quickly. No one ever looked forward to delivering the news that a loved one had been lost, especially when that loved one was a child. No matter the age, your babies are always your babies.

A rented SUV covered the remaining miles to the cabin forty-five minutes west of the city. I drove down the same narrow road, the dirt driveway through the woods, and pulled up to the house. To my surprise, Shane stepped out onto the porch wearing new prosthetics. He didn't even need his crutches. His concerned gaze transformed as I hopped out of the vehicle.

Thanos's dog rushed past him and ran up to me. I squatted down and grabbed the scruff of his neck while scratching his side. "Hey there, buddy. You doing all right with the old guy?"

The screen door creaked open and slammed shut. Lexi's father stood there, tall and defiant. Guess it was just how he held himself all the time. He turned his head, taking in the expanse of his front yard. I could see the question forming on his lips.

"Sir," I said, crossing the distance between the truck and porch. I dug into my pocket and wrapped my hand around the locket. My heart ached at the pain I was about to inflict. "There's no easy way to say this."

He pursed his lips together to keep them from quivering. Muscles rippled at the corners of his jaw. I couldn't imagine the thoughts racing through his mind. The day she was born, her initial steps, calling him "dada" the first time. Eucharist, confirmation, soccer matches and softball games. Her prom. Walking her down the aisle. Seeing her get into the FBI. His eyes watered and the steel facade cracked. He lowered his chin to his chest as tears streamed down his cheeks. Shane walked over, wrapped his arm around the old guy.

I grabbed his hand and dropped the locket in his palm. He stared down at it for a few moments while choking back sobs before finally opening it. It was a picture of her as a little girl, and him as a younger man. He was holding her, their cheeks pressed together.

"My God," he said. "She held onto this all these years?"

"One more thing." I jogged back to the SUV and popped the trunk. Disturbed dust swirled through the knifing sunlight. I grabbed a blue backpack and slung it over my shoulder.

"Where's her body?" he asked, wiping tears from his eyes. "Can I see my girl one more time?"

I let the pack slide off my shoulder and caught it with my hand. It hung there, dangling and twisting while I thought of the words to tell him he could never see her again.

"She did good for her country, right?" he asked.

"That she did. We found something that could have been incredibly damning to our country if the wrong person had hold of it. It's in the right hands now. They'll gather what they can from it and we'll be safer for it. Lexi's legacy will live on in all the lives that were saved because of her actions."

He seemed to believe my words, even if I didn't. I lifted the bag and extended it toward him.

"What's this?" he asked, taking the backpack from my hand, freeing me from the second half of Yashkin's blood money.

"It can't replace her, but perhaps you can do some good with it."

He unzipped the bag and stared at the cash for a few moments, then dropped it to the ground. "I suppose." He then retreated into his house.

Shane and I talked for a few more minutes. Turned out he and the dog hit it off, and he was taking him back to Chicago with him. I tossed the mutt a tennis ball, then climbed into the SUV and backed down the driveway.

My next stop was a good four hours away.

CHAPTER 67

I TRAVELED WEST ON 74 UNTIL I REACHED I-39, WHICH MERGED with I-90 in Rockford, Illinois. From there I made it to Madison and navigated from memory to the site of a steel warehouse. The snow had since melted. That was to be expected with temperatures in the high fifties. Police tape tied to stakes in the ground cordoned off the front of the building. The loft doors were secured with a thick chain and padlock.

My memory ran through that night once again. What if I hadn't found the paper sewn into Thanos's jacket? Lexi would still be alive. Yashkin, too, and he'd be no closer to the treasure he sought. Or would he? Had he known about the location, or had Rudin been following us? I was tired of the same questions and wanted answers.

I figured there was one man who could tell me.

David.

I had been gripped with pain that night, but not so much that I hadn't paid attention to the route Lexi took to reach David's facility. I drove along the country roads at a decent clip, paying attention to the landmarks that stood out in my mind's eye. The only difference now was the lack of snow cover. I only missed one turn. Five minutes later I realized it.

The driveway leading to the facility looked the same as I remembered. I pulled out my cell phone. Full signal. Not what I expected. But still it *looked* like I was in the right place.

I turned down the path to the house and eased forward. Last thing I wanted was some crazy woodlands character popping out with a shotgun, filling the SUV with buckshot.

I reached the clearing where the facility stood. Things were different though. The front door stood wide open. Windows were smashed. The antenna I recalled on the roof was gone, as was the satellite dish. Glancing at my phone, I saw it still had full signal. I got out and walked around to the entrance.

"He's gone."

I withdrew my pistol from its holster and spun to face the man.

"Easy, Jack." Charles held his left hand up. In his right was his sidearm, aimed at my chest. "Not here for any trouble."

"How'd you know I'd be here?"

"We've been monitoring you." He took a few steps forward. "You shoulda plugged Thanos when you first had a chance. Woulda been a whole lot less dead people."

"What do you know of it?"

He took a deep breath and shook his head. "We were conned, just like you. The Old Man ain't very happy about it, either. Turns out that guy Matt wasn't on our side. He was using us, using you, to get to Thanos. Everyone wanted the information that guy had."

"Yeah, well, you don't have to worry about him anymore." I looked at the facility. "What are you doing here, Charles? What does the Old Man care about this place?"

"I'm assuming you are now aware of who General Yashkin is, correct?"

I nodded, said nothing.

"This ex-spook, David Meadowcroft and Yashkin were working together."

I held up my hand, didn't need to hear anymore. Suddenly the answers I sought had no bearing.

"I'm not leaving with you," I said.

"Didn't think you would," Charles said.

"You can tell anyone waiting out there they'll die before they take me with them."

He laughed. "No one here but me, Noble."

"Why?"

"The Old Man is curious about what you found in Russia. Says it could be worth some serious coin to you."

"Second grade homework."

"What?"

"That's what we found." I pulled out a picture of the documents I had intended to shove in David's face and tore it into pieces. "It doesn't matter, really. Already turned it over to the Feds. It's being analyzed and shredded as we speak."

"That's a shame. I'll let him know." Charles turned and started toward the woods. At the edge of the clearing he stopped and faced me one more time. "If that should change, give him a call. Otherwise, we'll reach out to you sometime after you're back in the city."

I had no doubt about that.

No doubt at all.

The story continues in Noble Ultimatum. Continue for a sample or order now:

Join the LT Ryan reader family & receive a free copy of the Jack Noble story, *The Recruit*. Click the link below to get started:
https://ltryan.com/jack-noble-newsletter-signup-1

LOVE NOBLE? SAVAGE? HATCH? MADDIE? GET YOUR VERY OWN L.T. Ryan merchandise today! Click the link below to find coffee mugs, t-shirts, and even signed copies of your favorite L.T. Ryan thrillers! https://ltryan. ink/EvG_

NOBLE ULTIMATUM CHAPTER 1

"Why did you murder Frank Skinner in broad daylight, Mr. Noble?"

The man gripped his pen between his teeth as he slipped one arm free from his blue blazer, shifted his notebook to his other hand, then let the jacket slide onto the Victorian-era couch. He pulled the pen from his mouth, dabbing the end against his tongue. With it hovering over the blank page of his notebook, he stared unblinking over his gold-rimmed glasses at Jack Noble.

Jack held the man's gaze for several seconds before attempting a reply. When he opened his mouth to speak, he couldn't find the right words.

The man, whose name was Schreiber, tapped the end of his pen against his pad. The thump-thump-thump of a waltz. He glanced toward the narrow part between the drapes.

"That make you nervous?" Jack asked.

Schreiber nodded, tight and terse. His hair was pulled back into something akin to a man bun, only a little lower. "If you don't mind?"

Jack planted both palms on the hand-carved wooded arms of the chair he occupied and pushed himself off the seat. He took note of the other man stiffening. Jack would have been concerned if the guy hadn't. Schreiber's occupation was that of a journalist, not a soldier or a spy or a lawyer or a cop. He wasn't used to dealing with this element of society.

He didn't want to acknowledge people like me existed, but he sure as hell slept better because of our existence.

The meeting had been secured through back-channel communications. The risk in reaching out had been great. Jack trusted *maybe* six people enough to call upon while in his current predicament. The Agency knew the names of all six. The Agency presumably monitored all incoming and outgoing emails, messages, and phone calls of the six.

And that's what made the favor he phoned in all the more valuable. An old friend's mentor, who had nothing to do with the life Noble led, had arranged for Schreiber to book a room at the Hotel D'Coque in Luxembourg City. Noble spent three days tailing the man, first in his home city of Dresden, Germany, then as he made the trip to Luxembourg. If anyone else had followed Schreiber, they deserved to get the jump on Jack because he had failed to spot them.

Noble spread the blinds open another inch with his scissored index and middle fingers. Dark passing clouds diffused the light streaming through the window. Gusts of wind whipped dead leaves on the sidewalk into mini-cyclones, a hint of a late-spring storm brewing.

The busy street below was lined with four- and five-story buildings. Shops and lobbies on the ground level. Offices and apartments above. From a hundred-fifty feet up, the meandering pedestrians were nothing more than flat representations of themselves. Not real. Maybe that's what made dropping a bomb from thousands of feet up so easy to do. Noble scanned the passing throng for anyone who looked out of place. An individual overdressed for the heatwave. A guy lingering under an awning. Someone staring back at him from one of the many windows nestled in the steel and brick facades across the street.

The numbers offered anonymity. For Jack and for *them*. And make no mistake about it. The people hunting him were out there. Since he'd left Clarissa's hideout in Italy, the place she insisted no one knew about, they'd been a day behind him. Had she informed someone higher up the food chain about his presence? Or had they been watching her? He watched her sleep and told her where he'd be for a little while longer. She never showed, and he hadn't spent more than twenty-four hours in one location since.

A chance existed a few of the faces of his hunters would be recognizable. But agents came and went and died in the line of duty. Fresh recruits stepped up to take their place. The cycle repeated, depending on the state of the world, which, face it, had been shit for almost two decades now. Jack would lay odds it'd be some twenty-two-year-old fresh-faced kid wearing black glasses and carrying a Glock while possessing orders to kill on sight who would do him in.

"Mr. Noble," Schreiber said. "I was promised a story, an exclusive story. A CIA Director was murdered in the middle of a city street. *By you.* Are you going to answer my questions, or should I press the send button on my phone to have the police sent to my position?"

Jack let the sheer curtain fall shut and lingered there for a moment staring at the now-hazy street. They were out there. Somewhere beyond the veil. The room darkened after he pulled the right side of the drapes over the left.

Schreiber sulked back to the table and half-rested his ass on it. The guy didn't fancy getting too comfortable. At the moment, nothing stood between him and the door. As long as he wasn't too relaxed, he might be able to get to it before Jack felt like stopping him.

"Frank Skinner recruited me into the SIS in the days after I left the Marines and the CIA-sponsored program they forced me into before I had completed recruit training. He found me outside a dive bar in Key West. My first inclination was to turn him down. It's funny. A nagging feeling tells me that's what I should've done."

Schreiber dragged his pen across his notebook. Sounded like leaves scraping the street. A few seconds later, he stopped and glanced over his glasses again. "When was this?"

"Spring, 2002, I suppose."

"And what was your opinion of Skinner then?"

"Any opinion I had of Frank Skinner circa '02 has been affected by the events of the past decade. And those have been washed away by what's happened this year."

Schreiber focused on the tip of his pen for a few moments before asking another question. "A man with your skills, you could have done this at any time. Why in the middle of the day? In the middle of a street? Why in front of so many witnesses?"

Jack had relived that moment thousands of times. Truth drenched Schreiber's words. A planned hit would have served Noble better. He could have returned to the shadows, tracked Frank to his next destination, and taken the man's life in the middle of the night.

"Hate."

"Excuse me?" Schreiber said. "Hate?"

"Hatred. Pride. Hubris. Arrogance." Jack rose from his chair and walked back to the window, eliciting a groan from Schreiber as he pulled the curtain back again. Noble squinted against the sunlight knifing through a slit in the clouds. "Take your pick, man. If I could go back to that day, I'd kill him again, same place, same manner."

The room darkened again as he turned and let the shades fall in place.

"What specifically did Frank Skinner do to you?" Schreiber perched atop a stool with his right leg crossed over his left. His foot bounced.

"What didn't he do? I don't have all the evidence. OK? For all I know, every negative event that's taken place, every person I've lost, every time I've been in danger, I can attribute it all to Frank Skinner."

"So that's why you did it, then? That's why you murdered him."

Jack stuffed his hands in his pocket. The mousy man across from him again reacted by straightening up, eyes wide, pen clutched tight as though he could use it to knock away a bullet.

"I did it because the guy was a traitor to his country. He'd been working against the States for a decade, maybe more. I didn't murder him—and when I have all the evidence, everyone all the way up to the President will agree with me."

"Surely you are aware you can't act as judge, jury, and executioner, Mr. Noble."

"Surely you are aware I can snap your neck easier than you can a pencil, Mr. Schreiber."

Schreiber produced a tablet. He turned it horizontally in his palm and tapped on the screen several times. The muffled sound of a crowd of people speaking French floated out of the speakers.

He held the device up for Jack to see. There Noble was, in the middle of the road. Frank Skinner on his knees. A pistol aimed at Skinner's bloody head. The quick flash of muzzle blast followed by the eruption of gunfire. People screamed and raced past the cameraman, who only stood there for a few additional moments before running off. The image jumped and panned all around. The last thing Noble saw before the footage cut off was Frank Skinner collapsing on the ground.

Dead.

NOBLE ULTIMATUM CHAPTER 2

"What were you thinking at that moment?"

Schreiber rose from the stool, pen pressed to paper. He sucked his bottom lip into his mouth. His dangling mustache touched his chin.

Jack stared at the footage, now frozen on the image of Frank's slumped body. Noble stood over him, eyes cast down at the lump that used to be a man he trusted at one time. How long ago had that been? Had he ever fully trusted Skinner?

And what was he thinking after he killed Frank?

"I can't recall."

"You can't recall?" Schreiber deflated with a heavy sigh. "So, all I have from you is a confession? Should I call the authorities now?"

"You know you won't make it out of the room alive if you do."

He leveled his pen at Jack as though the thing were loaded with 9mm rounds. "That is exactly the reason I didn't want to take this meeting. You reached out to me, Mr. Noble. You wanted to tell your story."

Jack took a second to consider this and nodded at the guy. It had been Jack's idea. He wanted the truth out there. Schreiber needed to ask the right questions though.

"Look, you're wanting me to tell you what I was thinking at that time? I have no idea. Probably good riddance, Frank. Countless moments led up to me playing judge, jury, and executioner that day. I suppose I knew if I didn't do it then, Frank would get away with it. He'd find a way to silence me for good. Christ knows he's been trying for years."

"Can you explain what you mean there?"

Jack revealed a few events from the past. Things that were classified, but even the classified docs didn't tell the truth. "None of this happened during my time with the SIS. But that was a couple years later. Afterward, I worked on a contract basis. The first time I believed Skinner wanted me dead is when he offered me a job to take care of a supposed rogue agent named, Brett Taylor."

Schreiber listened intently as Jack listed events, frequently holding up a finger asking for time to jot down his thoughts on the matter. When Jack had finished, Schreiber set his pen and notebook down on the weathered coffee table between them.

"And what about the evidence that Skinner was working against the United States?"

Jack swallowed back the lump in his throat. This was the most he'd spoken at once in a couple of months. Clarissa had left shortly after he arrived at her hideout, and she hadn't come back. Everyone in the little village spoke Italian. Jack could get by with a few phrases, but that was it. They welcomed him into their homes, their bars, their cafes. But hardly anyone attempted to communicate with him.

"You have to take me at my word."

Schreiber scoffed. "At your word? I can't print any of this based on what you've told me. Your country thinks you are a murderous traitor. My country thinks this. The whole world thinks this, Mr. Noble. I need hard proof."

"I know you do. That's why I arranged our meeting."

"Whatever do you mean?"

"I need your help."

The slim man shifted his pen to his other hand and brushed his mustache inward with his thumb and forefinger. "I can't begin to understand what you mean by that."

This was the risk. Jack understood that when he first made contact. Schreiber was at the top of his game. He had contacts globally who could trade in favors and provide him with the intelligence Jack would use to piece together his case against Frank. Noble's word would never be enough. Not after the life he'd lived. But if this benign-looking journalist could gather the evidence, it could get Jack off the hook.

"I'm a wanted man. You know that. And with technology today, I can't get within a mile of the places I need to without being caught on a surveillance system. Facial recognition, license plate readers, they'd have me surrounded before I knew they'd spotted me."

Schreiber nodded at this. "I presumed that's why you chose Luxembourg.

An assumption they don't have that kind of tech, when, in fact, you can't escape it unless you stick to the smallest of towns. That is how you've managed so far, isn't it?"

"More or less."

"Have you remained in one place the entire time you've been off the grid?"

"More or less." Jack smiled. The gesture seemed to influence the journalist.

Schreiber took a deep breath and let his shoulders slump and head fall forward an inch as he exhaled.

"What is it I can do for you, Mr. Noble?"

Jack proceeded to tell Schreiber the names of five individuals placed in high-ranking positions in intelligence agencies in the United States, Great Britain, France, Russia, and Israel. Schreiber committed each to memory as well as the information he needed to procure from them. His reward for this would be uncovering one of the greatest intelligence scandals the world had seen.

"Why can't you go to these men directly?" Schreiber asked. "It's not like years ago where you'd have to expose yourself in order to do so."

"To get close enough, I'd have to. I can't take that risk."

"These men, they'd vouch for you?"

"It's not about vouching for me. Exposing the truth. That's what we're after. I can live the rest of my life on the run if need be. Prefer not to. Each of those five men hold a key. I also hold something over them. As soon as you mention my name and Frank's, they'll know what your meeting is about."

Noble returned to the window. He parted the drapes and curtains a foot or so. The sun had again retreated behind a silvery veil of racing clouds. Lightning flashed far off over the city skyline. The storm would arrive soon. Jack had use of the room for another night, but he wouldn't stay. Not here. Too exposed. Too much risk now that he'd met with the journalist. He had to work on a plan to get to the small country's border with Belgium. A friend there would allow him passage.

Schreiber cleared his throat.

"Our meeting is concluded now?"

Noble turned his back on the window. The thought that he hadn't studied the windows across the street passed through his mind, and he stepped out of the line of sight. He gave the journalist a slight nod.

"What if I don't do this?" Schreiber asked. "Suppose I go to MI-5 or MI-6 and hand all this over and let them do what they wish with it?"

Jack eyed him for several seconds, offered a shrug. "Then nothing changes.

Skinner remains a hero gunned down by his onetime protégé. No one will investigate his dealings over the past decade. Those who profited from those dealings will remain unnamed, planning God-knows-what against my country." He paused a beat, then added, "Yours too, I suspect."

"No repercussions from you?"

Jack felt his lip twitch into a slight smile. "You won't know that until it's too late."

The color drained from Schreiber's face as he fumbled his navy-blue bag open and stuffed his pen and pad inside. He retrieved his cell phone from the table.

"Don't turn that on until you are two blocks from here," Jack said. "They'll eventually figure out we were here. But we need as much of a head start as possible."

Schreiber stuffed the device into his back pocket. Like most phones Jack saw people handling, Schreiber's was too big for his front pocket with his keys and wallet shoved in there.

"How should we do this? Leave together? Separate?"

"There's one security camera on this floor. Turn left and go to the end of the hallway. I'll be right behind you. There are three doors in the lobby that lead outside. You take the one on the left and keep going that way down the street."

Schreiber nodded as he threw his bag over his shoulder and started toward the door.

"One more thing." Jack pulled a burner cell phone from his pocket. He handed the phone and two disposable SIM cards to the journalist. "It already has one in it. After our first call, you melt the SIM and replace it with the card marked with a red X. Got it?"

Schreiber took the phone and went to place it in the same pocket as his own cell. He handed it off to his other hand behind his back and tucked it away. "When will you call?"

"Two days. That should be enough time for you to make contact."

The journalist turned without responding. Noble grabbed his arm.

"Don't back out now, Schreiber. That phone rings, answer it."

Schreiber nodded without looking back. He headed straight to the door and exited the room. Noble didn't linger behind. He followed the journalist out and down the hallway to the gunmetal grey door leading to the stairwell. The sound of it opening echoed throughout the twenty-story steel and concrete chamber. It sounded as though there were an entire company of soldiers racing up or down the steps.

A few minutes later, they entered the lobby. Schreiber first, then Noble ten seconds later. They avoided eye contact, but Jack remained a few steps behind and to the right so he could keep the journalist in his peripheral. He lost a few steps when a woman looking the other way bumped into him. Once outside, he'd lose that view, and if the man decided to call it off, reach out to the authorities, Jack would be unaware.

He paused at the tinted door and inhaled the disinfectant-laden air. It carried a hint of lemon. The street outside was mildly busy. Enough people milling about that he would be able to absorb himself and become anonymous. He thought of his longtime partner and best friend Bear Logan. If the big shaggy man, who stood six-and-a-half feet tall, were there, they'd stand out amid the clean-cut pedestrians.

Jack pulled the door toward him. A rush of cool air whispered past. The incoming rain drenched the breeze. He stepped through the opening and was met with the crack of a gunshot.

Order Noble Ultimatum now!

Join the LT Ryan reader family & receive a free copy of the Jack Noble story, *The Recruit*. Click the link below to get started:
https://ltryan.com/jack-noble-newsletter-signup-1

ALSO BY L.T. RYAN

Find All of L.T. Ryan's Books on Amazon Today!

The Jack Noble Series

The Recruit (free)

The First Deception (Prequel 1)

Noble Beginnings

A Deadly Distance

Ripple Effect (Bear Logan)

Thin Line

Noble Intentions

When Dead in Greece

Noble Retribution

Noble Betrayal

Never Go Home

Beyond Betrayal (Clarissa Abbot)

Noble Judgment

Never Cry Mercy

Deadline

End Game

Noble Ultimatum

Noble Legend

Noble Revenge

Never Look Back (Coming Soon)

Bear Logan Series

Ripple Effect

Blowback

Take Down

Deep State

Bear & Mandy Logan Series

Close to Home

Under the Surface

The Last Stop

Over the Edge

Between the Lies (Coming Soon)

Rachel Hatch Series

Drift

Downburst

Fever Burn

Smoke Signal

Firewalk

Whitewater

Aftershock

Whirlwind

Tsunami

Fastrope

Sidewinder (Coming Soon)

Mitch Tanner Series

The Depth of Darkness

Into The Darkness

Deliver Us From Darkness

Cassie Quinn Series

Path of Bones

Whisper of Bones

Symphony of Bones

Etched in Shadow

Concealed in Shadow

Betrayed in Shadow

Born from Ashes

Blake Brier Series

Unmasked

Unleashed

Uncharted

Drawpoint

Contrail

Detachment

Clear

Quarry (Coming Soon)

Dalton Savage Series

Savage Grounds

Scorched Earth

Cold Sky

The Frost Killer (Coming Soon)

Maddie Castle Series

The Handler

Tracking Justice

Hunting Grounds (Coming Soon)

Affliction Z Series

Affliction Z: Patient Zero

Affliction Z: Abandoned Hope

Affliction Z: Descended in Blood

Affliction Z : Fractured Part 1

Affliction Z: Fractured Part 2 (Fall 2021)

Love Noble? Savage? Hatch? Maddie? Get your very own L.T. Ryan merchandise today! Click the link below to find coffee mugs, t-shirts, and even signed copies of your favorite L.T. Ryan thrillers! https://ltryan.ink/EvG_

ABOUT THE AUTHOR

L.T. RYAN is a *Wall Street Journal, USA Today*, and Amazon bestselling author of several mysteries and thrillers, including the *Wall Street Journal* bestselling Jack Noble and Rachel Hatch series. With over eight million books sold, when he's not penning his next adventure, L.T. enjoys traveling, hiking, riding his Peloton, and spending time with his wife, daughter and four dogs at their home in central Virginia.

* Sign up for his newsletter to hear the latest goings on and receive some free content ➜ https://ltryan.com/jack-noble-newsletter-signup-1
* Join LT's private readers' group ➜ https://www.facebook.com/groups/1727449564174357
* Follow on Instagram ➜ @ltryanauthor
* Visit the website ➜ https://ltryan.com
* Send an email ➜ contact@ltryan.com
* Find on Goodreads ➜ http://www.goodreads.com/author/show/6151659.L_T_Ryan